W9-CZK-606

The Passion of
Artemisia

Also by Susan Vreeland
in Large Print:

Girl in Hyacinth Blue
What Love Sees

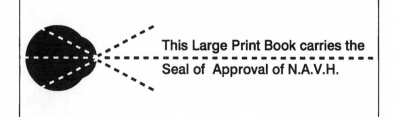

This Large Print Book carries the
Seal of Approval of N.A.V.H.

The Passion of Artemisia

Susan Vreeland

Thorndike Press • Waterville, Maine

Grateful acknowledgment is made for permission to use an excerpt from "Musée des Beaux Arts" from *W. H. Auden: Collected Poems.* Copyright 1940 and renewed 1968 by W. H. Auden. Used by permission of Random House, Inc.

Published in 2002 by arrangement with Viking Penguin, a member of Penguin Putnam Inc.

Thorndike Press Large Print Women's Fiction Series.

The tree indicium is a trademark of Thorndike Press.

Set in 16 pt. Plantin.

Printed in the United States on permanent paper.

Library of Congress Cataloging-in-Publication Data

Vreeland, Susan.
    The passion of Artemisia / Susan Vreeland.
      p. cm.
    ISBN 0-7862-3856-9 (lg. print : hc : alk. paper)
    1. Gentileschi, Artemisia, 1593–1652 or 3 — Fiction.
    2. Women painters — Fiction. 3. Italy — Fiction.
    4. Large   type books. I. Title.
    PS3572.R34 P37 2002b
    813'.54—dc21   2001057523

To Kip, *amore mio,*
for his understanding

About suffering they were never wrong,
The Old Masters: how well they understood
Its human position; how it takes place
While someone else is eating or opening
  a window or just walking dully along.

— W. H. Auden
"Musée des Beaux Arts," 1940

Author's Note

Any work of fiction about history or a historical person is and must be a work of the imagination, true to the time and character always, but true to fact only so long as fact furnishes believable drama. In order to serve my chosen thematic focus, I have combined actual personages into composite characters, eliminated others, and invented still others. Using what evidence is known, I have imagined the personalities and interaction of Artemisia Gentileschi, her father, and her husband. However, the trial record and her associations with Galileo, Cosimo de' Medici II, and Michelangelo Buonarroti the Younger are documented in art histories. All paintings referred to are actual works indisputably ascribed to her in roughly the same chronology. Like a painter who clothes figures from centuries earlier in the garb of his or her own time, so have I sought to render Artemisia Gentileschi in a way meaningful to us three and half centuries later, yet concordant with the soul and passions of the real Artemisia Gentileschi (1593–1653), for whom the story behind the art was always vital.

Acknowledgments

My deep-felt gratitude to Karen Kapp for introducing me to Artemisia; to Jim McCarthy for assistance in all things Italian; to Peggy Jaffe and the Tuscany Institute of Advanced Studies for the tastes and sights of Tuscany; to the Religious of the Sacred Heart of Santa Trinità dei Monti for hospitality, timelessness, and grace; to the Asilomar Writers' consortium, in particular Jerry Hannah and Grant Farley for their perceptive readings; and especially to my two *tesori:* my extraordinary agent, Barbara Braun, for her belief in me and her joy at my every step; and my gifted editor, Jane von Mehren, for her kind, astute, page-by-page tutorials in craft.

Contents

1

The Sibille

My father walked beside me to give me courage, his palm touching gently the back laces of my bodice. In the low-angled glare already baking the paving stones of the piazza and the top of my head, the still shadow of the Inquisitor's noose hanging above the Tor di Nona, the papal court, stretched grotesquely down the wall, its shape the outline of a tear.

"A brief unpleasantness, Artemisia," my father said, looking straight ahead. "Just a little squeezing."

He meant the *sibille*.

If, while my hands were bound, I gave again the same testimony as I had the previous weeks, they would know it was the truth and the trial would be over. Not my trial. I kept telling myself that: I was not on trial. Agostino Tassi was on trial.

The words of the indictment my father had sent to Pope Paul V rang in my ears: *"Agostino Tassi deflowered my daughter Artemisia and did carnal actions by force many times, acts that brought grave and enormous damage to me, Orazio Gentileschi, painter and citizen of Rome, the poor plaintiff, so that I could not sell her painting talent for so high a price."*

I hadn't wanted anyone to know. I wasn't even going to tell *him*, but he heard me crying once and forced it out of me. There was that missing painting, too, one Agostino had admired, and so he charged him.

"How much squeezing?" I asked.

"It will be over quickly."

I didn't look at any faces in the crowd gathering at the entrance to the Tor. I already knew what they'd show — lewd curiosity, accusation, contempt. Instead, I looked at the yellow honeysuckle blooming against stucco walls the color of Roman ochre. Each color made the other more vibrant. Papa had taught me that.

"Fragrant blossoms," beggars cried, offering them to women coming to hear the proceedings in the musty courtroom. Anything for a giulio. A cripple thrust into my hand a wilted bloom, rank with urine. He knew I was Artemisia Gentileschi. I dropped it on his misshapen knee.

My dry throat tightened as we entered the dark, humid Sala del Tribunale. Leaving Papa at the front row of benches, I stepped up two steps and took my usual seat opposite Agostino Tassi, my father's friend and collaborator. My rapist. Leaning on his elbow, he didn't move when I sat down. His black hair and beard were overgrown and wild. His face, more handsome than he deserved, had the color and hardness of a bronze sculpture.

Behind a table, the papal notary, a small man swathed in deep purple, was sharpening his quills with a knife, letting the shavings fall to the floor. A dusty beam of light from a high window fell on his hands and lightened the folds of his sleeve to lavender. "Fourteen, May, 1612," the notary muttered as he wrote. Two months, and this was the first day he didn't have a bored look on his face. The day I would be vindicated. I pressed my hands tight against my ribs.

The Illustrious Lord Hieronimo Felicio, Locumtenente of Rome appointed as judge and interrogator by His Holiness, swept in and sat on a raised chair, arranging his scarlet robes to be more voluminous. Papal functionaries were always posturing in public. Under his silk skull cap, his jowls sagged like overripe fruit. He was followed by a huge man with a shaved head whose shoulders bulged out of his sleeveless leather tunic — the Assistente di Tortura. A hot wave of fear rushed through me. With a flick of a finger the Lord High Locumtenente ordered him to draw a sheer curtain across the room separating us from Papa and the rabble crowded on benches on the other side. The curtain hadn't been there before.

The Locumtenente scowled and his fierce black eyebrows joined, making a shadow. "You understand, Signorina Gentileschi, our purpose." His voice was slick as linseed oil. "The Delphic sybils always told the truth."

I remembered the Delphic sibyl on the ceiling of the Sistine Chapel. Michelangelo portrayed her as a powerful woman alarmed by what she sees. Papa and I had stood under it in silent awe, squeezing each other's hands to contain our excitement. Maybe the *sibille* would only squeeze as hard as that.

"Likewise, the *sibille* is merely an instrument designed to bring truth to women's lips. We will see whether you persist in what you have testified." He squinted his goat's eyes. "I wonder what tightening the cords might do to a painter's ability to hold a brush — properly." My stomach cramped. The Locumtenente turned to Agostino. "You are a painter too, Signor Tassi. Do you know what the *sibille* can do to a young girl's fingers?"

Agostino didn't even blink.

My fingers curled into fists. "What can it do? Tell me."

The Assistente forced my hands flat and wound a long cord around the base of each finger, then tied my hands palm to palm at my wrists and ran the cord around each pair of fingers like a vine. He attached a monstrous wooden screw and turned it just enough for the cords to squeeze a little.

"What can it do?" I cried. I looked for Papa through the curtain. He was leaning forward pulling at his beard.

"Nothing," the Locumtenente said. "It can do nothing, if you tell the truth."

"It can't cut off my fingers, can it?"

"That, signorina, is up to you."

My fingers began to throb slightly. I looked at Papa. He gave me a reassuring nod.

"Tell us now, for I'm sure you see reason, have you had sexual relations with Geronimo the Modenese?"

"I don't know anyone by that name."

17

"With Pasquino Fiorentino?"

"I don't know him either."

"With Francesco Scarpellino?"

"The name means nothing to me."

"With the cleric Artigenio?"

"I tell you, no. I don't know these men."

"That's a lie. She lies. She wants to discredit me to take my commissions," Agostino said. "She's an insatiable whore."

I couldn't believe my ears.

"No," Papa bellowed. "He's trying to pass her off as a whore to avoid the *nozze di riparazione*. He wants to ruin the Gentileschi name. He's jealous."

The Locumtenente ignored Papa and curled back his lip. "Have you had sexual relations with your father, Orazio Gentileschi?"

"I would spit if you had said that outside this courtroom," I whispered.

"Tighten it!" the Locumtenente ordered.

The hideous screw creaked. I sucked in my breath. Rough cords scraped across the base of my fingers, burning. Murmurs beyond the curtain roared in my ears.

"Signorina Gentileschi, how old are you?"

"Eighteen."

"Eighteen. Not so young that you don't know you should not offend your interrogator. Let us resume. Have you had sexual relations with an orderly to Our Holy Father, the late Cosimo Quorli?"

"He . . . he tried, Your Excellency. Agostino Tassi brought him into the house. I fought him away. They had both been hounding me. Giving me lewd looks. Whispering suggestions."

"For how long?"

"Many months. A year. I was barely seventeen when it started."

"What kind of suggestions?"

"I don't like to say." The Locumtenente flashed a look at the Assistente, who moved toward me. "Suggestions of my hidden beauty. Cosimo Quorli threatened to boast about having me if I didn't submit."

"And did you submit?"

"No."

"This same Cosimo Quorli reported to other orderlies of the Palazzo Apostolico that he was, in truth, your father, that your mother, Prudenzia Montone, had frequently encouraged him to visit her privately, whereupon she conceived." He paused and scrutinized my face. "You must admit you do have a resemblance. Has he, on any occasion, ever revealed this to you?"

"The claim is ludicrous. I must now defend my mother's honor as well as mine

19

against this mockery?"

It seemed enough to him that he had planted the idea. He cleared his throat and pretended to read some document.

"Did you not, on repeated occasions, engage in sexual relations willingly with Agostino Tassi?"

The room closed in. I held my breath.

The Assistente turned the screw.

I tightened all my muscles against it. The cords bit into my flesh. Rings of fire. Blood oozed between them in two places, three, all over. How could Papa let them? He didn't tell me there would be blood. I sucked in air through my teeth. This was Agostino's trial, not mine. How to make it stop? The truth.

"Not willingly. Agostino Tassi dishonored me. He raped me and violated my virginity."

"When did this occur?"

"Last year. Just after Easter."

"If a woman is raped, she must have done something to invite it. What were you doing?"

"Painting! In my bedchamber." I squeezed shut my eyes to get out the words. "I was painting our housekeeper, Tuzia, and her baby as the Madonna and Child. She let him in. My father was away. She knew Agostino. He was my father's friend. My father hired him to teach me perspective."

"Why did you not cry out?"

"I couldn't. He held a handkerchief over my mouth."

"Did you not try to stop him?"

"I pulled his hair and scratched his face and . . . his member. I even threw a dagger at him."

"A virtuous woman keeps a dagger in her bedchamber?"

My head was about to split. "A threatened woman does."

"And after that occasion?"

"He came again, let in by Tuzia. He pushed himself on me . . . and in me." Sweat trickled between my breasts.

"Did you resist?"

"I scratched and pushed him."

"Did you always resist?"

I searched Agostino's face. Immovable as a painting. "Say something." Only two months ago he had said he loved me. "Agostino," I pleaded. "Don't let them do this."

He looked down and dug dirt from his fingernails.

The Locumtenente turned to Agostino. "Do you wish to amend your claim of innocence?"

Agostino's strong-featured face turned cold and ugly. I didn't want to beg. Not him. Santa Maria, I prayed, don't let me beg him.

"No," he said. "She's a whore just like her mother."

"She thought she was betrothed!" Papa bellowed from beyond the curtain. "It was understood. He would marry her. A proper *nozze di riparazione.*"

The Locumtenente leaned toward me. "You haven't answered the question, signora. The *sibille* can be made to cut off a finger."

"It's Agostino who's on trial, not I. Let him be subjected to the *sibille.*"

"Tighten!"

Madre di Dio, let me faint before I scream. Blood streamed. My new white sleeve was soaked in red. Papa, make them stop. What was I to do? Tell them what they want? Lie? Say I'm a whore? That would only set Agostino free. Another turn. "Oh oh oh oh stop!" Was I screaming?

"For the love of God, stop!" Papa shouted and stood up.

The Locumtenente snapped his fingers to have him gagged. "God loves those, Signor Gentileschi, who tell the truth." He leered at me. "Now tell me, and tell me truthfully, signorina, after the first time did you always resist?"

The room blurred. The world swirled out of control. The screw, my hands — there was nothing else. Pain so wicked I — I —

Che Dio mi salvi — would the cords touch bone? — *Che Santa Maria mi salvi* — *Gesu* — *Madre di Dio* — make it stop. I had to tell.

"I tried to, but in the end, no. He promised he would marry me, and I . . . I believed him." *Dio mi salvi,* stop it stop it stop it. "So I allowed him . . . against my desires . . . so he would keep his promise. What else could I do?"

My breath. I couldn't get my breath.

"Enough. Adjourned until tomorrow." He waved his hand in disgust and triumph. "All parties to be present."

The *sibille* was loosened and removed.

Rage hissed through me. My hands trembled, and shook blood onto my skirt. Agostino lurched toward me, but the guards grabbed him to take him away. I wanted to wait until the crowd left, but a guard pushed me out with everyone else and I had to walk through hoots and jeers with bleeding hands. In the glare of the street, I felt something thrown at my back. I didn't turn around to see what it was. Beside me, Papa offered me his handkerchief.

"I'd rather bleed."

"Artemisia, take this."

"You didn't tell me what the *sibille* could do." I passed him, and walked faster than he could. At home I shoved my clothing

23

cassapanca behind my chamber door with my knees, and flung myself onto my bed and cried.

How could he have let this happen? How could he be so selfish? My dearest papa. All those happy times on the Via Appia — picnics with Mama listening for doves and Papa gathering sage to scrub into the floor. Papa wrapping his feet and mine in scrubbing cloths soaked in sage water, sliding to the rhythm of his love songs, his voice warbling on the high notes, waving his arms like a cypress in the wind until I laughed. That was my papa.

Was.

And all his stories about great paintings — sitting on my bed, letting me snuggle in his arms, slipping me some candied orange rind. Wonderful stories. Rebekah at the well at Nahor, her skin so clear that when she raised her chin to drink, you could see the water flowing down her throat. Cleopatra floating the Nile on a barge piled with fruit and flowers. Danaë and the golden shower, Bathsheba, Judith, sibyls, muses, saints — he made them all real. He had made me want to be a painter, let me trace the drawings in his great leather-bound *Iconologia*, taught me how to hold a brush when I was five, how to grind pigments and mix colors

24

when I was ten. He gave me my very own grinding muller and marble slab. He gave me my life.

What if I could never paint again with these hands? What was the use in living then? The dagger was still under the bed. I didn't have to live if the world became too cruel.

But there was my Judith to paint — if I could. More than ever I wanted to do that now.

Papa rattled the door. "Artemisia, let me in."

"I don't want to talk to you. You knew what the *sibille* could do."

"I didn't think —"

"*Sì*, eh. You didn't think."

He wedged the door open and pushed the trunk out of the way. He brought in a bowl of water and cloths to clean my hands. I rolled away from him.

"Artemisia, permit me."

"If Mama were still here she wouldn't have let you allow it."

"I didn't realize. I —"

"She wouldn't have wanted it public, like I didn't."

"In time, Artemisia, it won't matter."

"When a woman's name is all she has, it matters."

2

Judith

A conversation at our neighborhood bakery shop ended abruptly with embarrassed looks when I came in with bound fingers. The baker's boys held up their hands with their fingers splayed in mockery. On my way home our tailor's wife leaning over her windowsill spat just as I walked by. Crossing the Via del Corso in the searing heat, I stopped to watch swallows careening among laundry strung from upper windows. *"Puttana!* Whore!" I heard. I looked down the street, but there was only an old woman selling fruit. *"Puttana!"* I heard again, a husky voice. I straightened my back and walked on, refusing to look around. From an upstairs window, a chamber pot splashed down not three steps ahead of me.

The trial didn't end. Whenever I was

summoned, I had to go and sit through more accusations and lies. It drove me mad that I couldn't work. When Papa pulled off the bandages to change them, the raw grooves around the base of each finger bled again. When they dried, if I bent them even slightly, the crusted blood cracked. I couldn't hold a brush or a spoon. Papa told Tuzia to feed me. Ever since Mother died, Tuzia had wanted Papa's love, not just his bed. She was jealous of his love for me. That's why she let Agostino in. Better to starve than to let *her* feed me, and so I didn't eat. Papa came home one afternoon raging that Tuzia had betrayed me in court. She had testified that she saw a stream of men enter my rooms, so he put her out on the street and asked our neighbor, Porzia Stiattesi, to feed me.

I tried to keep my fingers straight so they would heal and I could paint again. Still, they festered and oozed, and then the maddening itching began. All I could do was to pace the house, stare out windows, and study my rough sketches for my Judith, the heroine who saved the Jewish people. Papa had told me the story when he painted her. She stole into the enemy camp pretending to seduce the Assyrian tyrant, Holofernes, and get him drunk. She teased him, delaying the lovemaking, pouring him more wine until he fell asleep. Then she cut off his head and showed it to his soldiers the next day, and the army fled. That's the kind of woman I wanted to paint. Papa's Judith was so angelic and delicate she could never have done the deed without the intervention of God.

One morning a fishmonger came through our narrow Via della Croce carrying two baskets of dried fish. She had her sleeves rolled up and her muscular arms were thick and ropey like the veined arm of Moses in San Pietro in Vincoli. That's what Judith's arms had to be — thicker and stronger than I'd sketched them, with her sleeves pushed up too, ready for a bloodbath, stiff with determination and repugnance as she drove his steel blade through his neck. And Judith's maidservant, Abra, also had to have strong arms to bear down on the tyrant's chest. But more than arms, my Judith would have one knee up on the tyrant's bed, hacking like a farm wife slaughtering a pig.

The fish hawker sang out *"cefalo, baccalà"* and laughed uproariously at some children playing in the street. She was utterly free, and I envied her, for a moment. Not that I wanted to be a fishwife. I just didn't want to spend my whole life confined at home to

28

avoid humiliation.

I put on a shawl and tucked my hands inside, took side streets and crossed the large piazza to the church of Santa Maria del Popolo. Caravaggio's *Conversion of Saint Paul* hung in a small chapel there. I studied his chiaroscuro, how he used bright light right against darkness, and I yearned to try it myself. Saint Paul was lying on his back at the moment of his conversion, head and shoulders forward in the picture plane and his body foreshortened. I could do Holofernes like that, with his head practically bursting through the canvas toward the viewer, upside down, at an impossible angle if it were fully attached, but still living, taking his last horrific breath as he thrust his fist into Abra's chin.

I remembered being disappointed when Papa had shown me Caravaggio's Judith. She was completely passive while she was sawing through a man's neck. Caravaggio gave all the feeling to the man. Apparently, he couldn't imagine a woman to have a single thought. I wanted to paint her thoughts, if such a thing were possible — determination and concentration and belief in the absolute necessity of the act. The fate of her people resting on her shoulders. Not relishing the act, just getting it done. And his thoughts too. Confusion and terror. The world out of control. Yes, I knew about that. I could do that part.

But could I do Judith?

One day I was summoned to court and Agostino wasn't. Opposite where I sat in my usual seat, two women laid a cloth over a long wooden table and brought a basin of water and rags. What for? Some new torture? The older, larger one, whose fleshy throat hung down under her chin, stared at me with contempt, the wrinkles of her lower lids tightening. The younger woman, so thin she seemed only a bundle of bones, wouldn't look at me at all. I held my arms against my ribs. The notary sneered.

The Locumtenente cleared his throat to get order. "And so you say that you, a girl of a mere eighteen years, are no longer a virgin because of the action taken by Signor Tassi? Is that right?" he demanded in his relentless, implicating way.

I nodded. Admission that I wasn't a virgin, no matter the circumstances, would brand me forever as lacking in control, and that would make me unmarriageable.

"Say it for the record."

"Yes, that's right."

"What's right? Say the words."

30

"I am no longer a virgin."

The Locumtenente thumbed through some documents and raised his arm toward the two women. "These are midwives of much experience and," he paused to look at me, "unstained reputation. Diambra of Piazza San Pietro and Domina Caterina of the Court of Masiano. Signorina Gentileschi, you affirm with all your mind and proper being that you are no longer a virgin?"

I squeezed my legs together. "Yes, Your Lordship, on account of Agostino Tassi's forceful —"

"Signorina will be silent." He flipped his fingers at the midwives. "Proceed with the examination of the pudenda of Signorina Gentileschi, and let the notary observe." He stretched out his legs, leaned back and folded his arms across his chest.

I froze.

Murmurs spread through the courtroom. "Believe her," I heard Papa say. "She never lies."

The young midwife pulled the curtain, but it was so sheer I could see shapes right through it. The bailiff set up a screen between the table and the Locumtenente, but the notary walked behind it to stand right at the table.

I couldn't move. The courtroom hushed.

The older midwife marched toward me. I held onto the arms of the chair even though I could feel my scabs bursting open. She grabbed me by the elbow and pulled me toward the table. The cloth covering it was stained. By some other poor woman violated the same way? How had she managed to keep on living? Or was she shut up in a convent somewhere?

What could this prove? Agostino would only say that someone else deflowered me.

I sat on the edge of the table. Expressionless, the older midwife motioned for me to lie down and bend my knees. The bones in my legs melted. The younger one smeared rancid-smelling animal fat over her fingers and then she lifted my skirt. She looked down at me the way a new serving girl looks down to gut a chicken for the first time. Her greasy fingers wormed into me. I squeezed all my muscles against her. The feel of squeezing against Agostino shot through me and I shuddered.

"It will go harder with you if you do that," she whispered. "Loosen yourself and it will be over quicker."

I willed myself to relax. "Don't make me remember," I whispered.

She pushed farther. A bitter taste filled

my mouth, and my eyes stung. She withdrew and washed her hands in the basin of water.

The larger woman came toward me, pushing up her sleeves. Her fingers were thick and she was rougher than the first. I gasped, and squeezed my eyes shut. In spite of my effort, I felt that hot moment just before crying. I tried not to make a sound. I wouldn't give them that.

I kept my eyes shut until I heard her splash water in the basin. I pulled down my skirt, rolled onto my side away from the courtroom and drew up my knees. Oh, let the floor open up and swallow me. Just like I had wished when, as a little girl, I had opened the bedroom door with a fistful of dandelions for Mama, tufted seeds tearing away as I rushed into the room, and found Papa naked with his back to me and Mama on the bed, knees up, skirt raised, showing that secret territory between her legs. Shock had seered me. How I'd cried for days and wouldn't talk to her, wouldn't even let her near me. That was how they wanted to display me — as if caught in the act.

"It is as she has said," I heard the thin woman say beside me.

"State the report for the record." The Locumtenente's voice was casual, as if they had just performed some inconsequential, routine task.

"I, Diambra Blasio, have touched and examined the vagina of Donna Artemisia, and I can say that she is not a virgin. I know this because I have placed my finger inside her vagina, and found that the hymen is broken. I can say this because of the experience of being a midwife for ten or eleven years."

I tried to shut my mind to everything around me.

"And you?"

"I, Caterina of the Court of Masiano, have examined . . . touched her vagina . . . put a finger . . . deflowered . . . hymen broken . . . a while ago, not recently . . . my experience . . . fifteen years."

I waited there on the table until the court was adjourned, looked that notary dead in the eye, and dared him to lift one scornful eyebrow at me over that hook of a nose.

Papa and I were all the way home with our door closed before either of us said a word. "If Mama were here, you'd have been ashamed."

"I'm ashamed now."

"Of what? Your daughter lying there for all the world to see, or yourself?"

He shook his head, like a dog shaking off water.

"*Madre di Dio*, what's going to be next?" I said.

"But it proves it, don't you see? The damages I claimed."

"I am not a painting," I shouted. "I'm a person! Your daughter."

He tipped over a jar of brushes, gathered his painting things, and left. Just like that. Off to paint in Cardinal Borghese's Casino of the Muses in the Palazzo Pallavicini where he had been working with Agostino before the trial. Like it was any other day. As if nothing had happened. As if there would be no consequences.

I didn't want to be there when he came back. I put on my short gray cape and, as I left, I pulled the hood over my head even though the heat shimmered up from the ground ahead of me. On the way down Via del Babuino to Piazza di Spagna, I kept my head down so our apothecary might not recognize me from the door of his shop. Going up the Pincian hill, I straddled the ruts and avoided loose stones as I made a wide arc around the shiftless men who always lounged on this steep course between city and church. They'd be the first to shout some epithet at me. Toward the top of the hill, I climbed more slowly, up to the twin bell towers of Santa Trinità dei Monti.

Breathing heavily, I turned at the church and went up the long stairway next to it, which led to the convent. I pulled the bell rope.

I knew Sister Paola would come to the door. As one of the few Italian nuns in this French convent, it was her job to answer the bell, to sell the medicinal herbs the nuns cultivated, and to communicate with the outside world.

"Ooh, Artemisia! So good to see you." Her smile always reminded me of Cupid's mischievous grin in paintings of classical subjects, but now her face was drawn into worry lines.

"Have you been well?" I asked.

She opened the creaking wooden door to let me into the small anteroom. "As well as God wishes, which is good enough for me." Her voice rose and fell like birdsong. An otherworldliness hung in the air of the convent. I felt myself breathe more easily.

"And the garden? How is it doing?"

"It's glorious this summer. Come and look. Sister Margherita's rosemary and chamomile are in bloom, and my San Giovanni's wort is just about to bud. Sister Graziela's oregano is thick on the stalks and stretching up to God."

Walking behind Paola through the straw

scattered on the flinty stone floor of the cloisters, I noticed her shoes worn down at the heels. A sadness outside my own difficulties made me feel ashamed. Papa should have paid the convent more while I lived here those few years after Mama died.

"We even have lavender hanging to dry in the kitchen. It smells like Heaven itself."

We crossed the rose-colored stucco cloister and went through a corridor to the garden in back. Rows of herbs were in their leafy prime. A nun I didn't know was pinching off blossoms.

"It looks beautiful. Santa Maria must have smiled on it," I said.

"And it's making a little money for the convent too," Sister Paola added impishly, raising her shoulders and eyebrows and plump cheeks all at once.

"Beware of such dangerous forays into worldly enterprises," I said, putting on a stern look.

She giggled. "Oh, I give away the medicinal herbs to people even if they can't pay. True recompense is from the Lord." She smiled sweetly. "Do you want to see Sister Graziela now? We must go to vespers soon."

We went back inside. I knew how to find Sister Graziela in the workroom, but I let Sister Paola lead me there.

"Have you given up on me yet?" I asked.

"Certainly not," she said with exaggerated forcefulness. "We believe in miracles here. Someday I'll come to the door and there you will be, saying, 'I am ready now.' And I'll take you in to our holy sisterhood, and we'll all send up a *grazie a Dio*."

It might be easy coming here forever, slipping out of the world unnoticed, letting the trial go on without me, never having to face that beast of a judge, that sneering notary who pretended he was just doing his job, never having to fear encountering Tuzia or Agostino on the street. And Papa — I'd make him miss me.

Sister Graziela was alone, sitting on a tall stool by the narrow window where a shaft of pale honey-colored light shone on her cheeks and the tip of her pointed nose. Dust motes floated around her in a golden swirl. Her black habit and white cowl framed her unlined, oval face which glowed with contentment and absorption. Her downward gaze was fixed on painting the border of a page. She reminded me of Mary in Michelangelo's marble *Pietà* in St. Peter's. Like Mary, she was lost in peaceful thought, and, like Mary, she was beautiful to me.

She had placed the oyster shells I had given her years ago along the edge of her worktable. Each shell held pigments of the most glorious, pure, saturated colors — dark red madder, bright vermilion, the deep ultramarine blue of crushed lapis lazuli, the yellow of saffron, and a green as bright as spring parsley. It made me happy that she still used them.

She looked up. "Artemisia! Bless you for coming. I've longed to see you."

She motioned for me to bring over a low stool. She was illuminating a page with delicate vines and tendrils tied in intricate, loose knots and studded with bright red blossoms.

I could do that, sitting here with Graziela. If I lived here forever, I could do whole books. The convent would become famous for its illuminated manuscripts.

"It's lovely. I like the yellow bird."

"It's a Psalter for Cardinal Bellarmino, that hammer of the heretics who crushes anyone with an idea of his own. People don't make these books by hand much anymore, but this is a gift from the convent. We're hoping he'll take a moment from his Holy Inquisitions to pay attention to our request for roof repair. For years we've had buckets in our upstairs cells to catch the rain."

She waited for Sister Paola to leave. "I get so little done every day, just the smallest section." Her voice dropped to a whisper. "Always, it seems, it's time to go to Office just when I get absorbed in the work. Sometimes from one week to the next, it seems I've done nothing."

"I have something to tell you."

She laid down the tiniest brush I had ever seen and placed her hand gently on my arm. "We have known it."

"The trial?"

"Even though we're cloistered, the convent walls would have to be thick indeed for such a tale not to find its way in. We have been greatly grieved."

"You know everything?"

"We know more than we need to. Are you all right?"

I brought my hands out from under the cape. They were still swollen and oozing under the stained bandages.

She gasped. "Poor lamb. Where was your father when this happened?"

"He let them. He said it would prove my innocence if I kept to my testimony while the cords were on. I don't know which was worse, my hands or . . . today. Today they had two midwives examine me, you know where, with a notary watching. I know people could see through the curtain. They wanted to show me lying that way."

"Dio ti salvi." She held me and I laid my head on her lap. "It's just another way to break any woman who accuses a man. They are without conscience."

"They're beasts, all of them," I wailed into her habit.

"They may be, but they cannot destroy you." She cradled me, stroking the back of my head and my hair, letting me cry.

"My own papa let them."

"Cara mia," she crooned. "Fathers aren't always fatherly. They may try, but many fail. They're only mortal."

I turned my head to one side, and saw that my dress was smeared with the midwives' grease. I pulled it away from Graziela's black wool and noticed her shoes were as worn as Paola's.

"There is no way in to the fortress of the soul," she murmured. "Our Heavenly Father is the guard thereof. He does not betray us. Remember that, Artemisia. Though they might make you a victim, they cannot make you a sinner."

I could only sob.

"Paint it out of you, *carissima*. Paint out the pain until there's none left. Don't take on shame from their mockery. That's what they want. They want you to shrivel up and die, and you know why?"

41

I shook my head in her lap.

"Because your talent is a threat. Promise me — don't pray as a penitent when you have no need to be one. Don't plead. Approach the Lord with dignity, and affirm His goodness. No matter what."

"He abandoned me."

"Then love Him all the more. That will please Him most."

"But everybody thinks —"

"Don't care a fig for what they think. The world is larger than Rome, Artemisia. Remember that. Think of your *Susanna and the Elders*. When that painting becomes famous, the whole world will know your innocence."

"How?"

"Because in that painting you showed her intimidation at the lewd looks of those two men, her vulnerability and fear. It shows you understood her struggle against forces beyond her control. Beyond her control, Artemisia."

"You remember all that?"

"I'll never forget it. Her face averted and her arms raised, fending off their menace? The night after you brought it here, her face was blazing in my dreams. By the way you had her turn from that leering elder shushing her so she wouldn't cry out and reveal them, I knew then that you were being threatened."

"I painted that before it happened."

"Yes, but I could tell you were suffering some menace just as Susanna was. That's the brilliance of your skill, to have a masterpiece reflect your own feelings and experience."

"I can't even hold a brush now."

"You will. Nothing can stop you from bringing your talent to fruition. You are young yet. Never forget that the world needs to know what you have to show them."

"The world. What does the world care? The world is full of cruelty." I touched the rough edge of one of the oyster shells. "If I stayed in here with you, the world wouldn't matter."

"Artemisia." The word rang with a tone of authority. "One doesn't live a cloistered life to get away from something. One lives here to serve God because one feels an undeniable voice calling. Any other reason is illegitimate."

"I might discover a calling."

"You already have. Your art."

The bell rang for vespers which meant I had to go.

She walked me out through the cloister, stopped at the well in the center, and spoke softly. "You do not want to live where all you ever see is the same nine arches in each arcade, the same few frescoes, the same scraggly pear tree, the same crucifix every day for the rest of your life." She walked toward the tree and twisted a yellow-green pear until it came loose in her hand. "Here. Remember what I said as you eat it. You have your calling already. Don't pray as a penitent over someone else's sin. See yourself as God made you."

"Have you ever felt abandoned by God?"

Her chin pulled back a little, the only hint of her surprise. A disturbance passed over her face that I had never seen before.

"By God and man."

Outside the convent at the top of the stairs, I stopped to feel the wind in my face. There was something light and purifying about being up this high. After a few moments I heard the sisters singing the Magnificat which I loved. "My soul doth magnify the Lord." Sister Paola had taught me what the Latin words meant when I'd had my first lady's blood.

Before that, when Mother had told me I would bleed periodically, I thought she meant it would be God punishing me for pushing her away after I'd seen her in bed

44

that way with Papa. Later, in the convent when my first blood came, I was sure it was God reprimanding me for my unforgiving nature. I prayed to our Lady to forgive me for treating her that way. The blood still came, gushing like the Red Sea. I ran to Sister Paola thinking that I was dying, and told her everything. She said the blood was part of blessed womanhood just like forgiveness was, and that I didn't need to be afraid. She told me how the angel came to Mary and said, "Fear not, Mary, for thou hast found favor with God." Sister Paola said I had found favor too, because I was contrite, and then she taught me the Magnificat. Repeating the words to remember them, I had felt them all the way down to where the blood flowed. My soul doth magnify the Lord, just like Mary's soul. My soul, even my little soul makes the Lord more magnificent by something I had to offer. Maybe that's what Graziela meant today by my calling.

This late in the day the *ponentino* cooled the leaden air and ruffled my hair, and I imagined it coming all the way from Spain, skimming across the Mediterranean and up the valley of the Tiber to bless me here, high above the city's pulsing heat. Here the coarseness of the city couldn't crush me.

From the piazza at the base of the hill, streets spread out in three directions. The Via dei Condotti stretched straight ahead, lined with four-story buildings of pale peach and Roman ochre. Farther away the street did get narrower and the buildings shorter, just like Agostino had said they would when he taught me perspective, until street and buildings all came together at a vanishing point far away.

Why had I thought of him? I plunged down the steep path into the thick of streets and people.

When I turned onto Via della Croce, a woman I didn't know stood waiting near our house. She was as stiff as a Vatican guard, dressed in deep green with a black sash. As I came abreast of her, she said in a hoarse whisper, "Do not love him."

Another scandal monger. I turned my shoulder to her and she followed me to my door. I walked with a straight back, looking ahead only.

"I am Agostino's sister," she said behind me. "Listen to me."

I stopped.

She came up next to me. "I saw what they did to you today in court. I'm sorry."

I looked around to see if anyone heard.

"Do not love him," she said again.

"*Love* him!"

"He's been a scoundrel since the day he was born. He raped a woman in Lucca so that she was forced to marry him."

"He's married?"

"That didn't stop him from making a mistress of his wife's sister. And now he's hired two murderers to kill that same wife so he could marry you. As one woman to another, do not believe a word from him."

3

Agostino

One night when Papa was out, our neighbor Giovanni Stiattesi and I left the house after dark. We traveled without a torch and took only small streets, avoiding Piazza Navona and any torchlit doorways where music poured out. Papa might be in any of them.

Giovanni and Porzia had convinced me to see Agostino in the prison of Corte Savella. I thought maybe I could find out whether what his sister said was true. "You could tell him to his face," Giovanni had said with narrowed eyes, "he's a son of a whore." That was exactly what I needed to do, to see if I had the strength to kill him with words. Then I could trust myself to paint Judith killing with a sword.

We crossed the Tiber at Ponte Sisto in utter blackness, smelling the river beneath us. Giovanni held onto my wrist so as not to hurt my hands, which I'd left uncovered for Agostino to see, and with his other hand, Giovanni felt the stone balustrade.

"Why are you doing this for me?" I asked. Papa had told me once that Giovanni himself was a jilted lover of Agostino and his anger would serve our cause. He meant in pleading our case in court, though, not in a clandestine errand like this.

"I have no love for that man. You've been wronged. Reasons enough."

He led me through streets he knew to the back of the prison, and slipped the guard a coin. I waited in a stone corridor under a torch. The dank passageway smelled of burning tar. No one came for a long time and I began to pace. Finally, Agostino ducked through the door at the far end and swaggered toward me with his broad shoulders, open arms and exaggerated smile, like a warm host greeting an old friend.

"Artemisia, you've finally come! I've been waiting, dying for you a little every day." His voice echoed in the corridor with false sweetness. "*Amore,* I will marry you if you recant. I promised you then, and I will do it now."

"You think I came here for that? To marry a man who dishonored me?"

49

His dark eyes widened in arrogant surprise. "There would be no dishonor if you marry me. It will save you."

"You mean it will save *you*. Do you think I want to be married to a lecher? A scoundrel? A reprobate?"

"You know I love you. Remember all I taught you? You owe me something."

"Don't deceive yourself. I learned nothing from you I couldn't learn with my own eyes."

"How can you say that?"

"Because you can't paint people. You'll never last. You'll be forgotten the day you die, which won't be soon enough."

That got him. He was searching for what to say. "Then at least blame someone else. Say I wasn't the first so they'll drop the charges."

"I could slice your neck in two and the Holy Virgin would clap her hands."

"Say it was Quorli. He's dead now. How can it hurt?"

"What do you know of hurt?" I held up my hands with crusted blood lines around the base of each finger and raw, festering wounds between them. "These are the wedding rings you gave me. You sat there and let them do this, and yet you say you love me?"

He winced at the sight. "Believe me, I

didn't want to hurt you."

"Or the woman you married? You didn't want to hurt her either? Just strangle her kindly? With a rope and an apology?"

Agostino backed away in shock. Ridges formed across his forehead and his eyes sprang wide open. It was true, then.

"You're a monster and a murderer."

"Artemisia —"

"Bastard!"

I whirled around to leave, feeling blood surging to my fingertips, energizing me.

The next morning, I started *Judith Slaying Holofernes*. I could barely bend my fingers to grasp the egg-shaped muller to pulverize the pigments on my marble slab. Pain is not important. I have to ignore it, I told myself. Only painting is important. Paint out the pain, Graziela had said.

I couldn't keep my thumb in the hole of the palette so I put a stool on top of a chair to have the palette up high and close by. The smears of color made me breathe faster. Steeling myself against the pull of my skin when I held a brush, I swirled the shiny wetness of pure ultramarine onto my palette and added a touch of soot black to darken it for Judith's sleeves. Then, awkwardly, I took a stroke to rough it in, sketching with paint.

My heart quaked. I felt alive again.

Every day as soon as I woke up, I threw on my painting gown over my night shift, thrust my feet into my old mules, and painted from the first light, before hawkers shouting behind their creaking carts and old men arguing in the street distracted me. I loved those quiet morning hours stolen from the spectacle in court and I dreaded Papa telling me it was time to stop on the days I had to go.

I was frustrated that my hands wouldn't do what I needed them to. Holding the brush between straight fingers, I tried to work by moving my wrist instead of my fingers. Sometimes I lost control and the brush slipped out of my hand. For weeks, after court each day, Papa went to Cardinal Borghese's Casino of the Muses to work on the ceiling fresco, and I raced home to paint again until the late dark of summer evenings, fired by the thought that both Judith and I were involved in an act of retribution.

One day I painted two vertical furrows between Judith's brows, like Caravaggio had done to show that it was hard for Judith to kill, but then in court the next day, Agostino glared at me threateningly now that I knew he was a murderer. Back home that afternoon I painted the furrows out.

I wanted to catch Holofernes the instant he knew he was about to die, like Agostino's face when I had called him a murderer. I wanted ridges across his forehead, his eyes wide open, fixed in shock, but still conscious, the white showing below his pupils. I loaded my brush with sable brown. I had to bend my fingers to hold the brush tighter in order to have the control to do the fine edge around the pupils. Scabs cracked open, but I kept on working, loving what was appearing on the canvas — those dark, terrified eyes pleading at me.

When I drew my hand away, a few drops of blood had landed on the white bedcovers of Holofernes's bed. The deep brilliant red against the white thrilled me. I squeezed out more blood, feeling pleasure in the pain, and let it fall below his head, mixed vermilion and madder to match the red, and added more. Streams of it. A deep crimson waterfall soaking into luxurious, tufted bedcovers. Like the blood soaking my sleeve in court. Or the blood I had tried to staunch after the first rape. A smear of blood across Judith's knuckles too. If Rome craved spectacle, then I would give them spectacle.

4

The Verdict

The morning the verdict was to be announced, I opened the door to the street to buy bread from the baker's boy, and there, leaning up against the house, was a painting wrapped in a dirty cloth. I brought it inside and unwrapped it. "Papa! The stolen painting!"

"Are you sure?" He rushed into the room and grabbed it from my hands. "It could be a copy." He took it into the light, scrutinized the brush strokes, and saw something he recognized. "The very one. This changes everything. Hurry. We've got to get there early!" He threw on a sleeveless doublet over his shirt as he strode out the door.

We arrived at the Tor di Nona before the doors were open so we had to wait outside under that horrible noose, smelling the foul-ness of the Tiber's stagnant water. All summer and into the fall and not a drop of rain. Clouds of mosquitoes billowed up from the river.

Once inside, Papa demanded to see the Locumtenente. He pressed a coin into the bailiff's palm. "Before court convenes, if you please." Without a change of expression, the bailiff left. "You'll see now how things are done," Papa said. His pacing irritated me. The bailiff returned and ushered him down a corridor. I tried to follow but a guard stepped in my way and directed me back to the courtroom where people were being admitted. I took my usual seat.

The notary arrived, so prim and cold it made me sick. With his lips pursed, he began trimming his pens. Agostino was led in, and then immediately called back. Then the notary was called out too. People in the courtroom murmured and grew restless, arguing their predictions. I tried to shut out their gloating voices.

Only Porzia and Giovanni Stiattesi in the front row were silent. Porzia lifted her chin to give me courage. Giovanni picked at a sore on his lip. When he had testified a few weeks earlier, he revealed all that Agostino's sister had told me. Agostino had denied it, saying that his wife had disappeared. Giovanni insisted. Porzia testified the same. Nevertheless, the trial had gone on, sucking in more witnesses — other neighbors, Papa's plasterer, the apothecary from whom we bought our pigments, and a host of Agostino's friends all claiming to have had me. I'd had to deny each testimony, pierce the charade of one falsehood after another that tried to make my character the issue and not Agostino's deed. And Rome enjoyed it all.

A mosquito kept buzzing near my ear and I couldn't get rid of it. The room was stifling with all those people, and the wooden chair I sat in seemed much harder than it had before. Someone in the back shouted for court to begin. Others joined.

"Guilty. Hang him," someone shouted.

"Hang the whore," another voice bellowed.

"Hang them both together."

The whole room laughed. My face flushed hot, and I felt dizzy and faint in the airless room.

A door opened and the bailiff entered, then the Locumtenente, Papa, Agostino, and the notary. The court fell silent. Sweat dampened my shift.

I held my back rigid as His Lordship spoke. "In the foregoing case of Orazio

Gentileschi, painter, versus Agostino Tassi, painter imprisoned in Corte Savella, not disputing the claim and testimony of the girl Artemisia Gentileschi that she has been raped repeatedly by Signor Tassi, whereas the missing painting has been returned, and whereas the plaintiff has consented, and whereas the accused has already served gaol for eight months during the proceedings, the prisoner is pardoned. Case dismissed."

Shouts pulsed in my ears. Approval or outrage, I couldn't tell.

"However," the Locumtenente raised his voice, "due to his interference with the true and honest testimony of witnesses, the defendant Agostino Tassi is banished from Rome."

Pardoned? Did I hear that right, buried in all those words? I was struck dumb. *Whereas the plaintiff has consented* . . . Had Papa withdrawn the charge now that he'd gotten his painting back? Had he *allowed* Agostino to be pardoned? Blood rushed up to my ears and fury seethed in me. I levelled at that man who was my father a hateful look he'd never forget. He had no conscience, no honor, no concern for anyone but himself. I'd never call him Papa again. He would never hear me say the word he loved.

Numb, barely knowing what I was doing,

I pushed my way through the crowd. My skirt was stepped on. I yanked it free. Stumbling out the door into an inferno of glare, I turned in the opposite direction from home and lost myself in unfamiliar streets. I kept hearing the Locumtenente's words: *The prisoner is pardoned.* Heat waved up from the street. I passed the Forum and the Palatino. *Pardoned.* Free.

Banishment. That was ludicrous. Gratuitous. All Agostino needed was Cardinal Borghese to state that his ceiling was unfinished. Agostino could have sanctuary in the cardinal's residence. Banishment meant nothing in this city run by the pope. All that humiliation for nothing. *Not disputing the claim* . . . Small vindication, unheard in the roar of the pardon. There had been no statement of my innocence, no reparation of any kind. In the public eye, I was still a stained woman. What had I thought? That I'd be able to walk out of there as pure as Santa Maria?

Putting one foot dully before the other, I walked all the way to the southern edge of the city, to the Porta Appia, through the arch and out the Via Appia into the open countryside. Cicadas made their metallic scraping hiss, like an irritating ringing in the ear. Houses were abandoned. The stucco had fallen away, showing bricks and stones beneath. Arches led nowhere. Broken walls and sunken tombs were overgrown with anemone, blue cornflowers and orange poppies. It was a fantasy of ruin, a life lost in every stone.

I sat on a crumbling wall under the shade of a tall umbrella pine and tried to rub the ache out of my back. A thundercloud billowed on the horizon. Oh, why didn't it just come here and wash everything away — me, Papa, Agostino, the Tor di Nona, Rome itself. A smooth, white stone with a vein of sparkle glinted through the dust on its surface. I picked it up to throw, but I didn't know where to hurl it. What would a single stone do against the universe?

I kicked sand over an anthill and watched the blind frenzy of creatures of no consequence. Hundreds, thousands of ants — they reminded me of the thousands of nameless, hapless legionnaires who had marched to war on this road centuries ago, had fought and lay waiting to die, their parched lips unnoticed in greater pain. They were persons of no consequence. Armies dying like ants, ants dying like armies — it was all pitiful. Bigger things than my own life had happened here, and smaller.

I remembered a legend Sister Graziela

had told me about Christ walking here. Peter, fleeing Rome, had asked him, *"Domine, quo vadis?"* and Christ had answered, "I am going to Rome to be crucified a second time." Shamed, Peter turned back to face his own martyrdom, maybe from this very spot. I'd have to turn back too. I closed my eyes and breathed slower to let the new truth settle and find a spot to live in me — how hard the world was going to make me.

Graziela had said I might have to wait until my *Susanna and the Elders* would be famous for Rome to know my innocence. It might never be famous. I spat on the stone to get off the powdery film and started back, looking for Peter's footprints on the dusty cobbles.

I went to Santa Trinità instead of home, and found Graziela weeding in the herb garden behind the cloister. I bent down to help her, though I hardly knew which were plants and which were weeds. She didn't make me tell her about the trial. Her calmness helped to settle me. Finally I asked, "In the story of Susanna, what happened to the old men? When Susanna resisted and they spread the false rumor about her adultery . . . ?"

"She was brought to trial and convicted because the elders claimed they saw her fornicate with a young man in a garden." Graziela sat back on a low wooden box and brushed the dirt off her hands. "She was sentenced to death, but at the last minute Daniel demanded to know, of each elder separately, under what tree in the garden had she committed adultery. One of the elders said it was an oak, and the other said it was a mastic. That proved that at least one of them was lying. They were both put to death for false testimony."

"And so Susanna was saved?"

"Yes." Graziela put the weeds in a pile and we rinsed our hands in the stone water basin. "And you? What has happened for you?"

"There was no Daniel. I'll have to wait until my Susanna becomes famous."

The tiniest breath of a sigh escaped her, and her dark eyebrows came closer together. Her mouth was puckered in an unpleasant expression, and her jaw protruded from her wimple farther than I'd ever noticed. We walked back through the cloisters, our heads down, thinking.

I could say it. Right now I could say it — that I felt a calling. I wouldn't have to go back. Graziela would tell Sister Paola and she would burst into song. I smiled inside at the thought of her excitement. But a life of painting tiny tendrils on the margins of prayer books — without boldness, without interpretation, without drama — that wasn't for me.

When the great bell rang for vespers, Graziela stopped and pulled back her shoulders. Her fist clenched the crucifix on her rosary. "Though it would pain me not to have you visit, you might have to leave Rome. If you do, don't go out of any sense that you're being hounded out of the city. Go because the city is too small for your genius."

"Here." I put the stone in her hand with the crucifix. "I found it on the Via Appia. Maybe near where Peter saw Christ. It's smooth enough to burnish the gold on the pages of the Psalter for your cardinal."

We stood in the darkened anteroom and held each other for a long moment.

I went directly home.

"I can't live with you," I said when I came in the door.

"Artemisia, where have you been? I was worried. You can't just go wandering around the city by yourself."

"What does it matter now that my reputation's ruined?"

He had already hung the painting in the

main room and was sitting opposite it, drinking wine, his feet in velvet slippers on mother's cushioned footstool.

"I can't live with you as if nothing has happened, the painting back on the wall in a happy household. You betrayed me! My own father. You took away any chance to restore my virtue."

He scowled. "No. I —"

"Getting a painting back was more important to you than my honor. To you, I'm a person of no consequence."

"That's not true." His hand trembled. Some wine spilled on the table.

"Agostino's free now. How do you think I'll feel here at home while you go off every day to paint with him for some cardinal who pays no attention to legal judgments?"

"I thought you wanted it to be over."

"It won't *be* over. Not with Agostino pardoned. That doesn't exonerate me. It's impossible for me even to stay in Rome."

"In time, Artemisia —"

"Do you think I want to face neighbors and shopkeepers every day who believe that pack of liars in court? What kind of life will I have here being a target for chamber pots being emptied?" He reached out to hold my arm. I pulled away. "You think about that until the food runs out. Don't assume I'm going to face ridicule and scorn every time I go out to shop for food for my dearest papa."

"Artemisia, don't be foolish. It's just a brief unpleasantness."

"It won't be brief unless you do something." I gave him a long, cold look. "You have some amends to make."

He looked shaken, and spread his hands out on the table. "I . . . I'll arrange something."

5

Sister Graziela

Pietro Antonio di Vincenzo Stiattesi, Giovanni Stiattesi's brother from Florence, counted the coin of my dowry on the tavern table in the Borgo across the Tiber where Papa thought we'd be less known. I felt like a bartered goat. This stranger who was soon to be my husband didn't even look at me standing at the edge of the room, so I stole a few glances at him. His boot hose sagged and his codpiece cords were leather, not silk. I had never seen a codpiece except in paintings. They weren't in fashion anymore. What was he doing wearing one? If these marriage clothes were his best, I understood immediately why Father had been able to arrange this marriage of convenience. The dowry.

It was borrowed from the state dowry fund, he'd said, and from someone else. He wouldn't tell me who. If it were anyone else, he'd tell me. Like creeping ice in my veins, I realized that the money for the dowry must have been part of the negotiations behind closed doors while I and the Roman rabble had waited for a verdict. To be married with Agostino's money turned my stomach sour.

"My brother will be good to you. He is a painter," Giovanni whispered next to me.

"No proof of goodness in that," I whispered back, then felt shame for my rudeness. I knew better. I should be grateful.

With a hand calloused by the resting of a palette, Giovanni's brother swept the coins off the table into his pouch, and finally looked at me. His face was not unpleasant, slightly pocked and longer than his brother Giovanni's, with dark eyes set deeply in his head. I liked his dark curls. His small mouth had a tendency to move sideways. Perhaps in the years ahead I could take joy in such a mouth. I felt a small measure of relief. Some daughters, unwanted daughters, were married off to disfigured men, or old, crippled widowers. He smiled at me and I quickly smiled back. It reassured me for the moment. In such marriages as this, was love ever possible?

I thought of my marriage *cassone*, packed

and waiting in the carriage. Father had given me his tacking hammer and had told me to choose a few of Mother's things. I'd picked her yellow and blue faience pitcher and washing bowl, her bloodstone hair ornament mounted in gold with a pearl drop, her small onyx perfume bottle, her carved wooden memento box, one of a matched pair with Father's, and a brass oil lamp shaped with the figure of Diana whom the Greeks call Artemis, goddess of chastity. As an afterthought, I had packed Mother's dagger. She'd always kept it under her bed for protection when Father stayed out late at night. I didn't know what kind of a man this Pietro Antonio was.

A year ago when I'd assumed I would marry Agostino, I had painted on the *cassone* a scene of a wedding feast — a celebration I wouldn't have now. The *impalmamento*, the Mass of the Union, and the *nozze* were all to happen on the same day. There would be no banquet with crab apples, capons in white sauce, no tarts or marzipan, no wine, no toasts in our blushing honor, no music, no dancing, no happy friends bringing sweetmeats and wishing us well, laughing, teasing, saying pretty things, ushering us to the bedchamber and then reappearing at morning to learn that all was paradise. None of it. By noon my fate would be sealed.

There was just enough time, if I took the carriage. I grabbed my cloak and sidled to the door. "I'll meet you at the church. Santo Spirito."

"Artemisia! Where are you going? You can't leave here," Father said, but I was out the door.

"The convent of Santa Trinità," I told the driver.

Under the cold wet breath of gray clouds, I waited at the convent door. A pair of morning doves cooing softly went about their explorations together on the stairs. It was sweet how they pecked and explored but always stayed close to each other.

Paola opened the door.

"May I see Sister Graziela?" I asked with some urgency.

"She's in the church."

"Praying?"

"No. Cleaning. Come through here."

I entered the church through a side door near the altar. The air was cool, still, and waiting. I found Graziela scrubbing the stone floor behind the altar. "Your way of life certainly keeps you on your knees," I said.

"Oh, Artemisia, you scared me. I thought I was alone."

"Do you have to do the whole church?"

"Only behind the balustrade. Agility and humility go hand in hand, you know." She moved the bucket away from where she was working. "As well he should. What do you know of the man?"

"Only that he's a painter. From Florence."

"And you will go there?"

"Yes, today. They're waiting at Santo Spirito right now."

"Better soon than later."

"I thought I wanted this, but now I'm afraid. All desire I'd ever imagined has been sucked out of me."

"Not forever. It doesn't go away forever."

"How can I . . . I don't even want to be touched."

"As long as you hold on to your pain, you'll live a mean, bitter life. Leave it in Rome."

I felt uncomfortable standing while she was kneeling so I crouched before the sacristy steps. "Can I ask you a question?"

"You know you can ask anything. Softly. Someone may come in."

"What did you mean, abandoned by God and man?"

She dried the area with a rag and moved back to do more. "I was married once, but my husband died."

"I didn't know. I'm sorry."

"According to the law of forty days, the house we lived in was seized by my husband's brother forty days after my husband died, so I had to leave. When I went back to live at home, my father said he had no money to keep me." She scrubbed more vigorously. "He tried to find an old widower for me, but couldn't." Her voice dropped. "Because I wasn't a virgin."

"What did you do?"

"You can guess, can't you? I wasn't good enough for any man, so I was given to God."

Still on her knees, she scrubbed some more, talking to the floor and her scrub brush. "Piece by piece, I sold all I had for my dowry which I gave to the convent. All my clothes, some fine dishes and glassware, silver spoons and knives, pots, bed linens, pewter goblets, jewelry, a painting I loved." She stopped and leaned back on her heels. "It was of Venus and Adonis in a garden. Not by anyone important, but I miss it. I pleaded with my father to use the money for my keep. He protested that it wouldn't last my lifetime. So, when there were no more things to sell, I entered the convent as a postulant."

"You said once that you shouldn't enter a convent unless you felt some calling."

"Yes. True. But I didn't say when I learned that."

"Oh." That changed everything I knew about her. "Did you have any children?"

"No. We were married only five hundred and twenty-six days."

"How did he die so young?"

"You will have me tell all, won't you? Let it be a lesson, then."

She carried her bucket and scrub brush and rags to the sacristy step and sat down. She motioned for me to do the same. I was surprised because it was a disrespectful thing to do. The coldness of the stone seeped through my skirt.

Her eyes, every shade of olive green and gray, with amber lights, seemed to deepen, as though they were seeing many things again. "I loved my husband, and moved in earthly heaven in his presence. He had a lover. I like to think, even now, that it was someone he knew before he married me, but that may not be so. I existed only when he touched me, and waited, breathing somehow, for the next soft word."

"Did you stop loving him?"

"No. If it's really love, it doesn't change when you find out. Everything — eating, sleeping, waking, watching the rain — everything becomes shaded because you

71

know. You still have walks in the country and nights of love, but they're darkened by what's unspoken."

"So what happened?"

Graziela wrung out the wet rag into the bucket of dirty water, twisting the cloth with a force I'd never seen in her before. "The husband of his lover found out, and killed him. Dragged him into the Tiber, where all such men are bound." She stared down at the gray scum on the water. "A loss as vast as Egypt," she whispered.

"I had no idea. You seem so . . . peaceful."

"One can achieve that." She stood and lifted her bucket and brush and rags. "I'll be right back. Wait for me in the third chapel on the right." She pointed. "Volterre's fresco of the Assumption is there. Take a good look. I just learned that the standing figure in the long red *lucco* on the right is Michelangelo."

She'd been married, I thought as I walked down the nave. I'd known her since I was twelve, yet this I'd never known. No wonder she was different than the other nuns.

I looked through the wooden grating into the third chapel, and in the fresco there a man did wear a red cloak that hung straight to the ground. He had white hair, a white beard, and intelligent brown eyes. "Michelangelo," I whispered. He was not looking up in astonishment as the Virgin in blue was taken up to Heaven as the other figures were. He was looking out at me with an expression of tender concern, looking into me even, giving me a kind of benediction. I was going to his city to live and learn among his works. Below his full sleeve, his hand was gnarled and scarred from chisels. Love surged up in me for those hands. Even a scarred hand can bring forth greatness. There was a connection between us, between our spirits, I dared to think. No man might ever see it, but there, in the silent church, God could, if He wanted to, bless a union of souls.

Graziela found me. "Sister Paola is coming to say goodbye. I only have a minute." She reached deeply into her sleeve and drew out a tiny muslin bag. She untied the drawstring and tipped into her palm two gold earrings, each with a large creamy *perla barocca,* the luster covering a gnarled surface like a whorled walnut. "Imperfect. Like humans," she whispered. "I know it's vanity. I should have sold them with the rest of my things to give a larger dowry to the convent. Marcello gave them to me on our wedding day."

"How did you keep them all these years?"

She chuckled thoughtfully. "Nine years. It hasn't been easy. Sewn inside my underclothing most of the time. Once I had to keep them in the toe of my shoe."

She lifted one and let it dangle a moment. "If the beauties of the world were going to be denied me, then these, at least, would not be."

"The world in a pearl," I said.

I thought how the pearl's surface was secreted with infinite slowness to protect the live oyster from chafing and inflammation, like Graziela's serene calmness year by year smoothing but not completely hiding the rough territory within.

She laid one of the earrings in my hand. It felt warm against my palm. "I don't need but one," she said. "You can pin the other one on a dress."

"Graziela, no. I can't take it."

"Yes, you can. Let it remind you," she whispered. "Do not lose yourself completely to man or God. Do not delude yourself. You cannot afford to believe in illusion — for the sake of your happiness and for the sake of your art. As for the sake of your soul, trust that to me. I have many hours to pray, and it grows tiresome praying for one's own soul." She closed my hand around the earring. "You have work to do."

"Yes, I have work to do."

"Hide it under your bodice now, and remember, the real principles of living are not all in the Scriptures. They are in blood ties, histories, sayings, innuendoes, surreptitious looks, clandestine agreements, and hot clasped hands. When you learn to recognize them, life will become easier, rich in opportunities and rewards. Be wise, Artemisia. Be watchful. Look in their faces and show no fear."

I looked in her face now, and said her words over again in my mind. Their importance made them toll like deep bells that I knew would echo in the years ahead.

Sister Paola came hurrying down the nave, her short legs moving fast, her fingers on her cheeks, her face alive in a hundred expressions of joy.

"Ooh, Artemisia! I was afraid I missed you. Sister Graziela told me! I'm so happy, I could touch Heaven with a finger."

"I'm sorry to disappoint you, Sister Paola," I teased.

"I told you we believe in miracles."

"Because I'm getting married?"

"Because you'll be in the art center of the world. For you, what could be better?"

"That's generous of you."

They walked me to the door and Sister

Paola put the sign of the cross on my forehead with her warm finger, her cherubic face made even rounder with her happiness. Graziela held me by the shoulders and touched her forehead to mine. We stood there together awhile, our heads touching, our feelings pulsing breast to breast.

"You're doing that for my sake," Sister Paola said. "The only time her head will touch a wimple." We laughed a little, sadly. "Remember us, *tesoro*," Paola said.

"Locked close to my heart." I touched my bosom where I'd hidden the pearl. Graziela couldn't speak.

I pushed open the heavy door. It had begun to rain lightly, and I lifted the hood of my cloak. As the door was closing, I heard Graziela's soft, desperate cry, "Write and tell us what everything looks like."

I started down the stairs.

Sister Graziela was still grieving. After nine years. When had she discovered he had a lover? What surreptitious look had she passed over? In what private moment of horror had she happened to piece together bits of strange behavior, a stuttered answer, a shifted glance, an errand forgotten? Had she looked him in the face? The first meal she made for him after she realized — was it prepared with the same care as the one be-

76

fore? Had he once loved the sheen and heft of her hair, and did she cry when the sisters sheared it? Were such losses in my path too? If I remembered her words and watched enough, would I be spared the same — a life of contemplation and sacrifice and endless acts of humility?

All the way back to the church I held Graziela's still-raw heart in my hand like a relic.

6

Pietro

The carriage wheels clattered across the Tiber on Ponte Sant' Angelo where a row of eighteen gallows led to the fortress and prison of Sant' Angelo. Eighteen, the age I was when I went to trial. I was barely nineteen now. I wrapped the single earring in a handkerchief and hid it beneath the lining of my *cassone*.

I found Father pacing in front of the church. "What do you mean running off like that? Where did you go?" he demanded.

"To see the sisters. It's all right. I'm not late."

I gave my cloak to Porzia to hold. Father held my arm tightly and we marched down the dark nave and into a small side chapel lit by four candles.

I felt separated from myself during the

mass, as if I were a passerby witnessing something tawdry. I was seized by a longing for my mother, for her soft touch on the back of my head, her sad singing. It would have settled her to know I was married. Porzia smiled at me in an encouraging way, and I tried to make my face properly cheerful, demure and grateful, but the stone church was so cold that without my cloak on I shivered uncontrollably.

The Latin words of the priest passed over me in a blur of low tones which made me feel there was something furtive about what we were doing. I repeated the vows and tried to think about them, but when the priest came to "as long as you both shall live," I realized that these were the same words Graziela must have said. I could hardly get them out. I looked in Pietro Antonio's face as she told me to. His expression was serious, but without the tenderness of Michelangelo in his red *lucco* looking through me to touch my soul.

After it was over, Porzia put my cloak over my shoulders. "I'll miss you," she said softly.

"I feel like a part of my life is over," I said only loud enough for her to hear.

"A new life is about to begin for you.

Don't worry. Pierantonio's a good man," she whispered.

"I hope to God you're right."

Rain dripped down my neck, but still I hesitated before stepping up into the coach where the *cassone* had been transferred. Father flung his hands up, vexed by my faltering moment. I was only waiting for some affectionate gesture from him.

"Get in, get in," he said, and slipped me a small blue drawstring bag, weighty in my hand. I hid it in the folds of my skirt as I stepped into the coach. I noticed tight lines around his eyes and realized this was a hard moment for him. "I'll write to Michelangelo Buonarotti the Younger about you. Make sure you go see him." He closed the door, the coach lurched ahead, and this Pietro, or this Antonio, and I were off to Florence, where, I thought with relief, I would be free of dishonor.

Husband and wife. I kept telling that to myself as the coach headed north through the Porta del Popolo on Via Flaminia and into the countryside of ox carts and puddles. I had a rightful husband. *Madonna benedetta,* let him be kind. We rode facing each other in silence. Should I speak or wait for him to say something first? His unquiet eyes kept looking out the window, so I

80

looked too. What was it that held his interest so? Vineyards with leaves every shade from gold to russet? Orchards of almond trees? Blocky farmhouses behind the thin curtain of rain? Sodden sheep? It was as though landscape was more important than what was right before him. Me.

"What are you looking at?"

"Everything. Nothing. The poplar trees have lost their leaves. We'll have an early winter. It might even snow."

What an odd way to start a marriage. With the weather.

"Do they call you Pietro or Antonio?"

He turned to me at last. "Pierantonio."

"Hmm. Kind of long."

Slowly, he smiled in a wry, intriguing way, on only one side of his face. "So's Artemisia."

"Do you mind if I call you Pietro? I like that best."

"Call me what you'd like."

The need to say more necessary things hung like an iron weight in my chest. "What do you know about me?" I asked.

"I know what happened."

"The story talked about in the streets, or the truth?" I was filled with a burning urge to spill out to him the truth. "I am innocent. Though not a virgin, I *am* innocent."

He nodded, and I was grateful for that. "This man, Agostino —"

"Doesn't deserve the blood in his veins. He's a churl and a scoundrel."

"You were going to marry him?"

"Because I thought I had to. I don't care a pebble's worth about him, but I do care that I am considered innocent by the one man in the world who might matter."

The thought seemed to embarrass him and he turned to look out the window again. I straightened my back. Dignity, I thought. I wanted him to see in me some dignity. A quick movement passed over his lips. Maybe he understood. Or maybe he was merciful, not wishing to make me explain any more. Or maybe it meant that he didn't even care.

"Will we live with your parents?"

"No. They're dead."

"Oh, I'm sorry." I felt like a fool to have said that. I should have asked Porzia ahead of time.

"My uncle took Giovanni and me away to a hill town during the last plague, twelve years ago, but they had to stay. I own their house now."

I thought better than to ask any questions about it.

I grew hungry, but was afraid to mention it. I didn't want to make demands just a few hours into our marriage. I realized with a sinking desperation how completely a married woman gives herself into another's keeping — even to the eating of a morsel of bread. Had Graziela felt that way? Had my mother? It pained me now that I had not talked to my own mother more.

"Giovanni tells me you are a painter," I said after a while.

"I am."

"I am too."

"You?"

"Surely Giovanni told you." I pointed to my rolled-up canvases.

"There were two women painters in Bologna once," he said. "They painted flowers."

"I paint human beings." Curiosity streaked across his pocked face. "Would you like to see?"

Pietro nodded. I held them up and let them unroll in front of me. *Woman Playing a Lute* happened to be on top. He studied the whole canvas. "A graceful hand," he said. I let it slide to the floor and revealed my Susanna, too large a canvas to unroll all the way in the coach. He couldn't see the bottom where Susanna's foot dipped into the water of the stone bath.

"Oh!" His eyes opened wide. My heart beat more strongly now than during the wedding mass. "It's very good," he said with what I took to be mild surprise. He looked at Susanna's face and his expression darkened. "It has a lot of feeling. Her feeling, I mean. When did you paint this?"

"A couple of years ago."

"Before —"

"Yes."

"So young." He was thoughtful a moment, and then said, "You have a fine, subtle blending of color, especially in the flesh tones. As lustrous as glass."

"Do you want to know the secret? Varnish made from amber resin that lutemakers use in Venice. The colors just glide on. One part amber varnish to three parts walnut oil or linseed oil. Combine them over a slow heat and glaze the entire painting after each day's work. Then it's more stable and will dry quicker than oil alone. Glazing with just oil, the colors tend to slide down the canvas and bleed."

His face was tipped down at Susanna's belly but his eyes peered up at me as I looked over the top of the canvas, so the angle of his face gave him a covert, shadowed look.

"How did you learn this?"

"From my father. He just combines a drop of the varnish to each oiled color on his palette. The idea to do the whole canvas is my own."

He made a low, reverberating sound in his throat but it wasn't a word.

"You'll see. The brush doesn't tug as you take a stroke, and the colors are more brilliant. Now you know too." I smiled in what I hoped was a coquettish way. "It's my wedding gift to you."

He didn't smile back. He motioned for me to reveal the third canvas. Judith.

"It's not finished yet," I said, and let the Susanna fall.

He blew air out of his mouth with a "whooff!" His face contorted. "Not quite what I'd want hanging in our bedchamber, but very fine. A difficult composition." I caught his fleeting, astonished smile.

"Don't worry. I hope to sell it as soon as I am known."

He tipped his head to one side, as if to indicate the thought of me earning money hadn't occurred to him, but the deliberateness of that action seemed to be pretense.

"Or maybe I'll give it to Cosimo de' Medici."

"No! Don't do that."

"Why not?"

"You don't just give away a painting."

"As a means of announcing the presence

85

of another artist in the city? And to be hung among the great paintings that he must own?"

I could see he didn't like the idea. Be wise, Graziela had warned. "No need to decide now," I said. "It isn't even finished." I rolled up the canvases loosely. "I just want you to know that as soon as I am able, I intend to earn my own way."

"Fine with me."

We rode until dusk and finally stopped for the night at an inn. My back and shoulders ached from hours of tightening them against the damp. He helped me down from the coach and I was stiff from not moving. His cool palm was firm under mine. I liked the feel of it — at least on my hand.

The inn was filled with olive harvesters, vineyard workers, carters, farmers and their families. The sweat of their labors mixed with the smells of smoke from the fireplace, wet wool drying, and dung on their boots. I stood before the fire and let the warmth spread deliciously over my palms and creep up my throat. An ash flew into my eye. I turned around. In the blurred room, two squealing, giggling children and a dog ran around the tables and no one seemed to mind.

A young mother with her hair wrapped in

a cloth was nursing her baby next to a weathered crone slumped against the wall in a nest of blankets, wearing heavy socks but no shoes. Her gnarled fingers moved as though still performing some task while the rest of her sat dully blinking, oblivious to the boisterous talk and laughter around her. The spit and crackle of the fire lit only the right sides of the women's faces and necks. The whole human scene moved me. Rome seemed far away.

When the serving girl began to ladle something from an iron kettle, I squeezed between Pietro and another man on a bench before the trestle table. She passed bowls, tin cups, and earthenware pitchers of pale Umbrian wine down the line of people. The meal consisted of rabbit stew with onions, white beans and turnips, simple country food that smelled of sage and basil and garlic. With his head ducked low, Pietro ate fast, swallowing even before he chewed, and following with a gulp of wine. *"Buono,"* he said.

I couldn't cook like this. It would take half a day — all that gutting and skinning — and then how could I paint? Lavishing all that attention on a meal that wouldn't last seemed to be squandering life.

I looked at the rough, tired, noisy

Umbrian folk, and let their wine warm me and the stew fill me with things of the countryside. Pietro tore off a hunk of bread from the loaf.

"Good bread, eh?" I said. "The innkeeper's wife probably used grain from her brother-in-law's farm ground by her husband's father and baked this morning in a stone oven heated with wood from a forest owned by her own father and carted here by her cousin."

He laughed softly. "You know that for certain?"

"No. I just made it up."

Sitting opposite us, a scruffy man whose front teeth were missing said, "She's not far wrong. You better listen to her, young man."

"Is that so?" Pietro turned to me with a skewed smile.

"That's what my wife's been telling me for years. If men would only have ears like the jackasses they are, she says. So I say to her, that'll happen the day wives have mouths like jack rabbits. We've been saying it to each other for thirty years." He spooned in the juice with a sucking noise.

"Thirty!"

"Goes by fast as a bat's wing. How long have you been married, eh?"

Pietro and I exchanged sheepish looks.

"Four or five." He chuckled. "Hours."

"*Ehi! Madonna santa. Auguri.*" The man stood up and announced it in a loud voice to the whole room.

"*Auguri,*" they shouted.

Two young men sent up a whoop and everyone sang a ribald song about a milkmaid's knowing fingers. At the end, one round workhorse of a woman let out a piercing laugh like a chicken cackling. Pietro laughed too, and then noticed I was bewildered and so he stopped. He stood up, straddled the bench, and held out his hand for me. "Let's go upstairs."

The men grinned and whooped again, and the laughing woman squeezed my wrist after I got up and drew me down to her. "*Senti, bellezza,* you'll like it after he breaks you in." She cackled again, even louder.

To avoid her, I turned to go upstairs quickly, and everyone laughed again, thinking I couldn't wait. The heat of embarrassment rose in my throat and cheeks.

Pietro lit a lantern with a stick from the fire and held it before us as we climbed the stairs together. "Don't pay her any mind," he said.

Santa Maria, let him not be rough.

The upper chamber was unheated, so I undressed hurriedly, facing the wall, far away from the lantern. Even in this marriage of convenience, I had an obligation to comply, but I couldn't stand to think of his hand touching me where Agostino had forced himself, where the notary had looked. The thought made me queasy. I slipped into bed quickly. *Leave it in Rome*, I reminded myself.

His first touch sent a shock through me and I shuddered.

"You'll be warm soon."

Grazie a Dio. He thought I had shivered.

There was a softness in his voice. This would not be rape. It would not be by force unless I resisted. Let me not resist. Let me not cry out.

With his arm around my waist, he drew me toward him. Every muscle in my body was taut as a stretched canvas. He pressed himself against me. His skin was cold. Like mine. We had this likeness. The same damp cold I felt, he had felt too. It made me feel tender toward him.

His hands stroked my thighs. I squeezed shut against him. Try, I told myself. He waited. His hand between my knees urged me. Open. Open. A little at a time. It wasn't him that was making this difficult. It was me. I felt myself relax, a little at a time. Slowly, his hand moved up my leg and sent a quiver up to the center of me. A soft murmur, not words, just sound. Was it him or me? His weight didn't rest completely on me. He was being careful. In the surprising hope of becoming precious to him, I put my hands on his back. Let them not be too cold, I thought. I offered up my fear and he took it, gently enough at first, until he lost himself in a temporary madness and I braced against the slamming of his frenzy.

I ached so badly afterward that I had to hold myself, and then I felt a new sensation — his relaxing into sound and heavy sleep. No stealthy departure. No hurry. No crying. Just stillness.

Grazie, Maria. He did not make me feel ashamed.

7

Florence

Milk-white oxen wearing flowered wreaths and hauling carts of olives blocked the road, but Pietro didn't seem to mind. "I like that wooden chuk-chuk-chuk sound of the olive pickers, the way it echoes through the orchards," he said.

Out the coach window, netting covered the ground under olive trees made ghostly by vapors of morning fog.

"It seems like the whole world is outside with something to do," I said, happy to have a normal conversation.

"It's hard work looking up all day long for weeks. Giovanni and I did it at my uncle's orchard when we were young. Hard on the neck."

"Like Michelangelo painting the Sistine ceiling, probably. Or my father. He's doing a ceiling for Cardinal Borghese."

"Just as hard, only with olives you have to do it all over again every year."

I was pleased whenever I could make him smile, even though I was still suspicious of his honorable gesture of marrying me. To ask him what his reasons were seemed crass. Could gratitude be the seed of love?

While we rode, we ate salami, bread, green apples, and fresh *pecorino,* sheep cheese that the innkeeper had wrapped in a cloth. Simple enough. I could surely make meals like that.

I noticed a slim, square tower lifting its crenellated crown as if on a slender neck above a row of cypress trees. "What is the most beautiful thing in Florence?" I asked, thinking I might get a painter's description of a graceful church spire or a marble figure or a fresco.

He thought a moment, cut an apple wedge, and held it out to me on the sharp tip of his knife. "The women."

"You might as well have used the blade on my bare breast." I laughed softly to show I felt no injury, though my words were closer to the truth. Being careful of the blade in the jostling coach, I picked off the fruit.

He winced when he noticed the raw pink flesh at the base of my fingers and some deep scabs still there. "I'm sorry," he said, still looking. "Giovanni told me."

"Do you think the marks will ever disappear?"

"I don't want to say." With a wry expression, he pointed his knife toward the rolled-up canvases. "If you paint like that and earn lots of money, you can cover them with rings. Or if you had married a rich man."

"I'd rather marry a good man."

He smiled in an abashed way, cut another wedge of apple, held it with his fingers up to my lips, and watched me take it between my teeth.

In the afternoon two days later, the clouds broke apart and sunlight brushed with a light sienna the stone arches and crenellations of Porta Romana, the southern entrance to the city of Florence. Ochre buildings with red tiled roofs and shutters the color of cinnamon or basil lined the road. I felt myself getting as excited as Paola had been for me. Florence!

"This is Palazzo Pitti," Pietro said, pushing out his chest as we passed a stone palace, strikingly different than tradition because each of the three stories were the same height and had the same rough-hewn stone. It made the building look more formidable than graceful. "Il granduca Cosimo de' Medici lives here. Magnificent, yes?"

I nodded. "It's a beautiful color, so creamy. An impressive palace." It gained its impressiveness not with decoration or carvings, but simply by the repetition of its arched windows. To me, it looked austere, but I didn't dare say so. It was endearing that Pietro wanted me to be impressed.

"Have you ever been inside?"

"No." He shrugged. "The Medici are not what they used to be. This is Cosimo II, a far sight from his namesake."

We crossed a bridge into the city proper. Buildings taller than those in Rome squeezed the streets into tight corridors clogged with mule carts and fruit and fish stands. Paving stones sent up a racket of horses' hooves that echoed off stone walls, and chickens flew out from under carriage wheels.

Pietro asked the coachman to make one trip around the cathedral, the Duomo of Santa Maria del Fiore. When I caught my first sight of its ribbed terra-cotta dome, I forgave the palace for being so plain. "Someday I'll tell you the story of how Brunelleschi built the dome," he said, as full of pride as if he had been Brunelleschi's workman.

"The bell tower is a separate building," I said, astounded at its self-standing height. I craned my neck out the coach window to get a look at the top, which made Pietro laugh. The smooth green, rose, and white marble slabs glistened in the pale light, and the square tower seemed like a God-size reliquary made of precious stones. "Rome has nothing like this," I said to the sky.

"Giotto designed it," Pietro said. "It was finished long before the dome."

In the narrower streets off the cathedral square, throngs of people splashed through mud puddles and shouted to get through. The choking smell of horse manure was everywhere. Was I not supposed to notice that because of his obvious pride in his city?

"Don't ever walk on this street," he said as we rode through foul odors from butcher shops. "The paving stones are so slick with offal that women are always falling and breaking their hips. Go around. Later I'll show you my friend's *macelleria* on another street so you don't have to come here."

The street of the cheese shops, though pungent, wasn't so bad, and by the time we passed the spice shops, I was breathing normally again. Every shade of yellow ochre, sienna, orange, cinnamon, and dull green powders spilled out of large muslin bags

96

onto the street. The colors of my new city. In every piazza a sculpture, in every niche the patron saint of some guild. Everywhere I looked, art! A new life was opening for me.

Pietro directed the coachman to follow Corso dei Tintori, the avenue of the cloth dyers. Long lengths of wool and silk hung from every window and roofline. "The street is decorated for your arrival," he said.

"Like pageant banners." Women were buying and selling lengths of silk in a rainbow of brilliant colors. "Their clothes may be more elaborate and colorful, in finer fabrics, but the women here aren't any more beautiful than Rome's women," I said with what I hoped he'd take as a teasing smile. I screwed up my nose at the ammonia issuing from steaming vats in order to make him laugh.

Along the river, women and girls were rinsing heavy wool fleece in the greenish brown Arno. Just beyond this the coach stopped at a cream-colored stone building with a tile roof and faded olive green shutters.

"My house," Pietro said.

He opened the gate to a small courtyard with one fig tree, a few scraggly geraniums, and a square well that was surrounded by mossy green paving stones. The pail and rope told me what I'd be doing every day.

"I live on the third story," he said.

My. I. Maybe someday he'd say *we*.

More well off families lived on the ground floor and first and second stories, I assumed, just as in Rome. "An old woman named Fina who lives on the fourth used to keep house for me," he said. I guess that meant it would not continue.

While Pietro and the coachman carried up my *cassone* and our other bags, I looked around the three rooms that would be my new home. The large main room for painting and living had three sizes of easels and a wide bench which he probably used for posing since it was stacked with pillows, spreads, and draping fabric. Several straw-bottomed chairs were placed around a long rustic trestle table where his drawing and painting things were spread out. Not wanting to disturb them, I moved an iron lantern with oiled parchment sides to set down my bag and immediately got a splinter from the table.

Where would I store my painting things? On the windowsill, maybe, unless I wanted to mix them in with his on the table. In the years ahead, would we ever get to a state of no longer knowing whose brushes we were using?

The kitchen had a stone sink and an enclosed water bucket mounted behind it with a faucet. I assumed that was what I'd have to use to carry water up three flights of stairs from the well. Or would he do it?

The third room had a low, sloped ceiling so that we had to bend over halfway into the room. There was a bed with a straw mattress, two low chests, and a basin stand. The floors were terra-cotta brick in a herringbone pattern. On the side of the bed where he had laid his cloak, there was a small, thin goatskin on the floor, but not on the other side. I wished I had brought more of my mother's things, particularly her foot rug and her Roman-style folding camp chair. It had a cushion. Nothing here did.

Throughout the house the plastered walls were covered with unframed paintings — Holy Families, the Anunciation, Saint Theresa in Ecstasy — all of them voluptuous women with extravagant drapery in rich, strong colors. In one painting of the Annunciation, the eyes of Mary when she was told of the birth of the Savior had no specific emotion. I would have given her eyes astonishment by having them a bit more round and the irises lighter to call attention to them. His blending of color would be improved with the amber varnish, but I'd said too much about that already.

His paintings covered every wall, sometimes two paintings high. Where would there be room for mine? If I were fortunate, if I were skilled enough in this city of artists, mine wouldn't stay on our own walls.

"Florentine models?" I asked when he came in bringing the last of the bags.

"Of course."

"All right. I admit. They're beautiful."

Although he only smiled, I could tell I had pleased him. I had meant the women more than the paintings. Who were they? Was I looking at a history of his — should I call them associations? The women looked back at me holding secrets I doubted I would ever know. For the time being at least, Pietro's mystery made him alluring.

He opened the shutters in all three rooms and the double doors onto a narrow balcony overlooking the Arno. We stepped outside. A scant row of working people's low dwellings huddled against green hills on the other side. The gurgling of the river pouring over a low diagonal stone dam was soothing.

"Just think. That water will be in the sea one day, and then it could go anywhere in the world, and we're seeing it right now. It's a beautiful view."

"You may not say so when the river stinks.

It helps to keep a little sugar or cinnamon burning over the fire."

His little housewifely hint was sweet.

We looked down at couples arm in arm making an early evening *passeggiata* on the street separating our building from the river bank. The embarrassment of how I came to be married crept over me again, and I wished that Pietro and I could have chosen each other out of love like other men and women were beginning to do. That wistfulness must have shown on my face. He drew me back inside as if he'd read my mind, through the main room into the bedchamber, tipped me backward under the low ceiling, and lowered me onto the bed. With that amused sideways grin, he untied my bodice laces and quickly solved the mystery of my skirt hooks. Our lovemaking was wordless, swift, only a momentary closeness.

We fell asleep together, without a cover. When he changed positions, I woke up, startled, remembering where I was. My eyes traveled over his body silhouetted by a shaft of moonlight through the window. The straight ridge of his backbone, the rolling landscape of his back, the hollow in his buttock — all of him was surprisingly, painfully, unutterably desirable. I dared to touch his side. His skin was cool. It couldn't be love I felt so soon, but an admiration for the beauty of his form which made me tremble and lie sleepless. If I were to be granted love on top of all the rest, I thought my heart would split.

I learned in the weeks that followed that he was either hot or cold, with me fully, or someplace distant and unreachable. At those times, I trembled between sheets lest I seem a fool if he did not want me after I had made a gesture offering myself to him. His changeableness made me afraid to enjoy freely the times when he was fully mine.

Graziela had said I must not believe in illusion. In my first letter to her, I wrote,

I am trusting him only day by day and am trying to resist the allure of untested love. Even though I do see signs of affection, he still might want me only to grind his pigments, and clean his palette and hose. I want no more scars, even invisible ones, because of a man. Tell Paola she was right. The city is glorious with art and opportunity. So far, I am very happy.

Con amore,
Artemisia

And to Father, I wrote simply,

Thank you. I have high hopes. Florence has many beauties.

The finest times with Pietro were Sunday afternoons when we went to see the art of the city. Pietro decided each week what he would show me but he wouldn't tell me ahead of time. He wanted to surprise me. It was this playful aspect of his aloofness that fascinated me. On Sundays I woke with fresh anticipation of some new thing — a subject, a composition, a gesture, or an interpretation. If I used my eyes, and forced myself to go slowly and look with thoughtful consideration, I would encounter something wonderful. In this way, I learned the Florentine taste.

Dressed in new doublet and hose, new shoes, and a new hat in gathered purple velvet, Pietro held out his arm for me to hold with the air of a courtier who took delight in showing off his city's treasures. He told me histories and bits of information that made the artists human — how Ghiberti, not Brunelleschi, won the competition for the Baptistry doors, how Brunelleschi left the city in anger and went to Rome to study and measure classical ruins, how Donatello, his boy lover who went with him to Rome called him Pippo, how Brunelleschi challenged the other Florentine architects to make an egg stand on end, how he proved his own cleverness by tapping its narrow end on a table which broke it enough for it to stand upright, how that won for him the commission to build a self-supporting dome over the hole that had gaped over the cathedral for fifty years. And how Michelangelo regretted having kissed only the hand and not the face of the dying Vittoria Colonna, the light and solace of his later years. Through Pietro's stories, the city came alive for me.

"Masaccio was a bear of a man who died at twenty-seven," he said as we entered the monastery church of Santa Maria del Carmine one Sunday. Inside, he directed me to a small side chapel with frescoed walls. "This is the Brancacci Chapel, his patron's."

I stood transfixed before Masaccio's *Expulsion of Adam and Eve from Eden*. In a bleak, brown setting without any hint of a garden, Adam covered his bowed face with his hands. Eve's eyes were wounded hollows nearly squeezed shut, and her open mouth uttered an anguished cry that echoed through time and resounded in my heart.

The pathos of their shame moved me so that my legs were weak. I held on to the stone balustrade. Between Eve and me, I felt no gulf of centuries.

"I want to wrap her in my arms to comfort her," I said softly.

"Michelangelo, Raphael, and Botticelli sat right here drawing from this fresco," Pietro said as casually as if he had been among them more than a hundred years ago.

Nothing I saw the rest of the day could I even remember clearly when we fell into bed together. I couldn't sleep. I stared into the dark at Eve's tortured expression. That was what it must feel like to be totally abandoned, spurned, deprived of God. For all I'd been through, I had never felt such devastating despair.

The rhythm of Pietro's breathing pulsed Eve's pain into me and I flung myself over, unable to lie still. My thrashing woke him. "What's the matter?" he murmured.

"I can't get to sleep. I keep thinking of Eve."

He turned and drew me to him as if his sheltering arm would quiet me. "Try not to think, *amore*." We breathed the darkness in unison until I felt the wakening of his member brush against me. No, I thought.

Not now. How could I, now, haunted by Eve's anguish after her indulgence of appetite?

A surprising, furtive spasm quivered in me, and an involuntary squeezing deep inside. He turned me how he wanted me and rocked me, soothing me into compliance until I pushed the agony of Eve to the back of my mind and a sweeter agony took over. Afterward we slept as one.

Months later, alone one morning, I was cleaning brushes in turpentine and a wave of nausea rushed over me. The smell was overpowering. I opened the windows but I couldn't stand up a moment longer to breathe the fresh air. It wasn't fresh anyway. It smelled of the river. I sank into a chair and gripped the arms. My mouth tasted awful. The room blurred. I rushed to get a basin, and threw up.

I had expected blood for more than a month, maybe two. Even though I had known it would probably happen, I was stunned by the reality. A baby. It made me anxious. What if Pietro . . . ? I didn't even want to frame the thought into words.

Had my own mother felt this strange dizziness, this swelling — not just in the belly but in the throat and behind the eyes — the moment she suspected? But she had died in childbirth in a bed full of blood and screams. I was twelve and terrified. I had seen it all. I was enraged at father for killing her, or so it seemed to me, and silent for months until Paola's and Graziela's love slowly dissolved my stupor and I began to live again.

I couldn't allow myself to think about that. I wanted a child, and wanted Pietro to want one too. I wouldn't tell him just yet. Not until I was certain.

Every day, the same thing happened — throwing up at turpentine, even linseed oil. I couldn't mix my paints. But in the evenings, I felt fine. A couple weeks later, I seemed to feel a thickening and there was a definite tenderness in my breasts. It had to be.

That meant there were things to do. I washed my face, dressed, tied my hair in a knot and, on this important day, secured it with my mother's hair ornament. I rolled up my Susanna and my Judith and my *Woman Playing a Lute* and fastened them with a ribbon. I didn't know when my belly would swell, and presenting myself as a painter soon to be a mother would either be incomprehensible or laughable to some people. I had wanted to show the academy four completed canvases, and though I'd finished Judith, I had no other full-size paintings. I had some studies, but because I hadn't been painting from a model, they had no individuality.

"Whether I'm ready or not, it has to be now," I told Pietro.

He knew why I was rolling the canvases. The Accademia. We had talked about it before, but because it wasn't easy to share the intimacy of my hope, I hadn't said much.

"Why now?"

"There's a reason. I'll tell you tomorrow. I promise."

He gave me a dark look that I didn't understand. I opened the door, wondering if I was making a mistake.

"Tell me now."

If I did, he might not let me go. I wanted the two things, the academy and a baby, to be separate in his mind. I had to cajole him. I set the roll of canvases down by the door and bent over him where he sat, threading my fingers through his curly hair the way he liked. I kissed him on the ear and whispered, "It's a surprise. Just for you." He reached for me in a playful way but I dodged him, grabbed the canvases, and slipped out the door.

At the gate downstairs, I looked for good omens to reassure me. The geranium had exploded with scarlet blossoms. A chittering pair of finches in our fig tree urged me on. So did the bells of Santa Croce. The sky spread out in pale azure, smooth as spun silk. The air itself was sun-soaked and golden. Everything seemed laden with blessings.

With my canvases tucked under my arm, and a child in my belly, I stepped out into the street, into the throng of bakers' boys balancing boards on their heads to carry loaves of bread, handcarts piled with figs and grapes and melons, hawkers shouting their wares of cooking pots and knives. The cracking of whips and clatter of wheels passing on uneven paving stones fed me with the life of the city. My city now. City of Masaccio and Fra Angelico and Michelangelo and me. Artemisia Gentileschi. Maybe I'd call myself Artemisia Lomi, my ancestral name.

The closer I got to the Cistercian monastery in Borgo Pinti where the Accademia dell' Arte del Disegno was housed, the harder it was to put Pietro's look out of my mind. I was kept waiting in an antechamber lined with small paintings of Saint Luke, patron saint of artists. I tried to study them, but I couldn't concentrate. Now that I was actually here, fear made me hot and cold at the same time. This would be the first time I

showed my work to strangers of consequence on my own, without Father's en-
dorsement. I had to speak for myself. I went
over in my mind what I would say.

A round, yeasty-faced official came toward me. He wore a green damask waistcoat
without a doublet, as if he were in his own
home. "Yes, signorina?"

"I am Artemisia Gentileschi from Rome.
My father is Orazio Gentileschi. If you may
be so kind, I have some paintings to show
you."

"Ah, yes, Signor Gentileschi. I understand he was a good friend of Michelangelo
da Caravaggio."

"Yes, he was. I knew him too, before he
died."

"Under mysterious circumstances, I
might add. Most likely caught running for
his life after stabbing someone in a fight
over a prostitute. Booted, spurred, wearing
sword and poignard like a brigand. In and
out of jail for quarreling with police and in-
sulting a papal guard. And you say you knew
him well?"

"No, not well. I was a child, signore. My
father —"

I shifted my rolled canvases from one arm
to the other to bring him back to art.

"Your father sends his daughter to bring

us his paintings? Why doesn't he come himself?"

"No, signore. Not his. My own. I am a painter too."

His forehead contracted into a scowl. He gave a quick, impatient nod and I unrolled the canvases onto a long wooden table with adjustable top, and tacked them down. He tipped the tabletop up and stood back to look, but didn't say anything. He suffered a violent tick in his neck which I tried to ignore out of politeness. He peered down at my hands.

"One moment."

I sat down and waited until he returned with a thin man whose pale brown beard was shaped like a spade. They whispered rudely in my presence. With opaque eyes the brown of snail shells, the thin man looked sideways at my fingers too. I ordered my hands not to move. So that was how it was going to be. They knew. The world of art and artists was small indeed. That told me I needed to obtain a commission before my belly swelled. It would only confirm their judgments, and the Roman jeers of "whore" would follow me here. I folded my hands across my stomach.

The thin man said, "I am Signor Bandinelli, Luogotenente of the Accademia. My steward tells me you have brought these paintings. Your purpose in showing them to us?"

I stood up. "Why, to seek admission, of course."

"They are yours? Painted completely by you?"

"Yes, signore."

He turned to examine them. After a few moments, he cleared his throat. "Most women painters who aspire to professional esteem consider a conservative emulation of the masters sufficient for their hopes. To aspire to such expressive singularity" — he waved his hand backward at my Judith — "with *invenzione* like this, might jeopardize your precarious achievement, as well as your unprecedented petition, as a woman, to our Accademia."

"What's the point of repetition?" I asked.

"The point, signorina, is that deliberate flamboyance applied to biblical themes diminishes the spiritual content."

Look in their eyes and show no fear, Graziela had said.

"Perhaps the great moments deserving of celebration in art are not just moments of *spiritual* elevation." Whatever possessed me to counter him? As an afterthought, I smiled sweetly.

112

Bandinelli took his time studying Judith and her maidservant, Abra. He couldn't ignore that these were not weak women empowered only by the intervention of God. He had to see their strong arms and recognize their own control, Abra pinning down the arm of Holofernes while Judith held his head by his hair. Judging from Pietro's first reaction, I knew it was a view undesirable for men to contemplate.

"So this is Caravaggist? That shadow on her face?" the steward asked.

"Yes. For dramatic effect. To draw attention to the lighted side. And to suggest a clandestine act."

I hated myself a moment for explaining what should be apparent.

They passed over the *Woman Playing a Lute* without comment and peered at Susanna's nakedness with the same lewd voyeurism the elders did, as though titillated that it was painted by a woman with a shaded reputation. Signor Bandinelli knit his brows as if he was trying to grasp a thought. The painting must be too different. I had not given the focus to the old lechers ogling her at the bath like all the other Susanna paintings did, anticipating with glee their conquest while she waited for the inevitable. Apparently he didn't want to recognize that her anxiety was the true subject of the painting.

"For a woman painter to attempt originality in interpretation is unnecessary, and perhaps even hazardous," Signor Bandinelli said, and looked to the round-faced man to concur.

"I am not a stranger to hazard, signore," I said before the steward could agree.

I nodded to both of them, and when they only nodded back, I rolled up the canvases and paused a moment to give them one last chance to offer me a little shred of encouragement.

They looked at me blankly.

"We will, I am certain, see one another again," I said.

My heart quaked as I walked out the door.

8

Palmira

Pietro looked up from his drawing as soon as I came in the door. Slowly and quietly, he set down his charcoal. I let the rolled-up canvases fall to the floor and pushed them against the wall with my foot. I went into the kitchen and stared at the heel of bread left from morning. He came up behind me and laid his hands on my shoulders, and patted me a few times, as if consoling a sulking child. I ripped the bread in two.

"What did you expect? No patrons in Florence have bought your work yet, and the academy has never had a woman."

I whirled around to face him. "But they could. It's not a law."

His crooked, knowing smile made me feel like a fool. What a novelty, a wife who painted. How curious. How droll. She even thought the academy would want her. Foolish woman. He could laugh about it with his fellows in the tavern, and repeat the old saying: "A woman is like an egg. The more she is beaten, one way or another, the better she becomes."

I fixed a meager supper and went to bed early in sour silence.

Waking the next morning after fitful sleep, I ruminated in bed over what had happened at the academy, and where I had mispoken. *Woman* painter, they'd said. *Are they painted completely by you?* As if my father had held my hand while I grasped the brush. My disappointment made me feel queasy, and then I remembered: a baby. A warmth infused me, counteracting the nausea, an expectation, surprising and foreign. Was this the swell and urge of maternal impulse? I'd never felt it before this moment, never yearned for a child the way some women do, but now that it was here, definitely here, I was hot with anxious hope that Pietro would be happy too.

When Pietro stirred, I drew his hand to my belly and said softly, "How would it be for a son to learn painting from a father *and* a mother? Together."

He jerked upright in bed. "Is this the surprise?"

"Mmm, maybe. We'd be the first family of our kind in Florence."

"You mean a baby? When? Soon? A son. I'll have a fine strapping son."

"Half a year, I'm guessing."

"We have to get ready."

I laughed. "Not yet."

"We'll call him Pietro Giovanni Andrea Filippo Leonardo Michelangelo Stiattesi. A fine name for a fine son."

His excitement, and my relief, pushed my disappointment about the academy to the back of my mind.

Feeling a kind of glow around me, I tried to get as much painting done as I could in that half a year, but the turpentine made me sick and some days I couldn't work at all. I didn't want to give that any importance even though it seemed a bad omen — motherhood set against painting. Pietro took the painting he was working on and his paints and brushes to a friend's studio to finish it so the smell wouldn't bother me.

When Pietro left the house one day, I found I could paint if I wrapped a cloth folded into a triangle around my face to cover my nose and mouth. He came home and found me that way.

"Take that off," he said sharply.

"Why? I don't breathe the oil and turpentine so much with it."

"Take it off." He wouldn't look at me.

I didn't understand how that offended him. His dark expression made me afraid to ask. Did he not want me to paint? I put my palette and brushes and bottles of linseed oil and turpentine out on the balcony, closed the door, and untied the cloth.

"I don't ever want to see you that way again."

I busied myself in the kitchen, put out pasta with eggplant, and broad beans in oil for supper but didn't feel like eating any myself. I spread out the pillows and lay down on my back on the posing bench resting my hand on my belly to try to feel some fluttery movement. Both of us were quiet while he ate.

"It's just that I want to paint so badly," I said softly.

I heard his spoon clatter on the table. "When I was a boy, my mother, all the women who couldn't get out of the city, wore cloths like that at the first sign of the plague. The last time I saw her, she wore one, and kissed me through it before my uncle took Giovanni and me away."

I gagged on the saliva in the back of my throat. "I didn't know." A trickle of moisture crawled toward my temple. "I'm sorry. I won't do it again."

He came over to the bench and looked down at me and took my hand. "It just shocked me. I didn't want to think —"

"It's all right. My back aches too much to stand at the easel anyway."

The next day I drew in bed balancing my drawing album on my stomach and using Pietro's painting hanging on the opposite wall as a subject. When he came home he had a wooden cradle and a quilt in his arms. He put it down next to me, sat on the bed, and rocked it. They were both used, I could see, but to me they were signs of happiness to come.

"What's that? In the cradle?"

Nestled in the quilt was an earthenware jar with a cork lid. He lifted it out.

"What is it?" I asked.

He grinned and handed it to me. "You guess."

I shook it a little.

"No! Don't do that. The lid might come off."

"Is it something to eat?"

"No."

"Something for the baby to eat?"

"No. Open it."

I lifted off the cork. Inside was a fine yellowish powder. "It smells like flowers. Is it for the baby?"

He stood up, bent over and stuck out his buttocks and pointed there. He looked so funny I laughed even though it hurt my back. "When he gets sore, you put olive oil there and then sprinkle the powder," he said, making motions in the air as though he were sprinkling and rubbing it in.

"Where did you get this?"

"At the apothecary. Franco called it diapasm."

"How do you know so much?"

He grinned and shrugged and raised his chin. "Just intelligent, I guess."

It gave me an odd feeling, him knowing what I didn't.

"I wish I could do something more than just lie here," I said, trying to get comfortable by moving onto my side, but that wasn't any better. Pietro had tried to keep me occupied the last weeks by rotating the paintings on the bedroom walls, but even drawing had gotten tiresome, and for the last few days I had done nothing other than try to find a comfortable position.

"After the baby comes, you'll be so busy, you'll want to have a day of just lying in bed."

My time was close. A matter of hours. Fear had crept up from my toes farther each day to squeeze my belly, and now it took all my effort to push it back down. I looked up at Pietro hunched and pacing like a crow on a ledge.

"Stand still!" I held out my hand and he stepped over to hold it, the ceiling forcing him to bend his head down. I wanted to get a good look at him in case it would be my last.

"Do I send for her yet?" he asked for the fifth time.

"No." He meant the midwife. The neighbor boy was waiting down in the courtyard to fetch her.

"Maybe if I stood up, I'd feel better." He helped me up and slowly we walked into the main room. A sudden rush of warm fluid poured out of me. It embarrassed me and I crept back into bed. After a few moments I felt like a giant hand was inside me squeezing and ripping at the same time. I moaned until it let go.

Pietro knelt beside me and stroked my forehead with a cool cloth. "You're brave, *amore*."

"No I'm not." It irritated me. As if bravery were an easy thing. "I'm not brave at all. I have no choice."

"Then you're brave about not having any

choice." He smiled wanly and I knew that he meant it tenderly.

"I want this baby, Pietro."

The hand squeezed and ripped and let go, over and over for an hour. Then a pain that made the others feel like twitches engulfed me. I tightened against it. When a worse one came quickly after, I cried, "Now! Send for her now."

He sprang up and cracked his forehead on the beam, ran through the doorway, and shouted down to the boy. He was back before the pain subsided. Fear gripped me.

"If the blood keeps coming and won't stop . . . like Mother . . . If it's a boy . . . If it's a girl the same. Papa taught me the names of colors right away. Ah . . . Alizarin crimson. Venetian red. Scarlet. Madder lake. It's from a plant, Papa said. Vermilion. From Spanish cinnabar. Pozzuoli red. From a volcano near Naples. Titian's red. If . . . If I'm not there, you teach him. Or her. Teach her just the same, Pietro."

He took my hand. "You'll teach her. I'm sure of it."

"If I die, if I die, Pietro, give my paintings to my father. No. Not to him. He can look. I want him to look. To mother. No, that wasn't right. To Grazi . . . ahh . . . ela."

"Don't talk."

"One to her. And one to Paola. The rest to you."

The midwife and her assistant came in carrying a wooden tub and a birthing chair with grips and straps and a hole in the seat. It looked like a torture contraption designed by the Inquisition. I closed my eyes.

"Leave us now, signore," the midwife said. "Go build up the fire."

I screamed, cried, and pushed.

"No. Don't push yet," the midwife ordered. "It's a long time still."

For hours I tried to do what they said, tried not to push, begged them to let me, rested in between. Again and again. I didn't know where Pietro was. I didn't care. I heard myself scream whenever the pain came. Was it to go on forever?

"Get it over with," I yelled. "Give me something. I know you can make it stop."

"No, child. You were born into this world to bear this pain. Ever since Eve, it's woman's lot in life."

"No! I was born to paint!"

The worst, longest pain of all.

The midwife got me into the chair. "Here it comes. Push now!" she said.

All of me gritted and pushed down, squeezing. Pushing against the floor, it seemed. Sounds of wild animals came out of me. Finally, relief. Sleep. I wanted sleep.

I woke up in the bed. How had I gotten there? Waves of ache surged up from my belly to the top of my head. Holding her. A girl child. Such a color. Pale madder. A tiny fist of a face. A dear little translucent ear, perfectly carved in wax. And Pietro. Pietro was here. Pietro on his knees. Close to me. Crooning, *"Che amore di bambina."* Pietro, with a deep purple lump on his forehead.

We named her Palmira Prudenzia. Palmira for his mother. Prudenzia for mine. He didn't seem disappointed in the least that she was a girl. As for me, I was supremely happy. A daughter. A marvel. A miracle. Someday a beautiful woman. I felt her effect already, a herald of love. Pietro's lips were kissing my ear.

"She's destined for a palace," he said. "Look at her skin. Veins like threads of blue and red just like in the stone of Palazzo Pitti."

Eventually I wrote to Father.

You're a grandfather now. Her name is Palmira Prudenzia. She has lips the shape of a cupid's bow, a dainty, pointed chin, and skin as smooth as satin. Maybe Mother would have said she looks like I did. So far, her only talent is blowing bubbles, but who knows? She might be the first female artist to be born in Florence. You are fathering a legacy. We will take her to see the city's great art as you did for me in Rome. But of this you can be sure — she will not have her honor ripped from her in a public arena. I'll make sure of that.

The academy did not want me. Yet.
I am fine.

Your daughter,
Artemisia

He wrote back:

Dear Artemisia,
When you were born, I couldn't keep my eyes off you, your littleness and the newness of your hands. I remember watching for nearly an hour as your little pink fingers tried to pick up a bean. If I were in Florence now, it would be the same again for me. I would like to sing to her.

The academy is as tradition-bound as the church. It moves in paces of a hair's breadth, but they cannot ignore forever a talent such as yours. Have you forgotten to see Michelangelo Buonarroti the Younger? I should have heard from him if you had gone. He

lives on Via Ghibellina.
    Teach Palmira Prudenzia the name,
    Orazio Gentileschi

We took Palmira to be baptised on March 25, New Year's Day in the old Florentine calendar, the day when all the babies born in Florence during the year are brought to the Baptistry just opposite the Duomo. The line of families carrying infants wound around the octagonal building. Pietro held Palmira facing forward to get her first sight of Ghiberti's magnificent gilded bronze doors.

"According to the story, over these doors Ghiberti inscribed, 'Look at this beautiful work that I have done.' "

"We could say the same about Palmira," I said. Pietro smiled down at me, his dark eyes alight with pride.

A barefoot, ragged woman with wild eyes and stringy hair sat nearby on the steps of the Duomo, sobbing between Hail Marys. I had seen a few of these penitents of Florence, but never one so wild and desperate.

"She's here often, or at Santa Croce or San Lorenzo, working off some sin in howling penitence," Pietro said.

Is this what they had tried to make me become during the trial? I shuddered.

"Sometimes she's even on the Ponte

Vecchio," he continued. "Anywhere there are people. It's not genuine religion. It's for show. Don't pay her any attention or she'll scream more."

I'd never been inside the Baptistry. The throng of people squeezed through Pisano's door, the south entrance. In the press of families with babies, some of them crying, tightly packed around the font, Pietro and I stood like a normal couple, side by side, our bodies touching, offering our child to God. In that moment when Palmira was anointed, we were one — mother, father, child.

I held Pietro's arm and whispered, "She's now among all the great artists and sculptors and poets of Florence who were baptised right here in this same spot. God has blessed their work." My hope for her overflowed into tears.

Through the blur, I looked up at the overpowering Christ done in mosaic above the altar, and cringed under the judgment of his penetrating eyes. On one side of him, the good were being welcomed into Heaven, and on the other, the damned were being devoured by demons. Hell's torments were pictured as lovingly as the blessings of Heaven. Every kind of roasting, beating, boiling, disemboweling was displayed in detail with small glass squares in reds and blues and gold. Maybe it was superstition, but I held my hand over Palmira's head to shield her from the sight.

"Who created the ceiling?" I asked.

"No one knows," Pietro said.

It was from an age when artists worked anonymously for the glory of God. As real people, with loves and fears, parents themselves probably, they were nothing. To think that such fine artists were already forgotten. A vast emptiness engulfed me and threatened to spoil the joy of the day. No one even knew their names.

Palmira gurgled through babyhood in the cradle which we rocked with our feet while we painted. I felt a full and new contentment even though my time at the easel between feedings flew by in a matter of moments. Sometimes, like Father had written, I couldn't take my eyes off Palmira's shapely lips blowing bubbles or her tiny fingernails like flakes of candle wax, in order to do my work. Other times, when I was lost in the painting of something difficult, an eye or a hand or a foreshortened foot, her cries yanked me out of my concentration and it took extra time for me to find my way back to where I was. When she began to crawl, she tried to eat Naples yellow from a paint pot I'd set down too low on a stool. "Look, she's hungry to be an artist too," I said to Pietro. Palmira gave to our marriage a sheen of normalcy.

Pietro used us once for a Madonna and Child. He draped me in a borrowed blue velvet mantle banded in rose madder, while Palmira slept in the folds on my lap. He posed me looking down at her, which I never tired of doing. "*Che bellina.* My holy child," I crooned. From time to time her little legs thrust out against my belly. Pietro looked at us intensely, for hours, and I felt closer than I'd ever been to love.

In spite of such hope, sitting still so long made me restless. I wanted to hold her yet I also wanted to be the one painting her. How many women models in the last two centuries — Madonnas, Eves, Mary Magdalenes, Venuses, Delilahs, Salomes, Judiths — had yearned to be on the other side of the easel, I wondered. "Have you ever had a model who wanted to paint?"

"I never asked."

"But there must be some in this city. I wonder how I could find out."

"Ssh."

At the end of the session, I set Palmira in her cradle and took a look at his canvas.

Shock rippled through me. The shape of my face was too oval, my neck entirely too thin, my fingers too long and narrow.

"This isn't me at all," I said. "It's not a question of skill. You're a fine painter. This is intentional."

His face flushed as he studied the canvas.

"What am I? Only an armature to hang cloth on and reflect light? All you saw were the folds in the drapery. Pietro, why?"

He busied himself cleaning his palette and didn't look at me. "I have a reason."

"What is it?"

He let a moment of consideration pass, then set down his palette and strode toward the door. I rushed to block him.

"Tell me!"

"Are you sure you want to know?"

"Yes."

He looked pained. "Don Carlo knows you. You met him once, remember? He knows what you look like. He knows what happened in Rome."

"So?"

"Your reputation. I can't have a tainted woman for the Madonna."

"Tainted! Pietro, do you really think that?"

"Of course not, but it doesn't matter what I think," he said softly. "Don Carlo . . . The

130

painting would be scorned."

I felt weak and leaned on the table, my back to him. He came up behind me, put his hands on my shoulders.

"I didn't want to tell you."

I nodded. "Is it to follow me always?" I turned to him, feeling bruised, but not by him.

He drew my head onto his shoulder. "Someday I will paint you in a golden gown and everyone will know it's you. It will be so gorgeous I won't allow anyone to buy it. Not even Cosimo de' Medici. Not even," he flung his arm up, "the pope!"

I laughed softly at his flamboyance. Painting for ourselves seemed foolish. We both had work to do.

"Tomorrow we'll continue, eh?" I didn't want him to find another model and look at her the way I wanted him to look at me. Who knew where that might lead? Florentine women were beautiful, he'd said.

The next day and as long as he needed a rack for the blue mantle, I sat still and silent in hoped-for love.

He sold the painting for a fine price and we were happy. Now when we visited churches, he held Palmira, and I linked my arm in his. In the Uffizi, newly open to artists one day a week, Botticelli anointed us with the sweetness of life. In Venus riding on a seashell, I saw our child as a ripe and ravishing young woman mindless of her own beauties. In front of *Primavera*, Palmira's dimpled hand reached toward the figure of Flora whose flowered gown attracted her.

"How could this be that she has a preference among all the figures in the painting? She's only a baby."

"Not for long. She'll be wanting pretty dresses soon," Pietro said.

Was it this early that a person developed inclinations? Did the baby Michelangelo respond to Donatello's sculpture of the youthful David? Did his little arms that would someday wield a sculptor's mallet reach out every time he was carried by a niche with a figure in it? I wondered how young I was when my father first showed me the paintings of Rome. Did my eyes roam hungrily over colors and shapes?

Pietro and I painted side by side, with Palmira crawling between the legs of our easels. When she began to walk, she stumbled and tipped over Pietro's easel, which came crashing down on her. She screamed and we rushed to her. "Ssh, Palmira. You're all right. Mama's here. Papa's here too." Her little body heaved with her sobs and I pressed her against my breast, feeling a little helpless. Pietro held on to her bare feet.

The next day he built a baby-minder, a revolving pole from floor to ceiling with a sideways bar near the floor, about waist high on Palmira. When we tied her to the cross bar, she was supported and could toddle around in a circle and not be in our way while we worked, but still be with us. It moved me so much that he did this that I wrote to Graziela and Paola about it. To me it meant that he thought I could be a painter and a mother. Not many women could say as much for their husbands.

Inclinazione

Eventually I had enough work, and confidence, to show to Michelangelo Buonarroti the Younger. Because I could not write well in the florid style such a letter required, I asked Pietro to write a letter from me reminding Buonarroti of my father's letter and requesting an audience.

"Your father knows him?"

"Yes. From years ago."

"No."

"Pietro, please. I can't write that fancy language. Just tell me what to say. I'll sign it Artemisia Gentileschi, wife of the painter, Pierantonio Stiattesi. Then he'll know you too."

He relented. I trimmed a quill and wrote what he told me. "Go slower," I said, and labored over each letter.

A response came back quickly inviting me to the Buonarroti home on Via Ghibellina. Pietro read it, arched an eyebrow but didn't comment. I went alone, tripped on a dislodged paving stone, was splashed by a passing carriage, and arrived at a nondescript doorway in a narrow street, anxious and out of breath. A boy servant ushered me upstairs through a small empty anteroom to a rectangular audience hall with a coffered ceiling. A man wearing a green sleeveless *lucco* was carrying a sheaf of pages from a tall cabinet desk to a long table in the center of the room. The servant announced my name.

"Ah, signora, I've been waiting," he said, his voice coming softly from under his overhanging moustache.

"I'm sorry, Your Lordship. I didn't know the way."

"I meant, I've been waiting since your father's letter. You should have come to me directly when you came to Florence."

"I didn't know."

"No matter. Show me what you've brought."

He cleared off books and portfolios to make space on the table of polished wood with a border of inlaid stone. I laid out the new studies and drawings. He examined them all carefully, pulling at his tapered beard and murmuring. It sounded like appreciation. We tacked the Judith and Susanna on drawing tables. He tipped up the tabletops, stepped back, and I let the canvases unroll. His eyebrows shot up and a smile played about his lips. "Just as your father wrote."

"They please you, signore?" I dared to ask.

He chuckled and gave me a tender look, unmistakeable even through his bushy beard. "That's real flesh your Susanna is wearing. Those lines in her neck, the crow's feet at her underarm, the fold of flesh below her stomach — male painters wouldn't think of those details. And this Judith is an astoundingly complex composition, yet as real and true as if you had been there. Your interpretation will change how the world thinks of her."

My heart pounded against my chest so hard I thought he'd hear it. "Thank you, Your Lordship."

"I am in the process of turning the rooms on this floor into a memorial gallery to my great-uncle, il divino. This room will present an allegory of his virtues and achievements. Many artists will contribute. All these ceiling coffers will be filled with paintings."

I looked up to see deep recesses edged by heavy moldings of gold scrollwork on white.

"Might I commission you for a panel in *quadro riportato?*" he asked.

I lowered my head and gave a slow curtsey, as elegantly as I knew how. "It was my greatest hope."

"One figure. A female nude. I want her to represent Inclinazione, by that to mean his natural talent. A quality you share with il divino."

I couldn't control my face to reveal only modesty at that compliment.

He smiled in a fatherly way and looked at the Susanna again. "Yours will be the only female nude. Clearly, it's your gift and your advantage by reason of access. Life drawing of nude models is not permitted in the Accademia. Painters have to imagine women by using young male models, and their imaginations aren't trustworthy. In painting after painting, they create only the ideal. Your touches of realism are beyond their conception." His eyes wrinkled at the corners, as if in delight that he would have something no one else did.

He opened a copy of Cesare Ripa's *Iconologia*, just like Father's, and we found Inclinazione holding a compass and having a bright star shining above her like a guide.

"Place her against a deep blue sky. Give her a proud aspect. You shall have the model of your choice, and a liberal allowance for supplies. I will be pleased, I know."

"I will begin tomorrow. With all my heart."

My first commission! I felt like leaping and shouting the news all the way to Rome. I wondered if I would have been given it without Father's letter to him, but I couldn't think about that. In a rush of hope and excitement I threw myself into the preliminary sketches as soon as I got home. Pietro watched in silence from the edge of the room, arms folded across his chest. I didn't tell him what Buonarroti said about my inclination.

"Where can I find a female model?" I asked.

"At the academy."

I saw it as a wonderful opportunity to let the academy know that even without them, I had been commissioned by a man of importance. "I'll go there tomorrow."

"Who will take care of Palmira? I'm going to work." His voice was flat and final.

"I won't be gone long."

"I'm going to draw from sculpture at the Uffizi."

"They let you?"

"My friend is doorman there. He's going to let us in."

"Us?"

"Friends of mine."

"I can't take Palmira with me to the academy."

"Take her upstairs to Fina."

I had seen Fina almost every day on the stairs or down in the courtyard drawing water, and we always passed a few moments in conversation, but I had never been upstairs to her rooms. Whenever she saw Palmira she called her sweet, funny names like Stella del Mattino if it was in the morning, or Diva del Lungarno if Palmira had been crying. Sometimes she stroked Palmira's skin or tickled her softly. The first time I'd let her hold Palmira, Fina's whole face shone as though lit from within, and she whispered, "Fiore Dolce."

I ran right upstairs to ask. Fina had the door open and was singing as she was washing clothes. I was surprised at her strong contralto. She was obviously enjoying herself.

"Isn't it a perfectly beautiful day," she said, not as a question, but as an affirmation.

"How can you tell? You haven't gone downstairs."

"It comes in if you let it. The windows are all open. Have you been listening to that thrush?"

"No, I guess I haven't."

Fina wore the day on her face so that even her plain, puffy features were pleasant. "Your singing reminds me of my mother. She was always singing around the house. And my father too. Robust songs of adventurers and the campaigns of *condottieri* and drinking matches. But my mother's songs were from the troubadours."

"Singing helps to ease the way."

Apparently there was only a large attic room with bed, small table, trunk, oil stove, fireplace, sink, and washtub. One item stood out, a once-elegant straight chair, the seat and back of worn burgundy velvet with frayed silk fringe and brass studs. It hinted of better days. Clothes lay scattered helter-skelter.

"Are all these clothes yours?" I asked.

"Madonna, no! You take me for a lady of means? They belong to the family below you."

I helped her stir them with a wooden paddle as she poured heated water into the washtub. "You do washing for others too?"

"Yes, sure, for Pierantonio too until he married you."

"How long have you known him?"

"Since he was nothing more than a bulge in his mama's belly."

I was curious to know what kind of a boy he was and what else she knew about him, but that had to wait until I got to know her better.

She leaned out the window to wring out some clothes, and hung them on a line stretched between two horizontal rods attached to the building. "Signora Bruni on the ground floor doesn't want them hanging in our courtyard where people who come to visit her can see them, so I hang them here above the street. Foolish woman. Now everyone passing on the street sees them."

"I have a job for you, but it isn't washing clothes."

"I'm not good for much else. What is it you want?"

"You see, I'm a painter too, and I've just been given a wonderful commission to do —"

"A painter? Like that husband of yours?"

"Yes."

"For money?"

"Yes."

"*Mamma mia,* I suppose if it's for money, he'd allow it. Imagine, a woman painting for money. You sure you don't mean modeling? You're a beauty, you know."

141

"No, Fina. A painter. Is that so absurd?"

She tipped her head and her bottom lip protruded beyond the shadow of a moustache on her upper lip.

"I must go to the Accademia del Disegno tomorrow and he won't take care of Palmira while I'm gone. May I bring her up to you?"

"Oh, that's what you're after, eh? Of course. Bring her up. You know I love the little *principessa*."

"There might be more times too, Fina, if you don't mind. I'll pay of course."

The next day, the yeasty-faced steward at the academy looked me over, sniffed, and asked, "What is your business here?"

I was not going to overstep myself this time.

"I wish to inquire about female models, Your Lordship."

"We have a list that artists refer to as they need." He brought down a sheaf of papers tied together with a leather thong, and laid them on a desk. "You may add your name." He pushed an inkwell toward me. "If you can write."

Rub the mold off your brain, I thought.

"Your Lordship may recall, I am a painter. I wish to secure a model for a commission I've been given by Signor Buonarroti for the memorial gallery. Surely you know of the project."

He pursed his lips. "The list is only for members' use." He made a quick move to pick up the papers.

"Is Signor Buonarroti a member?"

"Of course."

"Then I am picking a model for Signor Buonarroti."

He took a noisy breath through his nostrils. "You may consult the list," he replied curtly.

I must not look smug, I told myself. Do not let my mouth form that gloating expression that Mama detested. Just do the business and say thank you.

Laboriously I copied twenty names and addresses and hired the academy *messaggero* to take each of them a simple announcement saying that I'd be choosing one at my home the following Friday.

Many women came that day while Pietro went out to a street barber and then to draw in the Uffizi again. One after another, I had them take off their clothes, but I was usually disappointed. I liked the face of one, the breasts and shoulders of another, the torso and belly of a third. Maybe that's how men thought when they looked at women on the street. I settled on Vanna, a lovely, light-haired woman with honey-colored skin, smooth, well-shaped limbs, and just the right combination of strength and fluidity and grace. The only concern I had was her constant sniffling.

I felt lighthearted and generous, and I had an idea that would keep Pietro at home instead of at the Uffizi and would give him an advantage over his academy friends. "My husband, Pierantonio Stiatessi, is a fine painter. Would you mind if he sketched you too, just while I'm doing the preliminary drawings? Nude, I mean."

She considered a moment. "Double the money?" she asked.

"Half again."

"All right. If you pose me and stay in the room."

"Of course."

"And neither of you can tell the academy."

"Understood."

In the morning, Pietro and I both sat behind our drawing boards propped on easels and waited as Vanna went through a ritual of undressing slowly, folding each piece of clothing neatly before taking off the next. She made it obvious that she was avoiding looking at Pietro, but by her languid movements she seemed keenly aware, in a primitive way, that he was studying her bare flesh. I murmured a few instructions, she moved accordingly, and I started.

Pietro didn't. Although I only looked at Vanna and my drawing, I could tell that for a long time he just sat there, immobile. I tried to read in Vanna's expression how Pietro was looking at her. What I recognized in the way she held her head, chin high but her eyes lowered at us, was confidence, pride in her beauty, even a tinge of haughtiness. Soon I was lost in my work and it was quiet except for the scratch of both our charcoals, Vanna sniffling, and Pietro clearing his throat every so often. After working awhile, Pietro moved his drawing easel away from mine to get a different angle. It was a good idea. That way we wouldn't be tempted to look at each other's work.

When I adjourned the last pose, Vanna's eyes lingered on Pietro as she turned and gave him her back when she got dressed. She accepted the coins from me in prim dignity.

"Do you want me," she stopped to sniffle, "tomorrow?"

"Yes, every day now."

That evening, Pietro and I studied the sketches. He used a heavier, more confident hand, and brought out the luxuriant sensuousness of the figure, but he missed seeing what I saw, the muscle of her breasts that started as high as her armpit, and the dimples in her hand. "You have a surer line," I said. "And you did better on the foreshortening of her foot. Look here, and here, in every one. Why is it so hard for me to get that just right?"

Slowly, he raised a shoulder, but he didn't offer any suggestion.

The next morning, Pietro set his drawing board on his easel and tacked down a sheet of paper. When Vanna arrived, there passed between them a look that set me on edge. Abruptly, he left the house, saying he had business elsewhere. It seemed so unreasonable for him to waste such an opportunity.

Vanna started to undress.

"You don't need to today. Just take off your shoes and raise your skirt. Sit here on the table so your feet will hang down."

"He doesn't want you to paint," Vanna said.

"How do you know?"

She shrugged. "I can just tell."

"You're not paid to tell. You're paid to pose."

All day I practiced only feet and ankles, and put everything else out of my mind. I drew feet sideways from the left, the right, three-quarter views from each side, and straight on, over and over, and then painted small studies. Eventually, they satisfied me, and I dismissed Vanna for the day.

Just after she left, Pietro came in flushed and energetic, flung his doublet on a chair and grabbed me by the waist and swung me around. "I've got a commission. I begin to-morrow."

"*Buono*. For whom?"

"A church in Monte Uliveto." He poured himself some wine.

"Then you won't be able to draw the model. What's the work?"

"Fresco."

"You've never done fresco."

"As an apprentice I did."

"Ceiling or wall?" I moved behind him as he sat, and rubbed his shoulders where they would be sore.

"Wall."

"That's good. Do you get to choose your subject?"

"No. It's —" He took a gulp of wine and looked sideways at my drawings of feet. "It's for fresco repair."

How would that benefit him? By the way he busied himself tearing off a hunk of bread and studying the drawings, I knew I

147

shouldn't question him, but I felt a vague unease.

In the weeks that followed he never left before Vanna arrived. They passed a few words, and then he was out the door. The job away might have been a coincidence, or it might have been an act of grace on his part to let me have privacy with her. I didn't ask. I worked. The simpler the background, Father had taught me, the more exact must be the figure, so with only sky and clouds behind her, I produced three times as many sketches of Vanna as I had for any other painting.

"Too many choices," Buonarroti said and chuckled. "You make an old man's head spin." He had spread out all the drawings on the floor of the large coffered room, and then walked back and forth studying them. The wooden floor creaked as I waited. He finally selected a forward nude sitting lightly on a gray cloud with her legs stretched downward resting on a white billow. Her front foot was foreshortened. A sudden happy warmth filled me.

"It will be placed right there." He pointed to a corner coffer directly above the entrance, wrote down the measurements and handed me the paper.

"Now, come with me. I have something to show you." He smiled at some anticipated pleasure and I followed him down the narrow stairs into a small enclosed courtyard bare of plants but with a well in the center. He walked over to a wooden crate resting on the paving stones. "This just arrived yesterday." He lifted the lid and brushed away straw. A bas relief of the Madonna and Child alongside a stairway lay in the straw. "His first work. Done when he was only sixteen."

"Michelangelo's?" I drew in my breath and could hardly believe it. The marble plaque was just lying there unceremoniously in a crate. I bent over it, daring to touch the crate, as if it were as holy as the manger. The Madonna had such modest grace nursing him, his head tucked under her mantle and his hand and arm flung backward in contended abandon, his fingers curled, just like Palmira's.

"He gets so much expression out of so little relief." My vision blurred. "She makes me feel that motherhood is sacred."

I noticed the Virgin's foot, and saw that the leg where it joined at the ankle was too thick for so short a foot. Even he had trouble with feet, when he was young.

"It was owned by the Medicis but Cosimo

is donating it to the gallery, so it has come home," he said softly.

I looked up at Michelangelo the Younger and he had that tenderness in his face again which reminded me of the fresco in Santa Trinità depicting Michelangelo. "Did he look like you?" I asked.

"You can see for yourself."

He took me into a small study on the ground floor. Baskets of letters on benches lined the room, and a portrait hung on the wall. The face had the same shadowed groove extending from the sides of his nostrils to the ends of his moustache, the same curves to the furrows in his forehead, the same three lines fanning out from the corners of his eyes, the same soft penetrating look as the man alive standing next to me.

"What a responsibility, to bear that likeness to the world. Did you know him?"

"He was an old man, and I a little boy. He told me once, 'Work, Michelangelo, work and do not waste time.'"

"Good advice for me too," I said, gazing at the portrait.

On the way home, it was *my* head that was spinning. I had seen Michelangelo's first work, had seen his face in fact, and his descendant wanted me to honor him with my own work. With a commission this important, and with the coins he gave me for supplies, I really was living the life of an artist in the greatest art city in the world.

I stopped at the shop of our apothecary, Franco. Bottles and jars sealed with wax lined the shelves, and withered roots and dried leafy branches hung from the ceiling. Trays of pigment cubes wrapped in paper and smeared with a thumbprint to identify the colors inside sat waiting for me in orderly rows. I could buy any of it.

"*Buon giorno,* signora. How is the little *bambina,* eh?" Franco asked.

"Growing fast. The joy of our lives."

"You came for more diapasm?"

"No. I came for pigments."

I picked alabaster for skin, and Spanish cinnabar for highlights. I selected some saffron strands to pulverize, and ochre clay to dry and grind. I put in my pile plenty of gray and white lead for clouds, and said, "I have a deep blue sky to do."

"I have some fine *azzuro dell' Allemagna,*" Franco said. His tongue licked up a few food morsels resting between his teeth and bottom lip.

"No, Franco. This time I want pure ultramarine."

He scrutinized me from under heavy eyebrows. "Lapis lazuli pebbles will cost you dearly. As much as gold. Is it for Pierantonio?"

"What does it matter?"

He hesitated, his tongue making another pass.

"If you have none to show me, just say so and I'll go elsewhere." I dropped my drawstring bag on the table loud enough so he would hear the coins.

He stuttered a moment and then turned to unlock a cabinet. He brought out a tied-up cloth, undid the corners, and spread out the stones. "From the Far East," he said, affecting a hushed, mysterious tone. "Just think how many foreign hands these have passed through to travel that distance."

"Yes, each one adding to the price. How much?"

"Which stone?" He touched the largest one as a suggestion.

"All of them."

His eyes opened wide, we settled on an amount, and he said, "May I ask who it is who shall receive such a painting?"

I gathered my purchases and drawings, turned back to him at the door, smiled wryly, and said, "Florence."

I hired a joiner to prepare the tall, narrow

stretcher according to Buonarroti's measurements for a life-size figure, and to build a larger easel and my very own cabinet for my drawings, brushes, and pigments. From now on, we were truly a two-artist family. Someday, maybe even three.

I primed the canvas, and ground the pigments ahead of time but did not add the linseed oil until the day I needed them. With Vanna posing, I began roughing in only the barest outline in paint. The weeks flew by in the joy of creating shape through color and shadow. I worked in a rhapsody, forgetting everything except the pleasure of laying on colors. I was working on her ankle when I heard Palmira's voice as if from a distant land. "Mama, I'm hungry, Mama."

I gasped. It was already late afternoon. "Oh, my darling, I'm so sorry. We'll eat right now." I hurried to get her a bowl of *pici* pasta left from the day before. I sprinkled raw broad beans with olive oil and laid out *pecorino* cheese and bell pepper for Vanna to eat with us too. I put honey on a slice of pecorino and handed it to Palmira.

"That's one good thing about having a child around," Vanna said. "She makes you stop work so we can eat."

"As good as one of those new chiming clocks." I pushed a plate of figs toward her. "Have you ever wanted to paint?" I asked.

"Never. Why go through all that agony? Men paint. Women pose. It's the way things should be."

"If you feel that way, why did you come when it was clear from my announcement that I was a woman?"

"I need the money. I am alone and have two boys. You know as well as I the alternatives."

Although I wondered what happened to her husband, if there had been one, I respected her privacy and didn't ask.

"Do you think you'll ever become famous being painted?"

"Yes, I do. They may not know my name, but they'll see me on a wall or a ceiling of a palazzo I could never get into myself to have a look around."

"And there's some satisfaction in that?"

"Yes. There is." She seemed at once defensive and wistful, a strange combination. "Someone who saw me painted there might recognize me in a piazza or on the street and take a second look. Or even speak. It could happen."

"Yes, I suppose. There are also the years to come."

"You mean when both of us are dead?" She pulled back her shoulders which thrust out her breasts. "I, as I am now, will last a great deal longer than any artist who paints me."

I had no way to answer that. What she saw was surface only. That which I contributed was, to her, incorporeal, and therefore of little consequence.

"Do your boys like figs? Take some for them." A haughtiness came over her features. "Please," I urged. "We have more than we can use from the tree in the courtyard."

"It's going to shock them with its reality, you know," Buonarroti said, looking at the finished painting propped on an easel in his audience hall.

"A naked woman sitting on a cloud has reality?"

He chuckled. "A woman. A real, rosy, flesh-and-blood woman. She's exquisite."

"I'm sure she'll be happy to know you think so."

"The academy, Bandinelli, Cosimo, they'll all see it and marvel," he said as he counted out thirty-four gold florins at his desk, put them in a brown velvet pouch and handed it to me. He grinned. "Do you want to know what part of her I like best?"

Her breasts? Hips? I didn't know. "Her face," I said.

155

"No. It's that plump left forearm with that endearing knob of an elbow. You are another Rubens. And I am the first person in Florence to recognize it."

"I'll be forever grateful."

With his back to me, he sifted through papers and quills in a desk drawer and drew out a paintbrush about the width of my index finger. The long handle was oiled walnut with a brass ferule, and the brush hairs were sable. He handed it to me. "Here. Don't lose it. It belonged to my great-uncle."

"Michelangelo himself?"

He leaned toward me in an amused, fatherly way, wagging his head back and forth. "He's the only great-uncle I have who painted. He'll have to do."

"It's a treasure! I won't ever use it."

"Oh yes. You must. Let this serve as a reminder that the blessing of God on genius is only given judiciously." He shook a finger at me. "Talent is not to be hid under a bushel." He looked back at my painting. " 'Every beauty which is seen here below by persons of perception resembles more than anything else that celestial source from which we are all come.' That's from a poem he wrote."

"God?" I teased. "God wrote?"

"No. Michelangelo."

"It amounts to the same thing."

At home I set out the thirty-four coins in rows for Pietro to see. I turned them so the lilies all faced up. I didn't show him the paintbrush. I heard Sister Graziela's voice. *Be wise.*

While I waited I felt something unsettling, unsatisfying that I did not feel when I had finished Susanna or Judith. *Inclinazione* may have been beautiful. It may have looked real, but it was missing something. For me, the pleasure had been visual, in creating shape and applying color, and tactile, in smearing the thick creamy paint on my palette, but the pleasure was not of the mind. The painting did not have *invenzione*. It did not tell a story. I had gotten paid for craft, not for art.

I would not write to Father about it.

"I can't believe it," Pietro said when he came home and saw the coins. His mouth seemed unable to close as he was counting. "Other artists commissioned by Buonarroti for single-figure panels received only ten."

"How do you know this?"

"One knows these things. It's our business to know."

That night in bed he lay as still as stone.

10

The Academy

I washed my hair, and used a twig to dig paint from under my nails. I wiped my old shoes with pork fat, and then I washed my good wine-colored dress. Sopping wet, the bodice didn't look bad, but the skirt looked like a rag. In a cold sweat, I took both parts upstairs to Fina.

"Bless you, child. You don't dunk a dress this fine into water. You just scrub the area you want clean. Now we'll have an awful time getting this to look decent again."

"Have I ruined it?"

"Put more wood on the fire."

She showed me how to press it smooth by using two iron pieces in the shape of pointed arches which she heated on the hearth. When I kept making more creases instead of taking them out, she elbowed me out of the way. "Hold up the skirt so it won't drag. My floor is none too clean."

It took most of the afternoon. "From now on, I'll pay you to do all our washing."

"Tell me, what's the occasion for such a dress?"

"The Accademia del Disegno has summoned me. 'Members ceremony and exhibition in commemoration of the feast day of Saint Luke,' the invitation said."

"Oh?" She looked at me curiously.

"Buonarroti, the man I did that painting for, showed it to members of the academy. I think I'll be admitted."

"And Pierantonio?" She scowled at the skirt as she worked. "He's invited too?"

"No."

"What does he think?"

"He hasn't said."

"Just be careful is all I've got to say."

"Careful. How can I be any more careful than I already am? I had to show him the invitation."

His eyes had narrowed and his mouth made that tight sideways movement when he read it. I'd said, "That overblown steward whose face looks like risen dough better not have put my name on the list of models. Do you think that's what this is for?"

Pietro had given me a look a person would

159

give to an annoying idiot in the street, and said, "How should I know?"

I helped Fina turn the skirt. "I'll be careful."

The exhibition hall of the academy was filled with men talking loudly in groups in front of paintings. Signor Buonarroti saw me at the door and came toward me holding out both hands.

"You will be a favorite here someday, mark my words," he whispered in my ear, and then he introduced me to the steward, the man who had tried to register me as a model.

"I believe we've met," I said. I couldn't suppress a wry smile when I offered my hand.

"Indeed."

Signor Bandinelli greeted me cordially, which surprised me, invited me to study the paintings, and moved on to greet others.

Signor Buonarroti pointed out il granduca, Cosimo de' Medici, dressed in a purple waistcoat with slashings showing emerald silk underneath, and matching green silk breeches and hose. Gold embroidery created a panel down the center of his waistcoat. He wore a narrow white ruff.

Oh, to do a painting with such exquisite

detail and that brilliant green, to build up the sheen with layers of glaze between paint no thicker than the silk itself, with brush hairs so fine their trailings would look like silk thread. But it was impossible. The only green that bright was made from Macedonian malachite, and could only remain that bright by leaving it coarse ground. That wouldn't do for silk because it would leave fine particles on the canvas. A shame. It was a spectacular portrait, but only in my mind.

Unfortunately for him, although Cosimo was young, still in his twenties, he was unattractive. His bulb-shaped nose cast a shadow on his mouth, and a rather silly looking miniature triangle of beard was tucked under his lower, pouty, rouged lip.

"Give him your most reverent curtsey," Buonarroti murmured. "Here we go." He took me by the arm. Hardly believing what was about to happen, I stepped forward, and il granduca took notice, but before Buonarroti could introduce me, the steward rapped his staff for attention.

The academy members arranged themselves in two rows facing each other with Signor Bandinelli at one end. I stood next to Buonarroti. Opposite us, a bearded, full-cheeked man dressed in scholar's brown smiled at me.

Signor Bandinelli cleared his throat. "Il granduca Cosimo de' Medici, members of the Accademia dell' Arte del Disegno, and guests. We are pleased to announce, on this feast day of Saint Luke, patron saint of artists and craftsmen, the new admissions to membership for 1615."

A fluttering in my stomach made me push my hand against my bodice.

"Members of the academy are held in the highest regard among the artists of the city of Florence, and are accorded the following privileges: instruction in drawing, painting, sculpting, architectural design, rhetoric, and mathematics; admittance to all occasional lectures, to the Uffizi and, upon application, to other private collections; and the use of studio space, academy library, costumes, props, and registered models. The following individuals, please step forward to receive their matriculation papers and sign our registry.

"Antonello Ignazio Barducci."

"Jacopo d'Arcibaldo Daviolo."

The steward handed out documents. At each name, the members tapped their staffs against the floor in approval, and said, *"Bravo!"* My toes cramped and I took only quick, shallow breaths.

162

"Antonio Guido da Fiorentino."

"Gianlorenzo Frapelli."

I held my breath.

"Francesco Alfonso Grepini."

My heart thudded to the pit of my stomach.

"Giacomo Luigi Romano."

I wanted to sink into the floor.

"And Artemisia d'Orazio Gentileschi Lomi."

For an instant, the sound of my name echoed in the room. Then the racket of staffs against stone, and the shouted word, *"Brava!"* My wild heart flew out of my chest and engulfed everyone. I stepped forward and signed with a big A, G, and L. I turned back to the men and met their smiles all around, from il granduca too, and especially the warm, proud face of Signor Buonarroti, looking like il divino himself. I wanted to hug them all.

No one mentioned that I was the first woman to be admitted. There was only that one word — *Brava.*

Was that resentment I saw in that man's stiffened back at the side of the room? In the arch of the brow of the man next to him? Was there anyone who did not tap his staff? Who was it I would have to win over with my words and not just my brush? Later, I'd watch for it later. Right now I was being congratulated.

"It is time for you to be one of us," Signor Bandinelli said. "The achievement of your *Inclinazione* alone makes you worthy of admission."

"That alone?" Apparently, he still didn't appreciate my Susanna and Judith. "I am most humbly grateful, signore."

Wine and sweetmeats were served and Buonarroti ushered me around the room and made sure everyone knew it was I who painted *Inclinazione*. Would I eventually find the entire membership to be more impressed by craft than by hard-won, thoughtful *invenzione?*

Just when we were about to approach il granduca, the steward stepped in our way. "Come with me, signora, for a tour." An oily command. With his palm out directing me, he gathered three other new members and took us upstairs to the library and studios and showed us the cabinets of drawings, the skeleton, the sculptural casts, and then iterated a long, detailed description of classes. None of that had to be done now. As quickly as I could, I paid my matriculation fee and registered for a class in writing and rhetoric. When I came downstairs, the gathering had dispersed. Il granduca was gone. It was over, just like that — a dream.

I held the document to my breast as I left the building, wanting to dance my way home. I'd write to Father. And Graziela and Paola too. But my excitement fought with the cold dread of telling Pietro.

I hurried back on narrow streets, weaving between two beggars in Piazza Salvemini. In front of Pietro's friend's *macelleria*, still-feathered chickens and geese hung from iron hooks, and the blood dripped into a trough that emptied onto the street. I stepped across it and went in and bought some boar sausage, something unusual for us, Pietro's favorite. Then, I walked on to a *vinaio*.

"A bottle of your finest grappa. For a celebration." My voice wakened the sleeping dog lying on the steps down to the wine cellar.

I picked my way past children playing in the street, past black-clad brethren of the Misericordia bearing a bier to Santa Croce. I crossed the large piazza diagonally. Because that wild-haired penitent was whipping herself and wailing by the church door, I didn't even stop at Michelangelo's tomb just a few steps inside the church as I usually did. He'd understand my excitement. *"Brava,"* they'd said.

165

What could I tell Pietro to soften it?

The lengths of colored silk on Corso dei Tintori seemed to be waving in my honor. I hurried down the Lungarno a short way, up the stairs, three flights, two, breathing hard, only one more, and heard Palmira crying. I opened the door. Huddled on the floor in a corner clutching my dressing gown around her, Palmira was hysterical. I ran to her.

"Oh, Palmira, *tesoro*. Where's your papa?"

My heart stopped. He wasn't here. God knows how long he had left her alone. He could have taken her to Fina.

I gathered her in my arms and kissed her reddened cheeks, her forehead, her ears, her little fists. Her tears salted my lips. "My little lonely one. *Poverina*. Don't cry." I felt her little body wracked with sobs. I held her close and rocked her. "Mama's here now."

She quieted, and her wet hand stroked the embroidery on my bodice. She walked her fingers up the braid at my neckline, but she wasn't willing to let go of her anger yet. Knowing she had my full attention, she sucked in a gulp of air and her bottom lip protruded. "I want a dress like this."

"You will have many. I promise you. Mama's in the academy now. Maybe someday you will be too."

I fed her half a hard-boiled egg and broth

with zucchini in her favorite blue faience bowl, and when she was finished she squirmed off my lap and put my dressing gown over her shoulders and pranced around the room dragging it behind her. Any other time, I wouldn't have let her do that, and she knew it.

I laid out the boar sausage for Pietro in thin slices like dark old coins touching each other around the edge of a pewter plate. In the middle I arranged pear wedges around the other half of the egg. "See how pretty? Like a star." Another plate for olive oil. And bread. How would I tell him? I couldn't allow my voice to sound exultant. I practiced saying it — "I've been admitted" — flat, like saying "It's going to rain," but I couldn't trust my voice. I sprinkled ground oregano on the surface of the oil, trailing shapes of an A and D for *Accademia* and *Disegno*. I put the document of admission with its large A and D next to the plate, and poured two glasses of grappa and waited.

"Hold still," I said to Palmira, and drew a humorous, exaggerated sketch of her with my dressing gown trailing off the page behind her.

"Is that me, Mama?" Her eyes sparkled with pleasure a moment before she remembered that she was sulking.

"It's my darling treasure. What is she called?"

"*Tesoro.*"

"What else?"

"Palmira," she said in a voice sweet as honey, and I knew I was forgiven.

I slid out one sausage slice and rearranged the others to fill in. I ate with tiny, delicious bites. I tried occupying myself by tidying my painting cabinet, but I kept taking one more slice of sausage, repositioning the remaining ones, and with every missing slice from the plate, the reason for Pietro's absence was clearer. He must have learned the news himself by now. I stirred the oil with a piece of bread so he wouldn't see the letters, pushed aside the plate, and took out writing paper.

Father,
I have news which should make you very happy. I have been admitted to the Accademia dell' Arte del Disegno, its first woman.

At first when I took the Judith and Susanna to the academy, they scoffed at me, saying women shouldn't paint any new invenzione. Then I took the paintings to Signor Buonarroti. Thank you for writing to him. He's a gracious, kindhearted man. He

*commissioned me for a large nude as part of
a ceiling in a memorial gallery for Michelangelo. Apparently members of the academy
saw it and they changed their minds. I must
not be too exultant. The future is still precarious.*

*Palmira Prudenzia is almost three now,
and is never still. She has Pietro's dark eyes
and brown curls. She's full of questions.
"How can I grow up faster?" she asked the
other day. So here I am, an academy artist
and a mother. I can hardly believe it. My
only worry is how Pietro will take my
academy admission.*

Ever your daughter,
Artemisia

Dusk came and dimmed the outside
world colorless. I lit a candle as well as my
mother's oil lamp, to make it a cheery place
to come home to. Many times Mother had
Father's supper ready and he wouldn't
come home until after it got cold. She'd sing
a song softly about the dancing lamplight to
make herself feel better, but to me, it always
sounded melancholy. The pears were
turning brown at the edges. I couldn't stand
to see them look so pitiful. I ate all but two
wedges. This was my celebration, after all.
The first woman in the history of the

academy deserved *something.*

I was giving Palmira the rest of the pear when Pietro burst in the doorway, yanking off his doublet. A bolt of anger flashed across his fine, small features.

"You could have waited," he said.

"Why did you leave her? She was crying when I came home. What do you mean, I could have waited? For what?"

"Until I was admitted." Flinging his doublet over his shoulder, he brushed past the table without looking at the document. The candle flame fluttered. I heard the door to our bedchamber close and latch.

"Pietro, what are you doing?" I pounded on the door. "*Per amor di Dio,* what does this mean? Don't do this to me." Palmira ran to me and hooked her arms around my legs. "You ought to be pleased. It will mean more commissions, for both of us." A muffled sob came through the narrow opening between doorframe and door. "What do you want?" I said to the door. "That I stop painting? Stop being what I was meant to be? Stop breathing?" I picked up Palmira, and paced from the main room to the kitchen and back.

Palmira nestled her head against my neck, as if she knew. I sat her on the sink counter and stroked her face with one hand, while I washed the dishes in the stone sink with the other. I made up Palmira's bed in the main room and gently laid her down. She tucked her curled fingers under her chin like a squirrel. I drew the quilt around her and whispered, "I swear, my precious, I will never allow you to be forced into a loveless marriage. You'll never have to marry out of convenience, never need to make the best of what circumstances give you."

I leaned against the wall. But wasn't that just life — making do with what circumstances give you? If it weren't for Agostino, if it weren't for Father, I might have been able to marry someone who loved me and would have been proud of me. Yet if I married for love, I might still be in Rome, might not have even been known to the academy. I thought of Graziela. Love marriages had no assurances either. The two things I wanted most in life — painting and love — and one had killed any chance at the other. Why was life so perverse that it couldn't or wouldn't give me one shred of good without an equal amount of bad?

I threw the dirty dishwater in the drip basin out the window with a great heave.

11

Judith

That dough-faced steward was not going to thwart my way to Cosimo de' Medici, and neither was Pietro. I began working on another *Judith Slaying Holofernes*, essentially the same composition but with different faces and richer dresses. This time, Judith's would be deep gold, which seemed to be a Florentine preference, and would have fuller sleeves pushed up in order to do her work. And because Florentines loved jewelry and decorative touches, I put gold braid on Abra's headscarf and gave Judith a bracelet with figures of Artemis in carved green stone framed in gold filigree. Since the making of fine cloth was one of the city's main industries, I used a wider picture plane allowing Holofernes's red velvet bedclothes to be more voluminous. I edged them with gold stitching. And for sensual appeal, I added the tinest speck of blood on the warm flesh of Judith's full breast, and more specks on her Florentine gold dress — all of this calculated to appeal to His Serene Highness Cosimo de' Medici.

The hardest part was to write the letter presenting the painting to him as a gift and offering my skill for future commissions. For three days I struggled to perfect the humble language of service. I sat at the table wasting paper with false starts, and watching Palmira play with a paper doll I had cut out of a ruined letter.

Instead, I wrote an easier letter.

Dear Graziela,
Palmira is three now and full of inquiry.
"Why do ants have fur?" she asked the other day. Fina, my angel helper who lives upstairs, taught her a song about a child carried to a far-off land by riding on a yellow bird, and now I hear it constantly. It reminds me of the birds on your manuscript edging. Are you painting any more Psalters? Have you gotten your roof repaired?

Pietro doesn't seem to mind that I paint, but he minds deeply that I have been admitted to the Accademia del Disegno before him. I have painted another Judith as a gift for Cosimo de' Medici. Forgive me,

173

Graziela, but I have made a cruciform of her sword. Let that puzzle them for centuries. If Cosimo accepts it for his palace, or commissions me for another, I fear stormy times ahead at home. Say a little prayer.

Ever your admirer and disciple,
Artemisia

When I finished, the letter to Cosimo came more easily.

A week after I had the painting and letter delivered, Cosimo invited me to the Palazzo Pitti, at my convenience, a genteel touch.

Pietro grumbled, "Of course. What do you expect when you give away your art?"

"You could do it too, you know."

"Push work on him? It's more gracious to paint for lesser patrons in the city and wait until he notices the work on his own."

"Wait? How long? We are mortal, Pietro. The sand falls through the glass every breath we take."

"Don't be morbid."

"I'm not. I'm being realistic."

Since it was early autumn, that brief, hazy, lovely time in Florence between summer's long sweltering days and November rains, I walked across the Ponte Vecchio rather than spending money for a carriage. The Arno

174

had shrunken to a sluggish muddy rivulet, and the normal reflection of ochre buildings that quivered on the surface of its green water was gone. Instead, weeds and dried grass edged the putrid ooze along the banks, and clouds of mosquitoes billowed up from the standing water. But that didn't darken my spirits.

If Pietro had been with me, he would have let the smell and the mosquitoes sink him into gloom. He might even have turned around, convinced himself that he would try another day, and then lose his resolve. He always did things that hurt himself, it seemed — like taking a job for fresco repair without pushing for a commission on new work. And he never used Venetian amber varnish when it was clear to both of us that it would enhance his work. I couldn't understand it. If a person loves something above all else, if he values the work of his heart and hands, then he should naturally, without hesitation, pour into it his whole soul, undivided and pure. Great art demands nothing less.

I waved my way through the mosquito cloud and went on.

The Pitti stretched out in stiff formality on the left side of Via de' Guicciardini. Even though I knew it not to be the case, the intimidating building seemed the home of a

175

despot rather than a family friendly to the arts. At the tall, heavy door, I gave my name to the porter who checked a list. He directed me upstairs to the *piano nobile,* the floor of audience rooms. I saw from a window that the palace was even larger than it looked from the street, having two perpendicular wings stretching back toward a grassy upward slope to form a U shape which enclosed a carriage courtyard.

I passed through the first windowed room full of antique sculpture and was ushered through a marble doorway into a room with elaborate white and gold cornices, the walls covered in deep rose brocade with paintings hanging everywhere. I could not look at them now. Courtesy required that I look at Cosimo. He and his guests were seated facing the courtyard eating what looked to be roasted stuffed pheasants surrounded by olives and artichokes. Pheasant feathers arched like a fountain in decorative display over mounds of quince, dates, figs, and almonds. In Rome I had not known food to be a work of art.

A steward announced me and I approached and curtseyed.

"So here is the feminine hand that wields such a powerful brush," Cosimo said, and extended a welcoming arm. "I had hoped to meet you at the academy."

"Your Serene Highness, I am greatly honored," I said, holding my curtsey and looking at the pattern of inlaid stone in the floor between us. "And I beg forgiveness for intruding on your guests."

"I am the one honored with such a gift, signorina."

How complimentary to address me that way. Apparently it was a Florentine pleasantry to reserve "signora" for matrons older than I. I wondered what he knew about me.

"You've given your Judith a hard face, you know."

"She is concentrating. Like all heroines, she feels profoundly her task."

"As you, no doubt, have felt about yours," he said with a chuckle. "And who, may I ask, was your male model who deserved such revenge?"

"It is not personal vendetta, Your Highness." Santa Maria, let me not offend him. "If it is to be called revenge at all, it's revenge against tyranny."

He gave that a slow, considered nod. "I shall find a fine place for your *Judith Slaying Holofernes* in the Sala dell' Iliade." He chuckled. "A place where my guests might need to be awakened from more passive pleasures. Be assured that it will be among good company, and further, that it must not be a gift. You shall be generously paid."

"Honored again, Most Illustrious Highness."

"But it must not be the sole representative of such a talented hand and mind."

Hope rose up my throat in waves.

"Let another one of equal skill accompany it and you shall be doubly rewarded."

"Another Judith?"

"Yes! Surely there are other moments to her story worthy of your brush."

"I will make it my most immediate task and pleasure."

"Why do pigeons fly, Mama?" Palmira asked, skipping along beside me the next day as I walked through the streets and piazzas and churches looking for an idea.

"I suppose to get away from little girls and boys who pester them."

How could I choose another moment with as much drama as the slaying? I thought of Father's version in which the two women huddled together over the decapitated head. I'd copied it when I was just learning to paint. The figures were strikingly posed, but that huddling wasn't what I wanted.

At one end of the Loggia della Signoria

stood Donatello's bronze Judith and Holofernes. I'd never cared for it. Instead of lying down, Holofernes was sitting up on the mattress while Judith's arm and scimitar were raised to strike. The figures were awkwardly positioned, the effect without grace.

I stopped before Michelangelo's David. His thunderous scowl looking out to the Piazza della Signoria seemed to shout to the giant, Goliath, *How dare you even think you can destroy me with your sword!* Now *that* was boldness. That was confidence. Florentines loved the David because he was the weaker force confronting and vanquishing a greater force. It was how they saw themselves against the world, and it was in Judith's story also.

While Palmira chased after pigeons, sending them flapping in the air, I stood in my favorite spot which gave me the profile I loved, David looking to his left toward Goliath. How could I use that wonderful curve to his neck? Looking to the side like that, he was alert to the danger but he wasn't tense, just ready, with his sling across his shoulder. If my new Judith could depict the moment after the slaying when Holofernes's head is in Abra's basket, the two women, facing each other perhaps, could be alarmed by some new danger, a noise in the camp. That would be a challenge — to paint a sound. Judith could look to her left toward the danger, just as David was, and she could have the same curve in her strong neck that David had.

Instead of the sling, she would rest her sword on her shoulder, on the lace edging of her white chemise, in fact. I liked that — the sword blade possibly cutting threads of the lace, the world of swords and the world of lace so different, yet touching dangerously. Yes. It would be new. It would be all mine. And it would not be for an age when women hide their skills in deference to men, even husbands.

Early one morning months into the work, I took Palmira with me across the Arno to Via Maggio, the street of the antiquarians which I knew she would love, and in a used-goods shop I bought an old, square metal table mirror in a wooden stand-up frame which had a tilting mechanism. I set it on the table at home and studied my neck and my Judith's neck, Vanna's neck actually, since I had hired her to model again. Vanna's neck as I had painted it was too delicate. Judith couldn't be that feminine and lovely. I was right in telling her to skip a day, even though she had still demanded to be paid. I set to work painting over Vanna's neck my own thicker neck and the first signs of my coming double chin.

When Vanna came the following day, Pietro hadn't left yet. She took one look at the painting and shouted, "What have you done? You've ruined it. That's not me!"

"No, it's Judith. But the eyes will be yours, and the mouth and hair."

She sniffed in a pouty way. "That neck is ugly." With big, watery eyes and a pitiful expression, she appealed to Pietro. "Don't you think it's ugly?"

"It's David's neck," I said before Pietro had a chance. "In the Piazza della Signoria."

"You expect me to be proud of that? People won't know it's me with that man's neck. Pietro, how could you let her ruin me?"

Caught between us, he shrugged and lifted his hands sheepishly.

"Vanna, please, blow your nose and take your position. I only need you for a few more days."

She thought a moment. "Double pay. I'll only stay if you give me double pay."

We all stood looking at each other, waiting for someone else to make the first move.

181

"Give it to her," Pietro muttered.

"All right, all right." I handed her Graziela's earring. "Put this on so I can see the shadow it makes."

I dismissed her as soon as I could, and used my own features in profile.

Painting the sheen and nap of Judith's brown velvet dress, the gold and black onyx beads sewn onto the intricate double panels of Florentine braid, Mother's bloodstone hair ornament edged in gold, the pommel of Judith's sword hilt shaped as a Gorgon's screaming head — all of it satisfied me, but when I got to Holofernes's head in Abra's basket, I had more trouble. Though I had in mind Caravaggio's Goliath, I couldn't make the greenish gray face look like anything other than Agostino's. That bothered me. I didn't want to paint out of hate. That would be cramped and mean-spirited and would limit my art and my expression forever. I worked and worried and it delayed my progress, but I could not let it go. I didn't want to be linked with Agostino's likeness forever, hanging among all those paintings created out of love.

I wrote to Graziela and told her I was paralyzed. How do I get rid of hate, I asked. I was restless until her answer came.

Cara Mia,

If that man has not separated you from the love of God, and he has not, then the only thing keeping hate of him alive is your thought about him. Only your pride keeps him in your memory and in your brush. Dissolve your pride, and you dissolve your hate. To be still possessed of the hate that pain made is not intelligent. Take care, Artemisia. It can sap your energy from what you know to be your purpose. By being troubled by it, you have already discovered it to be unworthy of your grander aims, and that, tesoro, is the beginning of humility.

Grazie a Maria, they have begun to work on our roof. Sister Paola wonders if you have visited Santa Trinità dei Monti in Florence. She wants you to know that the large crucifix in one of the chapels bowed its head to San Giovanni Gualberto who was kneeling in adoration. I long to know everything you've seen in Florence — every painting and sculpture, every church, piazza and tower, everything in sunlight, shadow, even rain. If you could spare the time and if it would please you, put your artist's eyes into words.

Sister Paola sends her utmost love, as I do.

Yours in Christ,
Graziela

A burning sensation behind my eyes blurred the words. I had not realized how much I missed them.

I wrote her back right away and described Michelangelo's first Madonna and Child in bas relief, his thick-muscled David, Donatello's winsome, youthful David, the Duomo, Masaccio's Adam and Eve, Botticelli's Venus. I felt inadequate to put into words the adoration these works of art stirred in me. I gave up and took a walk with Palmira and drew several little drawings of what I had tried to describe and one of Palmira chasing pigeons, and tucked them into the letter.

In between times at the easel, there was always food to buy, food to cook, one meal so soon after another, dishes to wash. I never knew when Pietro would be home and when he wouldn't. After he finished the fresco repair, he moved an easel and some of his painting things out of the house, I didn't know where. "So you'll have more room," he explained. A secret part of me withered like grapevines preparing for winter. He began to live like my father did, dressed more flamboyantly, and painted, ate, and caroused with his friends elsewhere than at home, missing the joy of Palmira's growing up. I remembered Father singing with Agostino or Caravaggio in the street as they staggered home near dawn all cock-a-hoop about what big things they'd been doing and what great painters they were, and Father banging his way through the rooms, knocking over a chair and falling, stinking, onto his bed. Was this to be my future?

The winter was particularly cold; it even snowed. Our well water froze and some mornings we had to strike it with an iron rod to break up the ice. Palmira had a fever, chills, and cough, and I was terrified. I stopped painting while she lay sick for a month. At first she cried a lot, choking on her sobs, and then she grew too weak for that. The thought of losing her haunted me day and night. Pietro stayed home more often to crack the ice and haul up water for me to dampen rags to cool her fever. He made endless, worried trips to the apothecary, and tended the fire while Palmira's wracking cough held me to her bedside. One night Pietro paced the room, picking up objects, setting them down, not knowing what to do.

"Sit here with us," I said. He hesitated. "It might help."

He brought over another straight-back chair with straw seat, sat down, and put his hand on the quilt over Palmira's leg.

"I remember once when I was sick as a little girl. I drifted in and out of sleep, and heard the soft murmurs of my parents' voices floating in a fog. I didn't know what they were saying, but it didn't matter. The blending of their voices sounded natural and loving and it comforted me."

A lock of Palmira's hair was plastered to her temple and lay near her eye. Pietro lifted it away and stroked her leg, awkwardly at first, and then lay his head on her bed. It was the tenderest gesture I had ever seen him make.

"Say something, so she can hear your voice too."

He turned his head sideways on the bed. Inadequacy flooded his eyes. "Palmira, your papa's here," he said. "You're going to be all right." I nodded encouragement. "I love you, little dove."

My heart swelled as if he'd said the words to me, and I returned the feeling, my offered cup of love full and running over. Wanting to make the moment last, I combed my fingers through his hair, which always soothed him. His eyes closed. When his breathing became deep and rhythmic, I leaned down next to him and laid my head on his shoulder and pulled my shawl up around us both.

We must have slept there awhile, a family, as close as on the day Palmira was baptised. When she stirred, we both woke up, and the stiffness in our necks and backs was nothing compared to the stiffness aching between us once again. Pietro looked at me with his dark, secretive eyes, astonished at his own affection. I kissed him just below his temple. One side of his mouth smiled in a soft, bewildered way.

Palmira's sickness finally let up in the spring, and Pietro was gone more often again. I didn't know where. I didn't dare ask. A new heartsickness welled up in me. I was a month behind in painting and still had Holofernes's face to do. Paint hard, I told myself.

But I didn't. Palmira was all the more precious to me because of the threat of losing her, so I spent more time with her. I felt unutterable comfort in her small, smooth hand in mine as we walked along the river. "Look, Palmira. Look at the light on the water. See how it dances? It's not just green. It's blue and brown and gray. Look at the colors move."

"I can't see it."

"Stand still and you will. Just look at one place."

187

But she couldn't stand still in her joy to be outdoors.

Across the river stood a three-arched crenellated tower. I made up stories about a princess imprisoned there whose sad lover was turned into a long-necked white bird that lived along the grassy bank below her tower, devoted still in his love to her. In summer when the water was shallow, we held hands and waded out on the diagonal dam. She loved to feel the cool water rippling across her ankles and to play at fishing with a reed.

I told her about Graziela and Paola in the convent on a Roman hill. In an open market I bought two wooden bowls and rigged them with twigs and paper sails. We fashioned dolls out of paper which Palmira colored black with a piece of charcoal from the fire, except for their faces and hands. She named them Sister Graziela and Sister Paola. I taught her the letters of their names and she wrote them on the backs. She would not say their names without the "Sister" first, as if they were titled ladies. I tied strings to the bowls and we floated them in the water and watched the nuns bounce and slide downriver as we walked along the bank, supremely happy in our play. Watching her tug Graziela's string, I realized that because Palmira got well, Graziela's words were true. I had not been separated from the love of God.

Only a couple weeks before the painting was due, without even thinking, I widened Holofernes's face and lengthened his nose. He became an Assyrian, and only an Assyrian. I took the greenish tinge out of his face so that it looked like smooth gray stone, or metal, the same color as the screaming head on the sword hilt, suggesting that's what he had been doing a moment earlier, though now he was peaceful. I let him rest in peace.

The painting was to be presented to il granduca at a court affair one evening in the Palazzo Pitti. Pietro did not attend. It was a shortsighted decision. There in the Palatina would be the whole Medici collection and all of Cosimo's present artists to talk to about composition, interpretation, and technique. He could have met a new patron. I would have introduced him to Cosimo as a fine painter. Pietro wouldn't hear of it.

They sent a carriage for me. When I stepped up into it, I heard something rip over my ribs. Fina had made me a tight new bodice of dark green with detachable sleeves, so if I were to be invited again, different sleeves would make it look like a new gown. I couldn't tell where the rip was. All I could do was to trust that it didn't show.

In the palace, colors of gowns, paintings and frescoed ceilings leapt out around me as I passed through the rooms to get to the large, square Sala dell' Iliade. The walls were covered with paintings three rows high, in no apparent order, all in elaborately carved frames, a feast for the eyes. My *Judith Slaying Holofernes* was there too, in an elegant gold frame carved in deep relief. It made me catch my breath to see it hanging in the presence of masterpieces. Who had painted them? Raphael? Titian? Tintoretto? Rubens? Andrea del Sarto? What a boon for me if I could just get someone to talk about them.

I curtseyed before il granduca. This time he was dressed with the colors reversed — emerald breeches and waistcoat, with sleeves intricately slashed to show purple satin beneath. I gripped a velvet chair back as my new Judith, covered by a drape, was set on a carved walnut display easel adjacent to my *Judith Slaying Holofernes*. The moment it was unveiled, I looked at Cosimo only. He pulled at the little triangular tuft of hair under his bottom lip in a self-satisfied way, looking from one painting to the other.

"*Brava*, signorina. *Magnìfico*," he said, and the whole assembly assented in one breath. "I have made a discovery. Here in Artemisia Gentileschi Lomi we have the rational mind of man and the sensuous hand of woman."

I couldn't help but look at my painting. Light from candles in the wall sconces showed off the highlights of Judith's face and throat, Abra's head wrap and sleeve, even the white piping between Abra's bodice and the gathers of her skirt. I noticed now more than ever the beautiful shape of a shadow coming to a point where her neck ended and her chest began. I was supremely satisfied.

"*Non c'è male*," I heard from somewhere in the room. I hated that overused Florentine expression, "not bad."

"But more than that," Cosimo continued, "with the two paintings together, we have two aspects to the feminine. We have the active and the contemplative. *Brava* again."

Others who now thought it better than "not bad" delivered compliments of "fine" and "formidable" accompanied by courtly bows.

One gray-bearded man nearing fifty, wearing brown breeches and standing separately, came toward me smiling. His long, straight nose, and that beard curved over his chin like the back of a pewter spoon, was familiar, but more individual than the beard was the wen high on his full cheek under his left eye. I was certain I had seen him somewhere before.

"You have a great future, signorina," he said, "which will, no doubt, match the great beauties of your person." The expression in his brown eyes was genuine.

What could I say after stumbling over my gratitude? "Perhaps you could tell me about this magnificent collection."

A fluttering of ladies in rasping violet, ultramarine and deep green brocade skimmed toward me across the marble floor like a swarm of iridescent insects on a still pond. They surrounded me, their tall wired collars quivering, and the man in brown retreated. "Do you come from Rome?" one lady asked, waving a painted paper fan on a stick.

"Or further south?"

I felt trapped. "I was about to ask that gentleman about the paintings. He seemed to know —"

"Who? Signor Galilei? No, he knows nothing of painting. He's the court mathematician. His head buzzes with only stars and numbers."

"Tell us, please," another woman asked in

a stinging whisper, "in the south, have you known, intimately, I mean, a man so swarthy as that man on the mattress?" The others tittered.

I held myself rigid as I said the single word "No," so as not to show that I even noticed the insult.

I was delivered home across Ponte Vecchio by carriage, without an escort. As we rattled across the Arno, I held to my nose a sprig of lavender given to each lady so as not to swoon.

No man had called me beautiful since — I hated to admit — since Agostino had.

Black velvet darkness enveloped the city. No moon. No stars. Only a few lanterns flickered on entries to the larger houses or illuminated the small niche carvings of protector saints. At Fina's, I half-wakened Palmira and carried her downstairs. Nearly four years old now, she was really too big for this. Her foot knocked against the same place on my thigh at every step.

"I had a dream, Mama. I was in the palace with you. In a beautiful red dress," she murmured.

"That's wonderful."

"With pearls sewn on." She was asleep again by the time I laid her down.

Pietro was not at home. I lit a candle and opened one of the doors onto the balcony, hoping for a breeze in spite of the rank odor. Somewhere on the riverbank, a bullfrog croaked, no more able to sleep than I was. Cosimo de' Medici reminded me of a lordly, emerald green frog, surrounded by flitting insects busy with their fan flipping. Standing next to il granduca, I had been at the very heartbeat of Florence, with masterpieces, painters, future clients all around me, and Cosimo himself asking for a Mary Magdalene next.

Yes, it was a magnificent victory, sweet as lily-shaped marzipan, but a temporary one. Strung like beads through the years ahead was a line of gala court occasions with harpsichord, poets and players, almond cakes and perfumed candies — which I would be invited to only when Cosimo had a painting of mine to unveil. Fine. That was just fine. I was doing what I loved, learning every day, and being honored for it. I hung the lavender from a ceiling hook among our iron pots. When it dried I'd grind it with mortar and pestle and add it to a dipper of well water, boil it a minute to make a sweet perfume, and I'd splash my throat and cheeks with it the next time I was invited. Maybe the court mathematician would be there too.

I swatted at a mosquito, but couldn't bear to close the door. I undressed and put on my night shift. The soft high chirping of bats swirling up from the river was the loneliest sound in the world.

What now? Write it all to Father? Yes, I could do that. He would revel in my triumph, even if Pietro didn't. But then Father had always claimed me as his product. "... *Carnal actions that brought grave and enormous damage to me, the poor plaintiff, so that I could not sell her painting talent for so high a price.*" That he considered me a novelty to sell still hurt me, but there was danger in bitterness. It might carve itself into my face permanently or show itself as woman's insolence, and a patron, taking offense like the academy had done at first, might cast me away. I could not afford to display resentment. Restraint had to be my public self. Besides, *he* was not selling my talents. I was. An enormous difference which might not have happened had I stayed in Rome — that is, had there been no trial. I'd never thought of it that way before.

Pietro did not come home. It would have been pleasant to talk over the evening in quiet tones — if not with him, with someone, that man who had called me beautiful, for example — to muse about the duke, the court, other possible clients, the music, the food, the finery, and, if it were Pietro, to undress bit by bit in candlelight while chewing on a fig, moments of the evening spilling out like plump grapes from a tipped bowl. Desirable certainly, but not essential. Painting was essential.

The eerie, whining night cry of a cat in heat startled me, made my heat-damp flesh go cold a moment. Made me conscious of a yearning issuing from some dark place, to touch, stroke, pet like a cat. And to be touched, to nestle myself in a palm, to arch against the pads of fingers, the push of flesh.

Restless, I lifted out Michelangelo's brush from the bottom of my *cassone* and unrolled it from the cloth. I'd never used it. I held it up to the air as if I were painting something, someone. Whom? The man with his head in the stars. The wide white collar that stood up in a curve over his shoulders, his straight, aristocratic nose, his intelligent, kind eyes. I realized where I'd seen him before — standing opposite me at the academy admission ceremony. Smiling.

I lay on the pillowed bench and touched the soft sable to my throat, the throat Vanna thought was ugly. So what if she thought that? Not everyone did. Besides, I had something that no one else did. The brush hairs, soft as cat fur, up my throat, around the back of my ear, their touch in my ear excruciating and titillating, il divino's own hand on this brush, down my neck, closing my eyes to candlelight, to anything that would distract me from the sensation, between my breasts, lowering the cotton of my shift, stroking softly in a big circle one and then the other, the circles getting smaller, hesitating, smaller and smaller circles, around the nipple, feeling the tingle deep in my belly, contracting, loosening, contracting, a rhythm lifting me, a wave about to crash, about to, then crashing. I trembled and relaxed, still and content and dreamy for a long time.

12

Galileo

San Giovanni's Day dawned in the splendor of immediate blue. Warm, silky June air invited me to pause and breathe deeply when I opened the doors to the balcony. Fina's beloved thrushes heralded the holiday of the city's patron saint.

"It's going to be a spectacular day. Are you sure you don't want to come with me to the Pitti?" I said over my shoulder as Pietro was pulling on his new cinnamon-colored hose. "Cosimo's invitation is for both of us. It will be a grand meal. There'll be music and Commedia dell' Arte, and afterward we can walk in the garden."

"I'll leave the garden and music to you," he said airily. "I'm going to the *calcio*." His lips twisted into a self-mocking smile. "To get my fill of barbarians cracking skulls for the year."

He made fun of the brutality, but still every San Giovanni's Day he went and did his share of shouting. In other years, I'd gone with him to the Piazza di Santa Croce to see the games — a tournament of four wild mobs pounding and kicking each other over a ball, each team named after a church in one of the four sectors of the city, creating a riot in the name of John the Baptist. Last year the Brethren of the Misericordia carried off two players on litters.

On such a holiday as this, and since my invitation was for two people, I felt I could bring Palmira. She would be thrilled. Besides, I didn't want Fina to be tied down at home when there were musicians and singing in every piazza.

Pietro sang in a bombastic baritone, tucking in his chin as the three of us walked downstairs and out the gate together. Everyone in the whole city seemed to be out in the streets. Where the Corso dei Tintori angled away from the Lungarno and we would go our separate ways, Pietro twisted Palmira's ear playfully.

"Be a good girl in front of the duke, eh!" And to me, *"Ciao, amore,"* with a kiss vaguely placed at my temple.

"Ciao, amore." He rarely said *amore,* and

so I savored it a moment. I almost decided to go with him instead, his mood being so blithe and loving, but an invitation to the Medici's palace was not to be taken lightly. We would both come home and tell each other what we saw and did. That would be like living the day twice.

It was a good thing the goldsmiths' shops along the Ponte Vecchio were closed for the holiday. Otherwise, I would have had a hard time getting Palmira across without a tedium of "oohs" and *"che bellas"* at every shop. This was her first time in the Pitti Palace, and as soon as we walked up the stairway, Palmira's little eyes opened wide. She was so awed by the beautiful clothing that she became quiet as a rabbit, only whispering to me to look at this or that dress. The people seemed much less real to her than the fabrics. I knew that when we got home, I wouldn't be able to get her to stop talking about all of it.

In the large Sala Bianca, her gaze was fastened on the dozens of double-tiered crystal *candelaria*. "Are they going to light them, Mama?"

"Probably not. People will leave before dark to go to the last game of the *calcio*."

On the credenzas there were trays of antipasti — melon wedges wrapped with prosciutto, and *crostini* spread with peacock liver paté, the tray decorated with a fan of peacock feathers. Palmira loved the exotic beauty of the display but was afraid to try one. Instead she ate the little pocket cookies filled with jam. The tables were arranged in a wide, shallow U facing the windows and the courtyard below. The open doorways to the terrace were hung with sprigs of lavender and basil to keep out the horseflies and odor from the carriage yard below.

I watched the Archduchess Maria Maddalena sitting at the center table. She wore a sheer black headdress, something like a nun's wimple, which came down over her forehead in a point. I couldn't understand why she had chosen such a severe style. It emphasized her narrow oval face to poor effect. A large, dark ruby hung from a gold chain that seemed about to strangle her. Her children came up behind her to whisper to her. She dismissed them, it seemed to me, rather than attending to them. Cosimo wanted my Mary Magdalene as a compliment to her. I knew nothing about her. How could I make the figure of a prostitute, even a high-class prostitute, honor her?

The meal consisted of roasted guinea fowl, beef tripe with bell pepper sauce, and spinach, finished off with baked peaches stuffed with almond paste. Palmira liked that best.

After the meal, I took Palmira out to the balcony which connected to a large terrace where Signor Galilei was standing with a group of men. I was sure it was him even without his brown waistcoat. Today he was as stylish as any courtier in a long blue sleeveless *lucco*. The white sleeves of his shirt puffed out like clouds. His gray hair threading through his brown glinted in the sunlight. Would he remember me?

The other men seemed to defer to him, letting him speak more, but when any of the others spoke, everyone still watched him to see his reaction. I listened a moment. They were engaged in a lively debate over the relative merits of sculpture over painting — far different entertainment from the rampage taking place on the other side of the Arno. This I could speak about. I left Palmira dancing her straw doll on the balustrade and stepped over to join them.

"Statues, being three-dimensional objects rather than two-dimensional paintings are more real than paintings," one gentleman said. "Therefore, they are capable of creating a more deceptive illusion — which is to say that sculpture is the highest of arts."

"I disagree entirely," I said, standing a few

steps away and behind Galilei. The moment he recognized me, his smile reached all the way up to the wen under his eye. He opened their circle to allow me to step forward.

"What does the signorina think?" one gentleman prodded, as if a lady venturing an opinion were a novelty.

I didn't know these men, but I plunged ahead, adopting their artificial style of speech. "Relief which deceives the sense of vision is within the reach of painting as well as sculpture because painting has all the colors of nature to give shape, whereas sculpture merely has lights and darks. Though sculpture has relief which is perceived by the touch, painting achieves a visible relief without that advantage. Therein lies the greater challenge, and therefore its superiority."

"The signorina is right," Galilei put in. "What is so impressive about imitating the sculptress, Nature, by using nature itself, stone, to create volume?" He turned to me for my agreement. "Of the two, painting is the superior art, but for one more reason. Being two-dimensional, painting is farther removed from reality, and the farther removed the means of imitation is from the thing to be imitated, the more worthy of admiration the imitation will be."

"Is that a general principle applicable to all the arts?" one of the men asked.

"Indeed. We ought to admire the musician who moves us to sympathy with an unrequited lover by representing his sorrows and passions in song much more than if he were to do it by sobs." His smile directed to me was playful. "Songs are opposite to the natural expression of pain while tears and sobs are very similar to it."

"Then in that sense, Signor Galilei" — I flashed him a sidelong look that suggested I was about to trump him — "music with the lute alone is higher than either song or painting by virtue of its greater distance from the human."

The men in the circle teased him for being overmatched. He waved his hand at them good-naturedly and asked me, "Even though I am sorely overpowered, might I have the pleasure of taking a *passeggiata* in the garden with my conqueror?"

I held out my hand to Palmira. She did a sprightly skip-hop to join us. "My daughter, Palmira."

"Ah, a lovely child. Her mother's image in miniature."

We walked downstairs and up a ramp to the entrance to the garden and a grassy ampitheater where some small boys were imitating the *calcio*. The greens of the cypress trees and ornamental box hedges were greener, the grass more velvety, the breeze fresher, the birds more melodious than anywhere I'd ever been.

"Everything seems brushed with a sheen that saturates the colors."

"That's the painter in you speaking."

Then he did remember me. "Where does this path lead?" I asked.

"To many delights, I hope. Specifically to several hedge labryinths."

"Oh, you'll like that, Palmira." In the meantime, there were plenty of people strolling so she would be content looking at their clothing.

"You were about to ask me something the last time we saw one another," he said.

"Yes, what you knew about the paintings in the palace, but now I need to know something else."

"What might that be?"

Palmira spotted a black and raw sienna butterfly and we stopped to let her watch it until it fluttered away.

"What do you know about the archduchess?" I asked.

"She's from Austria. Uncompromisingly religious. Fond of somber masses and endless vespers. Contrarily, she's a woman who feeds on the dramatic moments of Christian history, who loves its excesses and extremes. She would have followed Saint Francis if she'd been alive in his time."

"Or the example of Mary Magdalene? That is, if she had found herself in other circumstances."

"Even without those circumstances. There are women who take on the world's sins and make a practice of continual repentance."

"Renouncing the world and praying like a penitent while wearing their jewels?"

"Precisely."

"Thank you. That may prove helpful."

With his open palm Galilei directed us to take a narrower path between white flowering hedges. The sweet scent of jasmine was heady in the heat of the afternoon.

"Helpful for a painting?" he asked.

"Yes, a Mary Magdalene that the archduke has commissioned. I want to discover and display another side than the conventional belief of a sinner struck by unpremeditated conversion or spontaneous repentance. I think it must have been deep, prolonged, painful reflection that caused her great personal upheaval. Have you seen Masaccio's Adam and Eve in the Brancacci Chapel?"

"Of course."

"All of Eve's body is thinking and feeling. In the same way that Eve's body thought in Masaccio's hands, I want my Magdalen's body to think, too. I don't know yet what I want her to think, but I know it has to be more complex than anguish at her vision of herself."

"Might I suggest you see Donatello's carving in wood of the Magdalen in the Baptistry? It has an excessiveness the arch-duchess would appreciate."

"How can I, this time of year? I'd have to wait until March, the yearly baptism."

He stopped in the pathway to think. "With a little authorization from His Serene Highness, I'm certain you will be given admittance. I can easily obtain it and shall feel honored to accompany you today. You and your pretty daughter."

"Today? Won't that seem ungracious?"

"No. People will be leaving soon for the evening *calcio.*"

We cut short our walk, and he spoke privately to Cosimo. When we noticed some people leaving, we said our respectful good-byes, and rode across the Arno in an open carriage, another delight for Palmira. She'd never been in one. Galilei reached into his pouch and pulled out his fist. "Palmira, open your hand, if you please," he said.

She glanced up at me for permission and then did so. He dropped into her palm a hard, yellow-green candy, irregularly shaped. He offered one to me too.

"Citron. I have several citron trees at my villa."

Palmira pulled in her cheeks and made sucking sounds. "Why don't we have candies like this, Mama?"

"If we did, then these wouldn't be so special. Rarity increases the value of something."

Galilei looked at me for a long moment before he popped one into his mouth.

The river, less murky and more blue than usual, was crowded with every kind of boat surrounding a barge with musicians playing under gold banners. The *remaioli* had stopped their work of dredging sand from the riverbed and building up the banks. Today every sand gatherer used his slim boat as a floating house of revelry. On the far bank, we heard trumpets from the *calcio* procession. Palmira was beside herself with excitement.

At the Baptistry, we stopped and Signor Galilei stepped out. "I won't be long. I am somewhat acquainted with the sacristan." He went into a building on the piazza.

Palmira grew restless in the carriage so I

let her get out. "Stay close," I cautioned. Immediately she ran behind three pigeons. She could scurry away and get lost in the crowd just while I blinked. I followed her to keep her in view among the musicians, fruit vendors, and gamblers dicing at small tables. She was attracted by a *porchetta* wagon with the pig's head cut off like Holofernes's and looking at its roasted body. I didn't tell her the pig was stuffed with its own cut-up ears and entrails.

The ragged penitent sat moaning on the cathedral steps. Her anguish didn't seem false to me, as it did to Pietro. No woman would choose to live out her days that way and look so unkempt unless compelled to by something stronger than her will. Palmira's curiosity outweighed her timidity, and she approached the woman. The pathetic creature wailed louder and Palmira ran back to me crying. The louder Palmira cried, the louder the woman did also. I had to shake Palmira to get her to stop. "That's not kind. She's a sad old woman and you're not to pay her any attention."

"Look how dirty she is. Her feet are black, Mama."

"Yours would be too if we couldn't afford shoes. Now behave. Here comes Signor Galilei. He's doing us a favor so don't be contrary." I took out a handkerchief and wiped her face. "We're going to see where you were baptised as a little baby."

We followed Signor Galilei and the sacristan to the Baptistry and together the two men slowly pulled open one of the massive bronze doors just far enough for us to slide through sideways. We stood in the dim light coming in from the high windows until our eyes adjusted and I noticed features I hadn't at Palmira's baptism — the walls of green and white stone set in a geometric pattern, and the flat, fluted pillars. An enormous, ornate silver cross on the altar held Palmira's attention.

I left her there and crossed the open space with Galilei. Between two rose-colored marble columns stood Donatello's wooden Magdalen in old age. In one shocking moment I saw it all. An emaciated figure with wild, hollow eyes in deep eye sockets, and sunken cheeks, ravaged by time in the wilderness, her hands close together, praying. She was barefoot, standing with thin legs widely placed, naked, not artfully nude, clothed only in tangled hair that reached to her knees. Only two teeth stood like tiny headstones in her gaping mouth. Her shriveled legs so far apart and her clenching toes rooted her to earth while she longed for

Heaven. I shuddered.

"It's that lady outside!" Palmira shrieked behind me. She buried her face in my skirt and a burst of crying echoed in the empty stone chamber. Palmira would not be calmed no matter what I said. The only solution was to get her out of there quickly.

I looked at Signor Galilei helplessly, petrified with shame. "I'm sorry, signore. I think we must leave."

I grasped Palmira's hand and hurried her out, but I turned back for another look at the Magdalen. Pathetic woman, still driven mad by her sin seventeen centuries old.

"No need to take us home, Signor Galilei. We don't live far. I'm sorry to have inconvenienced you."

13

Venus

The next afternoon a messenger delivered a letter.

Honored Signorina,
I most humbly regret the trouble I caused you and your daughter yesterday. It was thoughtless of me not to foresee the reaction of a child to such a haunting figure, though I'm sure the presence of the unfortunate woman outside the Baptistry contributed to your daughter's distress.
*   Might I try to redeem my good intentions by inviting you to supper at the Palazzo Pitti on the occasion of the birthday of Cosimo's son Giovanni a week from Saturday? Cosimo has empowered me to send a carriage for you, and he asked that I tell you he would be equally delighted by your com-*

pany. I cordially kiss your hand; and, pray, continue to favor me with your good nature and brilliant mind, as well as with your pres ence to participate in our observations of the planet Venus that evening if the weather is clear.

Most humbly,
Galileo Galilei

The wax seal displayed an animal surrounded by laurel branches underneath a crown. The Lyncean Academy of Science, it said.

Observations of the planet Venus? Why that particular planet? What would Pietro think? What did I think? I wasn't sure. His interest in me must surely be only fatherly. After all, he was old enough to be my father. I had inconvenienced him, and I didn't want to appear ungrateful. And there were definite advantages to being in the presence of Cosimo's court. Every gentleman there would be a potential patron, including the young sons Ferdinando and Giovanni when they came of age. I answered yes.

By evening, I thought better of it. I didn't know Signor Galilei's intentions. If Pietro were with me, that wouldn't raise any suspicions. When he came home from painting, I told him about the invitation casually, as I was slicing onions.

"Would you like to go?"

"Let me see the invitation."

The knife slipped off the onion round. "No invitation. A messenger came in Medici's livery and recited it in verse. Quite clever."

I looked only at the onion and cut more carefully.

"When is it?"

"Saturday after next. Late afternoon and evening. To look through a telescope."

"No. I'm going to the horse races."

Horse races. That meant he'd either come back elated and generous with his money, or morose and tight-fisted.

The whole city was a cloudy oven on the afternoon of Giovanni de' Medici's birthday. Sultry heat waved up from the paving stones and bounced off stone walls. The air was so heavy it would weigh down a moth's wings.

In the Sala Bianca a steward directed me to sit next to Galilei at the end of the U-shaped arrangement of tables. As soon as he saw me, he stood up and bowed and drew back the chair for me.

"Have you forgiven me for abandoning you to the mercy of the sacristan?" I asked. "I am afraid both my daughter and I behaved badly."

"And I am afraid I have failed you again, signorina."

"How can that be?" I asked.

"The clouds." He glanced out the open window. "Venus won't show herself tonight."

"Perhaps they will blow away," I said.

Moving only one finger, he pointed to a banner hanging limp and unmoving from the opposite wing of the palace.

Nothing he said gave me any indication as to his intentions. More than once I found him not following the conversation at the table while absently scraping his thumbnail across the pads of his fingers. His mind *was* in the stars, just as those women had said.

Waiters served the antipasti of anchovies in olive oil and lemon, and fried zucchini flowers. People ate slowly, talked slowly, moved as little as possible. Even the laughter was slow and listless. No air entered through the open windows. Rivulets ran down the waiters' necks. Guests dabbed at their foreheads with napkins. Signor Galilei wet his handkerchief and laid it over my wrist to cool me.

We ate the *prima portata,* a savory pork pie with onions, dates, almonds, and saffron, while singers performed a rousing song composed by Lorenzo de' Medici. *Chi vuol esser lieto, sia di doman non c'è certezza,* they sang. Be happy now since the future is uncertain. What a song for a birthday. Others laughed and set down their painted paper fans to clap, but to me it seemed a grim augury. I thought of Pietro at the races, gambling. Signor Galilei, too, seemed to have dark thoughts at that moment, though I couldn't guess what they might be. His thumb worked rapidly against his fingers.

Cosimo escorted his son Giovanni along the tables, introducing him as if he were a little man, though he couldn't be more than seven or eight. When they came to me, Cosimo said, "This is Donna Artemisia Gentileschi, a great painter. She is working on a painting for your mother right now."

I quailed a little because I hadn't started it and feared he would ask about its progress.

"You will want paintings by her in your collection someday."

"Someday I shall be happy to paint for you," I said, and they moved on.

From where I sat I could see the dour Archduchess Maria Maddalena. She bore herself with pride, but she made no sweet gestures toward her boys that Cosimo's mother, the Grand Duchess Cristina, made freely. The mother's manner lacked the engagement and lively spirit the grandmother showed in honoring her grandson by reciting a poem dedicated to him.

I leaned toward Signor Galilei and whispered, "This archduchess of the egg-shaped face who queens the table with such gravity would not be flattered by emaciation and wildness of the kind Donatello's sculpture portrays."

"But what are you painting for, to flatter a patron or to express an idea?"

"My own idea, which is not of a woman crippled for life by exaggerated penitence. I had hoped to make her a heroine, but a penitent is not a woman doing a bold act for which she would later be proud."

"Then what will you do?"

I took a long, slow breath. "I don't know."

Next to me a lady waved her fan, and then thought better of the exertion and simply gazed out the window.

"The best paintings depict a specific narrative moment," I said, thinking out loud. "I had thought of depicting the moment of anxiety outside Simon's house when she was holding in her hand the alabaster box of costly oil, waiting for an opportunity to enter in order to wash and anoint the Master's feet, but now I'm not sure."

"You have read the Scriptures?" His thumb stopped moving.

"No. I just imagined that moment outside the house."

"But you have knowledge of the Bible."

"When my mother died, I was raised by the Sisters of Santa Trinità dei Monti in Rome."

"Is that to say that you take the Bible as literal truth?"

"I am not a theologian. I'm a painter. The Bible is a rich source of stories to depict dramatically in painting and sculpture" — I smiled here — "and in song, which you say is the higher art. As to the absolute truth of these stories, that is not my purview. I deal with the imagination."

"*Bene.*" He leaned back comfortably.

"And my imagination tells me that Mary Magdalene had a closer relationship with Jesus than her sister Martha had, bustling about serving food. He said to Martha that Mary had chosen the better way." I looked at the archduchess's hands weighted down with enormous rings. "That's what I'd like to show in some way, that Martha's active life with her concerns about propriety and things of this world was less important, at the moment the Master was teaching, than Mary's meditative life. The Magdalen was the sister who had the nature to dwell in a thinking plane occupied mostly by men."

He lifted his wine goblet but did not drink. "By men only?"

"Virtually so. Look at the disciples. Anyone who expressed a reasoned thought, even just an inquiring thought — all men. Biblical women *display* acts of faith and spirituality, but where have you seen them engage in speech or inquiry like Mary Magdalene did with the Master?"

"What about the Virgin?"

"What has she ever said from a spiritual consciousness? What evidence do we have of an inquiring, vibrant mind? Do we have a Virgin's Prayer like we have a Lord's Prayer? The Magnificat is the closest there is."

"Such an assessment would not gladden the Holy Fathers."

"It's not that she is undeserving of sanctity, but you have to admit, she has come down through the centuries in near silence. At least Mary Magdalene spoke with a mind aware of another perspective and capable of reasoning."

"If I might say so, you are like your Magdalen in that respect, which makes you an extraordinary woman, by your own argument."

"How's that?"

"A meditative mind. Looking at things from another perspective."

I nodded an acknowledgment at the compliment. "But it's difficult to convey any of that in a painting. And those not willing to reflect on a painting miss such suggestions."

After an interlude performed by players on stilts, waiters served the *seconda portata* — roasted pigeons wrapped in bacon, and after that, figs stuffed with musky black grapes. No one felt like eating. It still had not begun to cool.

"Signorina, or may I call you Artemisia?"

"Signora, but please, use Artemisia."

"Yes. I was much impressed by your participation in our debate over painting and sculpture."

"An interesting discussion, though not my usual fare." When had I had such a discussion with Pietro? I couldn't remember.

"Do you realize the magnitude of your success — the first woman in the academy? A woman kicking against the pricks of narrowness and tradition. A woman with a vision for herself. Very admirable."

I couldn't help but smile at such remarks. If it were cooler, I could have thought of a demure reply.

Guests strolled out to the terrace and garden in search of shade and a breeze. Galilei made no move to leave the table. He pulled out from his pouch a handkerchief full of the citron candies. "An old man's indulgence." With the handkerchief draped over his hand, he offered them to me.

"They're lovely. Each one is a different shape. Like molten glass." I picked one out. "Or raw jewels."

"The citron has done well this year. I grow them in terra-cotta pots at my villa. Oranges and lemons too."

"Candies growing on trees?"

He chuckled softly at his omission. "Made into candies by Sister Maria Celeste of the Convent of San Matteo in Arcetri." He laid the handkerchief on the table and watched them tumble out. "My daughter."

"Oh. I didn't realize you were married."

"I'm not." He let a moment pass. "Nor have I ever been."

It shouldn't have surprised me. Though not particularly handsome, he was an intelligent man capable of kindness, a man whose gallantry was sincere, a man easy for an intelligent woman to love.

"Strange, yes? For a man my age."

"Perhaps not strange for a man in love with the stars."

"I have another daughter too, and a son. Their mother and I are cordial, but have never lived together. She's married now and lives in Padua."

I shifted my gaze discreetly from the candies to his face to try to discern his feelings toward her, but his eyes were unreadable.

"We've spoken too much about my work. Tell me about yours," I said.

He studied me warily. "I believe you have a mind open to the universe of the eye, not cramped by the dictum of authorized belief."

"An artist's job as well as a scientist's is to study the universe of the eye."

"Then I shall tell you, though my detractors oblige me to be circumspect in pronouncing the results of my work as anything but theory." He leaned forward and spoke quickly. "By the magnified vision obtained through my telescopes, I have observed that the moon has hills and craters just like our Earth, and the sun has spots."

"Spots?"

"Fumes or vapors which show as darkened areas against the sun — and here's the point." He set his elbows on the table and moved his hands to demonstrate, forgetting the heat. "They travel across its surface, which suggests that the sun rotates, stationary, on its own axis." He stood the largest candy on end and swiveled it.

"Stationary! Then how can it rise and set?"

"That is only an illusion seen from Earth." He held up his index finger, disregarding my shock in his urge to explain. "And finally, the planet Jupiter has four moons" — he set four smaller candies around the large one — "despite those theologians who claim that God would not have permitted the elements of the planetary system to exceed the sacred number seven. We must acknowledge what our eye sees."

"And not take the Bible literally?"

"Certainly not in all matters. I have set forth that caution in a letter to the Grand Duchess Cristina, who has her doubts, although her son supports me. I was his tutor. He feels some loyalty."

"Can you see these moons in your glass? Maybe they are illusion too."

"They do exist! My telescope shows them moving across the surface of Jupiter, proving that . . . rather, suggesting that heavenly bodies can travel around other heavenly bodies than the Earth."

"That's astounding! A complete reversal. All we've ever been taught is that everything revolves around . . . us. Are you saying that all that our Holy Mother Church tells us isn't necessarily true?"

He raised his shoulders and pursed his lips.

"This is a wild and dangerous notion, signore. How can you be so certain?"

"Observation over time. And logic. If Aristotle himself were brought back to life so I could show him in my telescope, he'd rip his pages to bits as the primitive thinking of a narrow-minded egocentric."

"I would like to see these . . . moons." I pointed to the candies.

"I would show them to you tonight if the sky were clear. With clouds like this, they can't be seen. Sometime, when conditions are perfect, I'll show you. And the craters on the moon and the phases of Venus as well."

"Phases?"

"From sickle to full round."

"Then Venus is a moon!"

He smiled suddenly and tipped his head. "You might say that. A moon to the sun, which it orbits."

"You mean to say the goddess of love waxes and wanes?"

His expression changed rapidly — a touch of pique for diverting his thought, to which I smiled, then momentary doubt as to whether to follow my thought or his, and finally the effort to regain his ground.

"The phases indicate, don't you see, that Venus revolves around the sun, just as our moon revolves around the Earth." He set down a candy to represent Venus, and lowered his voice. "And because one planet travels around the sun, and since sunspots show the sun rotating on its own axis, it is possible that the sun holds all of us, all the planets, in its rotating grasp." He moved them in circles around the larger one.

"We are moving?" I looked out the window, and could hardly grasp the concept. "I don't feel us moving."

"Nevertheless, Artemisia, we *are* moving, and at tremendous speed. We only experience the illusion of standing still." He said it tenderly, as if laying out the rules of walking for a child.

I pointed out the window. "Then why is that banner hanging down and not billowing sideways? That woman on the terrace, why isn't her hair blowing?"

"Other forces prevent that." He leaned back in his chair. "You have a keen, original mind."

I smiled at that. "Where art and science touch is the realm of the imagination, the place where original ideas are born, the place where both of us are most alive." In spite of the incredulity of his ideas, an affinity of the mind drew us together. I had to look away not to show my admiration.

"Both the artist and the scientist would

do well to have a healthy skepticism for traditional thinking," he said.

"I commend you, signore, for your risk," I said in a whisper.

"Galileo please, not signore."

We walked outside and stood by the balustrade looking off to a row of darkening cypresses like shadowy church spires pointing to his sky. "We are both taking risks," he said. His expression clouded. "I must go soon and put my discoveries before the pope. To liberate him from bondage to Aristotle and Ptolemy, and to seek his protection in the event that I may need it."

"Rome! You'll put yourself in the lion's jaw?"

"I'm afraid I am already there."

"And shall I worry for you when you go?" I put out my hand to stop his answer. "Regardless of how you answer that, I know I will. You are too trusting. Anyone with new ideas has enemies. The papal realm is one that can twist your meanings against you faster than the snuffing of a candle. It is a dangerous city. Rome can brag about your ideas one day, and oppose them the next. Rome can admire strong individuals, but enjoy their fall."

"How is it that you know this?"

"You forget. I am a Roman."

We were silent a long time, each thinking about our own Rome in the coming darkness.

A few of the guests approached us. "No stargazing tonight, signore?"

"Heaven doesn't always grant us what we wish," Galileo answered. He went inside and brought back a lute.

"The lute," I reminded him, "is the highest of arts. Higher than painting. Higher than sobs. Play something melancholy. For your going away."

The notes hung in the thickening darkness just as I knew this evening would hang suspended, like a star behind clouds, in my memory.

As people left, Galileo walked with me downstairs and helped me into one of the waiting carriages. He laid his hand on mine on the edge of the carriage door. "Be assured, I will send you word as soon as I return." His soft, burdened eyes glistened in the circle of light from a carriage lamp.

"In the meantime," I said, "I'll try to feel the Earth move."

14

Mary Magdalene

During midday rest, I asked Pietro as he was lying down with Palmira half-asleep next to him, "What do you think is the primary requirement to be a painter?"

"To be a keen observer — first, last, and always."

"And what if what the painter sees is unpleasant?"

"He must look anyway."

"Do you mean she must not avert her eyes even though she flinches?"

"What's all this about?"

"My penitent Magdalen." I gathered my lead pencils and a small bound album of drawing paper. "Will you stay here awhile with Palmira? I'm going to find that penitent woman."

"What for?"

"I'm not sure. I'll know when I see her. I'll be back before you finish napping."

She wasn't at Santa Croce. I circled the Duomo and the Baptistry. Why was it that she was gone right when I needed her? I found her at San Lorenzo. I positioned myself so that she was in my line of sight between the horse and wagon.

Bare shins to the ground, rocking back and forth, the woman moaned her remorse, feeling a shame so sharp as to make her lose all propriety. What could she possibly have done that was so heinous as to earn her a lifetime of self-mortification? No one short of a tyrant deserved such unremitting agony. I cried there with her, for her, for Eve, for sorrows past, for sorrows yet to come. I put my pencil away. It was wrong to draw live pain. If there had been an artist at Bethany, it would have been wrong to intrude his chalk or charcoal on Mary Magdalene's weeping as she washed Jesus' feet. Some things were too raw for art until time dulled their sharpness.

I retreated between buildings and turned toward home.

If the moment of conversion leads to that abject misery, I didn't want to paint it, but the moment just before — now that was intriguing. The moment before renunciation when Eros still holds her, when her mind reels with what dark future she might have if she followed the drift of her life, at that moment she might dread having to give up things she still wants. Then she could still be in a gorgeous gown that these Florentines would love. Her unconfined hair could show a barely repressed sensuality. I'd give a suggestion of the wild abandonment of Donatello's Magdalen by having one unconsciously bare foot — not a pretty foot, a working woman's foot — show beneath the hem of her gown.

I walked faster, fired by the idea.

She must be ironic, contradictory, and ambiguous. She'd have furrows in her forehead, tears in her eyes, the upper and lower eyelids red and swollen in shame for her past, yet she'd still be in sumptuous silk, still wearing jewelry, just having prepared herself, with her mirror nearby, for the next philanderer. The ambiguity would be in her tears. What were they really for?

Near home, on the Corso dei Tintori, burnished gold silk hung drying from the upper windows. Panels of it lay stretched on wooden forms. The ideal color for the Magdalen! A young woman was lifting more of it from a vat, and the sun reflected off the

liquid and shone on her thick, bare fore-
arms. I watched her awhile, a big, beautiful,
golden-skinned girl, broad-shouldered,
curly-haired, with her face screwed up in an
expression of agony. If I could get her to
look that way again and gaze outward instead of down into the steaming vat . . .

I approached her. "That color is gorgeous. Doesn't it make you love what you're
doing?"

"No, signora. Would you like to breathe
ammonia fumes and scald your skin day
after day?"

Her eyes were red and watery. Perfect. It
would look like she'd been weeping.

"What would you rather do?"

"I'd rather weave, or stitch."

"Something sitting down?"

"Ah, yes."

"How would you like to get paid for just
sitting still?"

She eyed me suspiciously. "I'm a good
woman, signora. I'm not a —"

"I'm a painter. I'd like to paint you. You
are beautiful."

She scoffed at that. "My father won't believe me."

"Let me talk to him."

She led me into the back of a narrow shop.
His answer was a resounding no.

"Who would tend your vat?" he asked her, ignoring me, it appeared. I couldn't be sure. One of his eyes wandered away and gazed in another direction. I wondered how the world looked to him, and felt sorry if it careened off in a distortion.

"I'm sure you could find someone at one-third the cost of what she'd earn from me."

"She won't take her clothes off, no matter how much you pay," he snarled.

"On the contrary, I would like her dressed in a gown of that exquisite gold silk. The same as you have drying now. The color looks as though it was woven of filaments of pure gold. I'm sure it's the finest in the city, yes?"

"Of course it is. People in my family have been dyers here for two hundred years."

"And wouldn't you like Maria Maddalena de' Medici, the archduchess herself, to know the dyer who produced so magnificent a color? It's for her that I'm making the painting. What is your name, signore?"

"Marco Rossi."

"And your daughter's name?"

"Umiliana."

"*Bene*. It's settled then." I held out my hand. Scowling his suspicion, he slapped it as if I were a man. I smiled at him and turned to Umiliana. "Wash. Your hair too.

Come on Monday morning. It's just down the Lungarno, not as far as Piazza Piave. Look for a wooden gate carved with the design of a lion's head. You'll see a square well and a fig tree in the courtyard. Pull the bell rope that has three knots in it."

On Monday, Umiliana brought me a peach. I split it three ways, for Palmira, Umiliana, and myself.

"I am sorry, signora. I didn't know you had a child. I should have brought one for her and one for you."

"Nothing to be sorry about. Look at this luscious color inside. Almost like the gold silk. A seamstress is coming today to take your measurements, and we shall send her to your father's shop to buy the silk."

"That will make him very happy."

"Your hair is so smooth today," I said.

"Because I didn't work this morning. It's the steam that frizzes it."

"Ah, but that's what I want. Hair a little out of control. Make sure before you come every day that you hang your head over a hot vat."

She did, faithfully, though she didn't think it looked as nice. During the week I tried her in many poses, and she proved supple, curious, anxious to please.

Every day she asked, "Do you have the dress?"

Palmira was just as excited about it as Umiliana was. "Will it come tomorrow, Mama?"

"Don't worry," I told them both. "It will come."

When it was finally delivered and I laid it out on a cloth on the trestle table, Palmira jumped up and down, and Umiliana whistled through her teeth and stepped back away from it. Her eyebrows were stuck in arches high on her forehead.

I laughed. "*Dio mio,* don't be afraid of it, Umiliana. Here, let me help you put it on."

A hush came over her as she quickly let her own clothing fall to the floor and raised her arms over her head. Palmira watched with big, envious eyes as I lifted the dress over Umiliana's head. When we had it fastened, Palmira could hardly contain herself. She squealed and shook her arms in admiration. "She looks like a queen," Palmira shouted, and then curtseyed to her. Palmira waved her arm elegantly at Fina's worn velvet chair I had borrowed. "And this is her throne."

"Bring my mirror, please, sweet." Palmira skipped away and came back with it held importantly in both hands.

An abashed, shocked smile spread across Umiliana's face. "I'll never have a dress like this, you can be sure of that."

I tugged down the neckline to bare one shoulder. "Nor will I, probably."

"What will happen to it when we're finished?" Umiliana asked.

"Oh, I'll have to sell it, I suppose."

"Seems like a lot of trouble just for a painting." She trailed her finger over the braid on the bodice as she gazed into the mirror.

"Not when it's so important to the message of the painting."

"I wish Giorgio could see me in it."

"Giorgio?"

The dress had made her bold, but suddenly she retreated into shyness. "My —"

"Ah. Of course." I smiled. "When we're finished, he can come to look at the painting before I deliver it. But that won't be for a long time."

"Good."

I seated Umiliana by a table, three-quarter view, with the folds of the luxurious, ballooning skirt taking up a good two-thirds of the painting. The wooden-framed mirror on the table gave me an idea. What if the mirror suggested not the woman she is now, but what she would become — gray and hollow, with a ravaged face, Donatello's version? Let the viewer guess whether that would be her if she didn't repent, or if she did. That would be the *invenzione*. I posed her left hand as if pushing the mirror away into a shadow, shielding herself from the ugly trick of time.

"Put your right hand on your left breast. Up further. No, not clutching, just resting there. Good. With your thumb in the cleft."

"It feels silly."

"It looks like you're distressed. That's just what I want. Now look as though it's a sweltering day and you have to put your arms into that steaming vat. How would your face look?" She screwed up her face. "Too much. Ah, yes. Like you've just heard a sad story. The saddest story you can think of. That Giorgio left you."

Her face became distraught, but then she broke into a giggle at herself. "I'm sorry, signora." She composed herself and tried again.

"That's good. Now look out instead of down. At that crack in the wall running down from the ceiling. Perfect. Hold."

Over the next few weeks I learned — and so did Umiliana — that she could hold a pose without a break for hours, including that expression of distress. It was just right for a Mary Magdalene fearful of renouncing everything she had known.

One morning after she saw Pietro leave the house with paint smears on his work clothes, she remarked, "Two painters in one house. Strange."

"Isn't there more than one dyer in your house? My father is a painter too. We do what seems natural."

"Then how does anyone start doing anything different?"

"By being a different sort of person. By not fitting in. By having strong likings all one's own."

I worried for a moment what this period of more genteel employment would do to her when she went back to the vats. It might make what she hoped for out of life impossibly far from what she would get, and I would be responsible. And yet, the persistence of hope tapping us on our shoulders is a good thing because it reminds us of the larger picture, and keeps us breathing on our worst days.

"How does someone know which one of you to ask to paint something?" Umiliana asked.

"By looking at our work, I suppose."

"Where is his?"

I waved my arm at the walls. "Here. All of these are his."

She looked at them as if for the first time. "Who's better?"

Palmira's head popped up at the table.

"Neither of us," I said.

"Don't you have fights over who is better?"

Watching us, Palmira let her porridge drip off her spoon.

"No, not fights. Here, let's get started."

"How do you know who's better between any two painters?"

I considered a moment. "Sometimes it's impossible to tell. Different painters are good at different things." I looked at a Holy Family that Pietro had done which had been on the wall since the day I arrived. Mary was lovely, with all the sensuousness in her downcast eyes and bare neck that a virgin shouldn't have. I regretted that it had never moved me. She wasn't an individual.

"The line between defeat and immortality is sometimes as thin as thread. One never knows how close one stands. A person could be highly talented when viewed alone, but when placed next to brilliance, his work would appear mediocre. It's all marvelously complicated."

That was probably more than she needed

238

for an explanation, but I couldn't resist her curious mind.

In summer Umiliana brought fresh rosemary and marjoram from her mother's garden. In the fall she brought fresh *pecorino* that shepherds from the mountains brought down to Giorgio's cheese shop while it was still soft. In winter, pears, apples, and chestnuts for roasting.

"Not much accomplished today," Umiliana often said cheerily as she looked at the canvas at the end of the afternoon.

On the last day, I inscribed *Optimam Partem Elegit*, Latin for "Choose the better way," on the mirror's frame in florid gold lettering.

"There you are, as beautiful as Botticelli's Venus," I said when we finished.

"Isn't there something else you have to do to it tomorrow?"

"Only to sign my name."

"May I watch that?"

It suddenly occurred to me that in all these months, she'd been on the other side of the easel and had never actually seen me apply paint to canvas. Inadvertently, I had kept her out of the core of the process. "Of course." I mixed a tiny bit more gold paint, turned the painting sideways, and wrote "Artemisia Lom" on the side support of the chair. "Artemisia Lom," I said in case she couldn't read.

"Your name is Lom?"

"Lomi. It's my ancestral name. It needs one more letter. Stand here, right in front of me. Give me your hand." I put the brush in her hand and clasped mine gently around hers to write the *i* together. "Now, all by yourself, put a little dot right above the last letter."

Heavy responsibility puckered her mouth while her hand, steadied at the wrist by her other hand, moved slowly through the air toward the canvas. She turned to me afterward, pulling in a long breath which closed her nostrils. Her eyes were moist. "Thank you."

That such a simple thing could mean so much. She had treasured this entire experience. I held her in my arms, and over her shoulder I saw Palmira watching us, uncomprehending.

"Who's that person you said?" Umiliana asked.

"The painter Botticelli. His Venus is in the Uffizi. I don't suppose you've ever been inside."

"No."

"I'll write a note as an academy member explaining that you are my model, and you go in there and take a long look at everything. It's a sin to live in this city all your life and not see its paintings and sculpture."

"I see statues all around. I don't like them. Everybody's always doing something mean. That man in the Loggia della Signoria holding up a woman's head with snakes for hair, and all that ropey stuff hanging out her neck. Ugh! I look the other way every time I go by. Why is every one of them so cruel?"

"That's true, Mama. Why are they?" Palmira demanded.

It surprised me that she would take notice. I didn't realize she'd been listening.

"I can't answer that. Just what the sculptors chose, I suppose." I was glad Umiliana had never seen my Judiths. "All right then. Forget the sculpture. Go to look at the paintings, and study how graceful the women are. Pay attention to how they're standing and sitting. You may need to know someday. And after that, you can invite Giorgio. But be sure to go there first. I'm going to ask you what you saw."

The next day I went to the academy to see the steward. "Do you still have your list of models?" I asked. "I'd like to add a name."

He tipped his smug, round face to the side and allowed himself a pinched smile, as if he

241

had won some kind of victory. "Certainly, signora." The words dripped off his tongue like oily epithets of vindication.

He reached up to get the sheaf of pages and handed me a quill. I wrote in big, clear letters, *Umiliana Rossi, Corso dei Tintori,* and turned it back for him to read. "She's excellent. You see that she gets some work!"

His smile fell into a straight line.

15

Pietro

It was cold. It was February. It was already getting dark. I had run out of Roman umber and Naples yellow. I poured out onto the table all the coins from Father's blue drawstring bag, replenished by three commissions from Cosimo after the Magdalen, for which he paid generously because it pleased the archduchess. Even so, the bag was depleted now.

Attracted by the noise, Palmira came over from the fireplace and helped me stack coins of each type to count them — six Venetian zecchini, five piastre, one giulio, one scudo which was seven lire, and four lire. Four lire could feed one person for a week.

Palmira's index finger pressed on the shiny silver giulio and drew it to her edge of the table. "Can I have it, Mama?"

"No. I need it."

Her little fist closed around it and disappeared under the table.

"Give it to me," I commanded.

She put her hand behind her back and shook her head.

"Palmira, let me have it."

She ran from me and I followed her, out the door onto the balcony.

"Naughty child. Give it to me." I grabbed her by the shoulder and struck her on her backside. She screamed, squirmed out of my grasp, and flung the coin far over the balcony.

"You're mean," she said with a hateful look and stomped back inside, hooked her foot on my easel and tipped it over. My unfinished Saint Catherine fell to the floor. Palmira stood over it, half smirking, half fearful.

"That was a spiteful thing to do! You ought to be ashamed. Go to bed."

"I don't have to. I'm eight now."

"No, you're not! Not yet. You're seven and a half! I don't even want to see you. Go to bed!"

She raised her foot as though she would step on the painting.

"No!" I screamed, and lunged for her. She ran into the bedroom and flung herself on the bed. I slammed the door closed after her and leaned up against the wall.

Was this the end? Was this what it all led up to? A foolish argument with a child? I set Catherine back on the easel — the saint who painted and who bought paintings by women for her convent in Bologna. If only she were living now.

Maybe I truly wasn't good enough to live by painting. Maybe Father had filled me with the wrong ambitions. Maybe I was living a fool's dream.

I put the coins back into the little bag and tried to think calmly. I shouldn't spend for anything other than food until I had a new commission, but Cosimo didn't want any paintings now that he was intent upon enlarging the Pitti. I'd been without a commission for half a year. Still, I had to keep painting in order to have work to show. I'd buy only a quarter cube of Naples yellow.

Seeking a new patron in the same city might be considered disloyalty or lack of appreciation, but working for a church wouldn't. The next day I left Palmira with Fina, glad to have some time without her, wrapped my unfinished Saint Catherine in a cloth, and took it to Santa Maria del Carmine where there might be space to hang a painting in the cloisters.

I asked a young priest if I could speak to the monsignor, and waited in the Brancacci Chapel, my favorite because of Masaccio's Adam and Eve. Now, as if it had never been there before, his fresco of Jesus sending Peter to find tax money in the mouth of a fish touched me to the quick. The face of Christ was untroubled and assured even though his disciples looked at him in alarm and puzzlement. Jesus was calmly pointing to the lake, and Peter echoed the gesture, but his face was saying, incredulously, "There?"

What depth of faith Christ had to look in such an unexpected place as a fish's mouth. No shred of doubt. No self-pity that he was poor, that he had to pay the tax, that he didn't know where his disciples would get their next meal. Oh, for that utter trust in a Heavenly Father. I squeezed my eyes shut and tried to feel His guidance. When I opened them and saw that trust painted on the wall, I realized that for once in my life, I was using a church and its art for what it was intended. Regardless of Galileo's logic, the highest of arts, I realized, is to uplift the spirit, whatever means one uses.

The monsignor approached me looking concerned. Even that comforted me. I introduced myself and offered him my painting, explaining that it was Saint Catherine.

"It doesn't look finished."

"No, it isn't. I just thought . . . I love Masaccio's frescoes. It would please me to think that a painting of mine could be nearby . . . when it is finished."

"Aren't you the wife of Pierantonio Stiattesi, the painter who worked on the frescoes in Monte Uliveto?" the monsignor asked.

"Yes."

His lips pinched in judgment. "The wife who is a painter."

What did he want? For me to stay home to pluck geese and shine silver spoons?

"Stiatessi is a member of the academy now."

"Yes. We both are."

"I understand he has been ill-used."

"By whom?"

"By you, of course, if you are in fact his wife in the eyes of the church."

"I am. I've done nothing against him."

"Nonetheless, we have no space here for your painting. I'm sorry."

"Monsignor, I have painted for the Medicis."

"The Medicis are not the church." He put his hands up his sleeves, as if to signal the end of the conversation.

I was bewildered. Hesitating, I glanced at

the fresco again. Anything I could say would sound self-pitying. I acquiesced with a nod, picked up my painting, and left.

Who did I have to turn to? It should naturally be Pietro, but ever since he was admitted to the academy, he spent less time at home. Without knowing what that meant, I didn't want to ask. I didn't know what my appeal would uncover. Father would help me, but in his last letter he said he was leaving Rome to live in Genoa. I had no way to reach him there. I was too embarrassed to ask Buonarroti for another loan. I never knew whether Pietro had repaid his share of the last one. Galileo was my only hope.

I walked home along the river, slowly in spite of the drizzle. Galileo had his own troubles. I hated to disturb him. When he had come back from Rome several years earlier and we had taken a walk in the gardens of the Pitti, he said he had bowed to Cardinal Bellarmino's command. He was made to promise not to defend Copernican theory. His cheeks had lost their fullness, and he spoke more softly than before.

"It grieves me to think that the church is hounding you," I'd said.

"I'm told you have had your own unfortunate experience with a papal court," he had said.

"I hope you learned more valuable things than that in Rome."

"Yes. I learned that Rome respects a scientist only if his ideas do not raise one speck of doubt about entrenched beliefs."

What could I have said to cheer him? I understood only too well the bite of wrong judgment.

"Pope Paul has assured me of my protection."

"Still, this is not the end."

"No. It is not the end."

At home I set my unfinished Saint Catherine back on the easel and took out Galileo's last letter from my memento box.

My Dear Artemisia,
The frigid tramontana blows so fiercely that I fear to go out at night even to look through my telescope for an hour. I missed seeing the comets because of the clutch of illness. The invitation I extended to you so long ago languishes. Know that I keep it folded in my mind, and that some day you shall be a welcome guest at my villa in Bellosguardo where there is an unobstructed panorama of the skies. In the meantime, I am studying the tides, and I am reasonably happy.
                    Your admiring friend,
                    Galileo

I had tried to give him encouragement in my letters, telling him not to worry about explaining everything to us. It might not be a bad thing for us to have some mystery left to ignite the imagination with.

Now I wrote:

My Most Illustrious Friend and Scholar,
I think of you often and trust that the pursuit of your many interests has brought you joy.

At the risk of you thinking that I write only when I need something, might I ask you for one favor? I believe it to be within your power and I hope in the light of our friendship that it might be your pleasure and not too great a trouble to give me this aid.

The first Judith I painted for Cosimo — you may remember it, the one in which she is slaying Holofernes — Cosimo said he would pay for, but he has not. He is young, and all his passion goes into building now, so he has forgotten. You have influence with him. A private word, as his former tutor, might do much to remind him of his promise. I wouldn't ask, but I find that I am in need.

I have been searching my mind for many months to remember what I had heard of Cardinal Bellarmino. I know now. He's called "the hammer of heretics." A nun in

Rome told me that. Take great care, my friend.

I kiss your hand and shall live in gratitude to you —

Always,
Artemisia

It wasn't long before a nice sum was delivered, but after I paid my debts to the joiner, the tailor, and the apothecary, and bought staples for us to eat for a good while, I had to be frugal again. I didn't know the future.

It had rained some every day for a week, and I spent the time teaching Palmira to read and write more than the sisters' names. I wrote silly notes to her — *Look in the mirror. There is a chicken in your hair* — and hid them in the house for her to find. Then she wrote back to me — *A horse is under your skirt* — and made me stop what I was doing to search for her note. It entertained her at first, but soon she became peevish and impossible trapped in the house.

Nothing was further from my desire than to go out in the rain, but I bundled her up and let her take her straw doll and small rubber ball. We hurried through rain-darkened streets to the Loggia della Signoria where there would be a roof over us, room for her to run figure eights around the statues and bounce her ball against the wall, and sculptures for me to draw. We arrived wet but exhilarated.

I had already drawn the three intertwining figures of Giambologna's *Rape of the Sabine Woman* from the piazza. Now I circled the statue, the first sculpture designed to be viewed from all sides, to see what new thing I could discover from another angle.

The man abducting her was clearly in motion, stepping over all obstacles, even a fallen old man from whom he had probably taken her. One muscular arm was trying to control her at her shoulder, the other around her hip and thigh. I had never noticed before how his fingers pressed so deeply into the flesh of her thigh. This hugely muscular man had to use all his strength to contain her mighty struggles. It wasn't just her open mouth, frightened eyes, and her frantic gesture for help, but that grip on her thigh that showed she was being taken against her will. That iron grip would be the focus of this drawing. I would call it my *Pietà*.

"What are they doing, Mama?"

"The men are capturing her. They want her to do something she doesn't want to do."

"She looks scared."

"She is."

I sat down on the cold stone floor and began to work, musing that the sculpture I chose was one depicting rape. When had my own rape ceased to hurt me so that I would choose this to draw? I suppose it was when Pietro and Palmira came to teach me how to love. I could study this Sabine woman who lived nineteen centuries ago and feel empathy for her, but now her struggle did not devastate me, did not make me wince as I had the first time I'd seen her. I had walked by this sculpture a thousand times on my way to the vegetable market and I had not become rigid with anger. Those atrocities against women had not ceased to exist in the world, but life marches on. Onions and white beans must still be bought.

Palmira watched me through round, fearful eyes. "Why don't you paint anymore?"

"Oh, I'd rather just draw."

"That's not the reason." It came as an accusation.

"No? How do you know, my little worrier?" I pinched her nose and she backed away. "Here, let me teach you something."

She shook her head, and ran out into the piazza in the rain.

253

"Palmira, come back."

She did, but not before she got drenched.

A woman in a full-length hooded cloak dashed into the loggia and lifted off her deep red-violet hood to shake off water.

"Vanna!" I hadn't seen her for years.

She was more startled by my presence sitting on the floor than I was by hers. In an instant her beautiful face turned surly.

"Why did you use a common wool washer with rough hands instead of me?"

"What do you mean?"

"For your Mary Magdalene. Some tart from the vats with raw skin. And other women for Diana and Persephone and Aurora. Four Medici commissions, four chances for me to be in his palace and you didn't use me once."

"How do you know whom I use or what I paint?"

"Pietro told me. He tells me everything," she crowed, her nose in the air. She hesitated an instant, caught in her own gloating. "He knows about your bad reputation. You and that greasy coachman. A commoner! You don't know two nuts' worth about being a painter, *or* a wife."

In that instant, I knew. She was Pietro's lover.

When she saw I was speechless, and realized what she had revealed, she lifted her hood and darted out through the rain and into the corner entrance to the Uffizi. In a gorgeous ruby cloak no model feeding two children could afford, her phantom figure passed before the marble loins of David. A specter.

Surreptitious looks. Hot clasped hands. Clandestine meetings. Pietro had a mistress who was going right now into the Uffizi. Pietro drew with his friends in the Uffizi, more frequently of late. Right this instant, she was rushing to him in the blaze and swell of passion, unsettled by this chance meeting with "the wife." And the little girl. Grown older now, and pouty. Should she warn him that the wife knows? No. He might renounce her. Not with the woman and her child just outside. Think about it later. At his studio. After trailing fingers down his spine, his muscled sides, the twin valleys of his loins meeting in a dark tangle, kissing his loins, trailing her tongue, making him arch and rise and rise again, delirious with desire for her.

Stop! I told myself. Think rationally.

I couldn't be here when they came out of the Uffizi. "Palmira, come. We're going home."

"We just got here."

255

"Get your ball."

I held my pencils, album and her doll beneath my cloak, grabbed her hand and ran. "Count the puddles," I shouted, to give her something to think about. I yanked her around them, past the vats, empty but for rainwater, the dyers inside on such a day, and through our gate. We collapsed together out of breath in our stairway.

Upstairs, I took off her wet clothes, dried her briskly, wrapped her in my dressing gown, spooned hot broth into her mouth, and cut for her a few wedges of apple. "Are you a little sleepy? Sometimes broth makes you sleepy." I made up her bed and tucked her in. "This is how to get warm," I said, rubbing her body through the quilt.

"Why did we run, Mama?"

"The rain, sweetheart."

"But we were already wet."

"Ssh, now. Take a nap. I'll be upstairs at Fina's. You can come when you wake up." I hummed a lullaby, and when she finally fell asleep, I went upstairs. Fina was washing her few dishes.

"Awful day," I said.

"Where's Palmira?"

"Sleeping in a warm bed. We got soaked today. We never should have gone out." I felt my chin quiver.

"What's the matter? What happened?"

"Oh, Fina, you know, don't you, that mine was a marriage of convenience?"

She dried her hands on a scrap of towel. "I surmised as much."

"And that he has a mistress?"

"Yes," she said quietly after a moment.

"More than one?"

"Are you sure you want to know?"

"Yes."

"He's had a string of women. I haven't kept track. It's a blessing that his poor mother did not live to watch it."

"Do you think he keeps another residence?"

She closed her eyes and lifted her shoulders. "It's possible. Anything is possible."

"Why did he marry me in the first place? Do you know?"

She took a long breath that raised her chest. "Because he was in debt. The dowry."

"Yes, but why else? Why not someone in Florence?"

"Because of his reputation. Women claiming that he was the father of their children would have issued objections if he posted any banns in Florence. The only way he could get a wife was to find one out of Florence."

"A fool! Fina, I've been an utter fool." I

slumped on her sad velvet chair and fought back tears. She pulled up a stool next to me and drew my head onto her soft bosom. "Would he have been mine if I had given up painting, do you think? He's never done or said anything that suggested he wanted more than what I was to him already. He let me in only so far."

She stroked the back of my head. "He can let any woman in only so far. That's why he leaves them and goes on to the next when he's uncomfortable. It isn't your fault."

I chuckled gravely. "Maybe his mistress will discover that."

We were still awhile and I felt the comfort of her heart thumping softly against my cheek. When she stirred to light an oil lamp, I thanked her and went downstairs. Palmira was sound asleep.

Graziela had said that when I felt abandoned by God, I had to love Him all the more. I had to affirm God's goodness. I'd do that later. Tomorrow I'd affirm His goodness. Give me one night of bitterness, one night of self-indulgent pity, one night to get it all out.

I didn't know two nuts' worth about being a wife? Was Vanna right? Those times when Pietro and I were most together, in bed, his need had entered me and found a likeness, like a looking glass in a dim room, yet neither of us spoke of the inner place where this need dwelt. If I had, would it have been any different?

I knew I shouldn't write to Graziela in such a state, but I couldn't help myself.

At first I tried to watch, to be cautious, but in the end I did the very thing you told me not to do — I gave myself to a man. To an illusion, just like you said. A man who was giving himself to another. I never really had his love. What I had was only what I hoped to have. And now what I have is the first glimpse of a sad and penetrating loss, and why? So that one day I can paint it?

But I will not give myself to God or convent, no matter if I only have a single coin. Even though I have no patron, no money, and no real husband, I have a place to live. My dowry grants me that. And I have talent that shall not be hid under a bushel. I will write letters. I will secure a new patron. I will earn my way. I will go on as if nothing happened. I will find a new life.

As I was sealing the letter with candle wax, Pietro came home wet to the bone.

"Nasty weather," he grumbled, and hung his dripping cloak on a peg. "Writing to someone?" He sat down at the table.

"Just to Sister Graziela." I moved the letter to the edge of the table and put an apple on it from the basket. "She wanted me to describe more art." I dried his hair with a towel. The black curls I loved smelled of unfamiliar hair oil. "Do you think it'll stop raining tomorrow?" I asked. An inane comment.

"No."

I heated the broth and added onions and stale bread. He cast furtive looks at the letter while he ate.

"What did you do today?" he asked, reaching for an apple, choosing the one I'd put on the letter.

"I tried to teach Palmira how to read and write better." I showed him her notes. "She's been terribly restless, but she's sleeping now."

He smiled as he read them, and then he touched the edge of my letter to Graziela, either absently or intentionally, testing me, knowing why I'd written it. I froze, staring at his fingers resting on the letter.

A sudden burst of rain beat against the closed shutters and seeped in along the window frame. It diverted us for the moment. We packed the leaking places with paint rags.

"At least it's washing the streets and buildings," he said. "When it's finally over, the city will look cleaner."

I grabbed at an idea.

"Is it possible to go up to the lantern on top of the Duomo?" I asked.

"I don't think so."

"What about the bell tower?"

"What for?"

"To look at the city. To see it clean."

"It's a long way up."

"All the better."

"I suppose there has to be a staircase inside for the bell ringer," he said. "If we give him a couple lire, he might let us up."

"I want to see if up that high we can feel the Earth move."

Pietro looked at me as if I had lost my mind.

"You know that philosopher mathematician, Galilei, in Cosimo's court? He said that the Earth moves around the sun, and other planets do too."

"He'll find himself in trouble someday. Once a priest at Santa Maria Novella preached against all mathematicians as the devil's workmen. Everybody knew he meant Galileo."

"Recently?"

"No."

"If we're moving, maybe we can feel it that high up. Let's do it. Tomorrow. Sunday."

"It will probably rain."

"That doesn't matter. If we don't do it now, then we may never."

He looked at me in the strangest way — as if he realized I might know, or that our arrangement of convenience might come to a crashing finish. For an instant, I thought I might have seen pain in his eyes.

Could I actually be fully his? Every day? Every hour? Him the only focus of my life? A painter or a wife. A wife or a painter. Which did I really want to be? Going up there might tell me.

"I want to get above all this. . . ." I waved my hand vaguely. Let him decide what I meant.

"Palmira too?"

"No. Let's leave her with Fina. Tell her we have some painting business."

One side of his mouth lifted in a soft, sad half-smile. "Like our excursions when you first . . . came here."

"Yes, just like that."

"Do you still want to go?" he asked, opening the shutters in the morning.

I got up to look. The rain was lightly pocking the river. "Yes."

We didn't tell Fina where we were going, and she gave me the most uncomprehending look. It made me giddy inside, as though *we* were doing something clandestine. I put on my hooded cloak and we walked quickly with our heads down. We waited in Piazza del Duomo under the loggia of the Brethren of the Misericordia for the bell to chime noon. Rain pelted the stones in the piazza harder now. The marble facing of the square tower shone wet like polished gemstones.

"I wish Giotto had lived long enough to see it finished," I said, "to climb to the top just once before he died."

"Strange how a person can live in a place all his life and never think to do this," Pietro said. He was indulging me in this with all good humor. It was good of him, and wrong of me to transfer my hate of Vanna onto him.

When the bell ringer opened the tower door, we dashed out to stop him from leaving.

"We are artists," Pietro said, "and we'd like to take a look at the Duomo from the top of the tower."

"For a drawing for the Accademia del Disegno."

He looked at me suspiciously. "Both of you? Artists?"

"If you let us just step inside —," I said.

He moved back to let us get out of the rain. I opened my cloak and showed him my insignia from the academy. Pietro pressed two lire into his palm.

"You picked a wretched day to do a fool thing like this."

"What does it matter to you?" Pietro said, a bit surly.

The bell ringer shrugged. "Suit yourself." He waved us up.

We ascended the steep stone steps inside a double wall closing us in on both sides and closing out the world. The stairs went around the perimeter in a large square until the first *piano,* and on this level open arches between delicate twisted columns let us see out. The tower of the Palazzo Vecchio was all the more magnificent because the structure supporting the upper tier of crenellations was much taller from this height than it appeared from the ground. Houses, streets, and people looked unreal, like boxes and puppets.

"Maybe this is what it looks like to God," I said.

Pietro smiled at the notion.

Above the first *piano,* steps went in a tight circle at the corner in order not to obstruct the open arches. Pietro lifted my cloak so it wouldn't drag against the three-hundred-year-old stone steps. I had to stop and rest on the way. He let me lean on him. His chest heaved under my cheek.

At the second open level, wind through the arches buffeted us. We disturbed a family of pigeons in a crevice and they flapped and flew below us. "Strange to look down on birds flying, isn't it?" I asked. We were almost at eye level with the base of the barrel vault that supported the big brick dome of the cathedral.

"Imagine the excitement of people to see that dome rise," Pietro said. "When a boy was born, it wasn't there, and when he was old enough to notice, the dome started to grow, and when he had a boy of his own, the stone ribs met and the dome was closed. What a time to live." He put his hand on my shoulder as we looked. I didn't move so his hand would rest there a moment longer, until we started up again.

"You know, this tower was finished a hundred years before the dome was," Pietro said. "How many times do you think Brunelleschi climbed these very steps to get a look at what he was building?"

"Not every day!"

"No, but I'd wager at least once a month. I would have."

We didn't stop at the open third level, we

were so eager to reach the top. We were breathing heavily. Once I didn't lift my foot high enough and it caught on a step which pitched me forward. Pietro grabbed me from behind and kept his hands just under my breasts, holding me against him until I breathed normally again.

A couple more spirals, Pietro opened a door, and we stepped out. Rain lashed against us, and pricked my cheeks like needles. Our cloaks flapped and billowed and threatened to blow away unless we held onto them. To be so high, with nothing more than a waist-high wall blocking us from being blown right off the tower frightened and thrilled me at the same time.

"Look!" I cried. "You can see the pattern of bricks on the dome." We had to shout to make ourselves heard.

He took me by the hand and we walked around the square, looking in all directions — at the dome of San Lorenzo, the white facade of Santa Croce, the roof of Vasari's Corridor over Ponte Vecchio, the Pitti Palace and its gardens, and beyond that, the gray and ghostly hills — all of Florence in one sweep.

"Think of all the thousands of people who have lived here and have never seen this," I said.

More slowly, we walked around the square again. He leaned over the ledge.

"*Attenti!*" I shouted.

My panic for him made him stand back and look at me softly. "It's all right. I'll be careful."

The ledge was slippery. He leaned over it again. I held on to his arm with both hands. "Oh, Artemisia!" he cried in awe. "The people down there are so small! The stones of the piazza are like grains of salt. You've got to see this. Here, I'll hold you."

He put his arms around me so that I felt safe, and I leaned only a little over the ledge. Wind whipped back my hood and rain soaked my hair. "Ohhh!" Blown every which way, rain glazed the city's walls, the medallions on the walls, the niches, the statues in the niches. "Hold me tighter!" I cried, feeling dizzy, and when he did, I leaned out farther. My hair came unpinned and snapped back at him.

I had the sensation that the whole stone tower was swaying in the storm. I closed my eyes. "The Earth *is* moving," I shouted. "It's not an illusion. Can you feel it, Pietro? Galilei was right! Just think. We're whizzing through the universe."

He pulled me back and turned me, and my cloak blew out behind me. His lips were on mine, wet and smooth and luscious, sliding over my throat, my eyes, and mine on his, juicy and urgent in the shivery thrill of the unexpected. Don't ask why, I told myself. I ran my hands through his wet hair. He took hold of my wet breast, pressed his loins hard against me, making me quiver and press back.

We let the rain blow on us, rinsing our hearts of suspicion and hurt, and held each other in the swirl of wind and feelings, our knees weak, his eyes slicked with rain, both of us lifted by the storm above all earthly injury, both of us longing for what was possible once, both of us desperate for what we knew was lost.

We made love that night with all the urgent, bittersweet misery of lovers soon to part. There were no words between us. I commanded my mind to think of nothing but the present moment, in fact not to think at all, but just to feel — his hands like a sculptor's stroking his creation, his tongue on my throat, his hand up my thigh, then his knee urging me to open, to ride out the sea of storm with him again and again until the swells subsided.

I fell asleep thinking of the incomprehensible, baffling order of the universe that kept planets in their courses, birds in flight, and towers from tumbling down. In this universe where I knew now we were not the center, where I was as insignificant and unremarkable as a grain of salt seen from a tower, God still allowed me to take my next breath.

16

Graziela

"Watch me, Mama."

I was pulling up a bucket of water at the well while Palmira hopped in a circle around a dandelion growing between paving stones, singing a song about the moon that Fina had taught her. I commended her halfheartedly, and then noticed globes of dandelions all over the courtyard, like pale moons on stiff stalks — Galileo's moons of Jupiter that I never got to see.

I picked one, held it to my lips ready to blow off the tufts, and went through my litany of wishes — that some day I could see Galileo's real moons, that Palmira would grow up to be a fine, respected painter, that Umiliana was working as a model now and would never have to go back to the vats. And then I admitted the wishes I felt more

270

sharply — that I had never hired Vanna, never, out of generosity, let Pietro draw her nude, that our time in the tower had meant more to Pietro than a fleeting burst of passion, that he would recognize he was wrong not to love me, that he would come home tonight and tell me that he'd left her.

Too many wishes for one mere dandelion. Under present circumstances, I knew if I had only one wish, it would have to be this — that I could earn my way.

I closed my eyes, and felt the wish as truly as I could above all others, though I had to push aside the bell tower and Pietro's firm hands on my buttocks pressing me against him. I blew the dandelion, and thought, God still allowed me to take my next breath, yes. Wind did not blow us off the tower. These things should have made me feel cared for, but they didn't.

When I opened my eyes, I saw a small ragged boy standing outside our courtyard gate.

"I have a message for Signora Gentileschi," he said in a high-pitched voice taut with responsibility.

"I am Signora Gentileschi." I reached my hand between the wooden slats, expecting a letter.

"It's only here," the boy said, and pointed

to his mouth open in a perfect O. "I'm supposed to tell you to go to the Church of
Santa Trinità and ask for Sister Veronica."

"When?"

"Now."

"Why? What else do you know?"

"Nothing, only Sister Veronica said for
you to come alone."

I thanked him and offered him a dipper of
water through the slats of the gate.

"I want to go too." Palmira flung herself
backward against the gate.

"No, you'll have to go to Fina."

She stamped her foot. "I *always* have to go
to Fina." She mimicked my intonation, but
allowed me to drag her upstairs.

The Church of Santa Trinità was up the
Lungarno past the hide-tanning neighborhood. I tried not to breathe its rotten sharpness. I'd been to Santa Trinità once to see
the enormous cross for Sister Paola's sake.
Now, when I opened the heavy door, I was
happy to breathe the musky scent of wax
and incense. A nun standing near the tray of
candles greeted me and introduced herself
as Sister Veronica.

"I am Artemisia Gentileschi."

"May I show you the church?" she asked.

"Please."

We walked down the nave. To the right of the high altar she drew me into a side chapel. "These frescoes illustrate the life of Saint Francis. They're by Ghirlandaio." From her wide sleeve she pulled out a tiny cloth drawstring bag. She lowered her voice. "Sister Graziela of Santa Trinità in Rome sent this hidden in a shipment of dried herbs. Her note instructed me to give it to you, with apologies if it smells like oregano."

I smiled and held it to my nose. "Yes, oregano, and rosemary too." I slipped it up my sleeve.

"And here in this panel you see Saint Francis performing a miracle, restoring a dead child after he fell from an upper story. Right here in Piazza Santa Trinità."

"Oh, yes. I recognize the church façade there in the painting."

We made a circuit of the church and at the door I thanked her and passed her a lira. "For your order."

She bowed her head in thanks.

At home I untied the string and tipped out the earring — Graziela's pearl drop. On a scrap of paper edged with Graziela's leafy tendrils were the words, "Sell the pair. Buy paint."

A warm wave passed through me. I touched the earring to my lips and closed my eyes, sure that I had never understood love till now.

Some weeks later, just when I thought I'd have to appeal to Pietro for money — I couldn't bear to sell Graziela's earrings — I received a letter from a Genoese merchant, Cesare Gentile. I tore it open eagerly. He had seen my work at the Pitti, he said, and was interested in having me do a large painting of one figure, a female nude, the identity to be decided upon my arrival in Genoa. He offered me a moderate sum, a room and studio in his palace, and possible further commissions if my first pleased him. A cry and a sigh escaped me.

Ce-sa-re, imperial and grand. Gen-ti-le, kindly and tender. His name seemed a good sign.

"*Grazie a Dio!* Palmira, we are saved." I grabbed Palmira's hands, leaned back, and we swung together in a circle until her little feet lifted off the floor and she squealed.

"What about Papa?" she asked.

"Pietro can come too, if he wants."

But it was my own papa her question reminded me of. Father was in Genoa. Writing to him occasionally was one thing. Living in the same city was another. How could I act as though nothing had happened between us — especially in front of Palmira?

I'd have to try.

I looked up and saw behind her my unfinished drawing from the loggia, the Sabine woman celebrated at the moment she was being raped. Just like Rome, Florence was a man's city, made of stone by men like Lorenzo il magnìfico and Brunelleschi, with reputations as solid as stone. Stone that was cold right through your shoes in winter, blazing hot in summer. The only woman they liked was the pathetic, penitent Magdalen. This was not a city kind to women.

Maybe Genoa would be different.

Genoa didn't have Pietro.

Neither did I.

17

Pietro

"Your reputation is spreading," Pietro said archly, after I showed him the letter from Genoa. There was a tautness to his lips which I took to mean artistic jealousy, until he added, "Naturally a nude. It's what you do best."

It wasn't art he meant.

Apparently those false rumors had reached him too. Unless, of course, that was where they began. The thought shocked me until I considered it. He'd never forgiven me for being admitted to the academy before him, never gotten over the sting of my success before his. Were the rumors a calculated attempt to win commissions away from me? To regain his stature as an artist and a man? Was he capable of that? I looked into his darting eyes.

Yes.

If the rumor hadn't begun with him, he would surely have confronted me with it more forcefully than with this feigned innuendo. Any man would. All he'd have had to do was to suggest the rumor to Vanna, and she'd have made sure it spread through the academy.

He tossed the letter onto the table in front of me as if it were worthless.

"I have no choice but to accept," I said flatly.

He scowled. His two-day growth of whiskers darkened his face and made him look fierce and haggard. "Choice?" He raised his voice. "You are my wife."

I sat up straight. "I am a painter first."

"A painter first?" He took off his doublet and flung it against a chair.

"Listen to me, Pietro." I leaned forward and spread out my fingers on the table. "We will both bow equally at God's feet on our day of judgment, and if either of us hides our talents, we deny God the full expression of Himself."

"Where'd you learn that? From your Roman nuns?"

"From the Magnificat. 'My soul doth magnify the Lord.' That's for all of us, Pietro. No matter how small, I am going to

277

add my piece to the mosaic of the world's art. Just like you are."

"A painter first." He sneered and walked to the sink and rinsed his face.

"All my life I have wanted to be both. And I have been both. I'm not a failure at either — no matter what Vanna says."

He swirled around. "Vanna!"

I laughed bitterly. "You think I don't know? You think I'm so lost in painting and Palmira that I don't notice you being gone? My heart cracks a little every night I blow out the lamp alone. Count the number of times and you'll see a heart in shreds."

"Vanna's Vanna, but you're my wife."

I leaned forward. "How long, Pietro? How long do I wait until you notice the difference between us?"

"*Dio mio!* Don't twist things to make it seem that I've left you. You're the one leaving," he added petulantly.

"Has there been any goodness in our marriage, for you?" I asked softly. "What did that mean in the tower, Pietro?"

He jerked his shoulders as if shaking away flies.

I held the letter from Genoa over Mother's oil lamp, high enough so it made smoke but didn't catch fire.

"If what we felt in that tower meant something to you, then I'll let this letter burn and never count the loss."

He looked furtively at my hot, trembling hand.

"Tell me, Pietro. What did it mean?"

His mouth stretched to one side as it always did when he didn't know what to say.

"Nothing? Was it nothing that made you get drenched in a storm? Nothing that made you climb halfway to Heaven on a whim of mine? Nothing when you covered my throat with kisses, pressed your hardness against me next to God's own dome?"

For one fraction of a second, he looked me in the eye.

He couldn't say.

I set the letter down.

"To me it meant possibility. It meant a discovery of love laid right in our hands. In our grasp, Pietro." I balled up my fist. "Right under this roof. Was it so with you, even for a moment?"

His shoulders lifted but no words came.

"It's not that you want me to stay then. It's only that you're hurt that your wife is leaving. There's a difference, you know."

"Don't quibble, Artemisia." He yanked a chair back from the table and sat.

"If there has been — any good at all — then come with me."

He snorted his mockery of the idea. I knew what repelled him — the humiliation of his wife having a wealthy patron when he didn't.

"You can come later if you don't want to come now." I put my hand on his arm. It tensed under my fingers.

He stared at my painting cabinet. "I can prevent you from going, you know."

"For what purpose, Pietro? If that bell tower and that night meant nothing to you, we are not husband and wife beyond a document of convenience."

His fingers traced the body of Artemis on my mother's oil lamp. He noticed me watching.

"Take it. It's yours," he said.

He stood up, walked to the wall, straightened a painting of his, walked to the opposite wall. He took one long breath, let it out in one great gush. And then he picked up his doublet and left. Not angry, not with door slamming or extravagant gesture, just a slow, old man's movement toward the door. He stood with his hand on the latch a moment, pushed open the door, and looked at the threshold. He was there, and then he wasn't. My last brief look at him showed a handsome, tormented man weighted down by secret obligations.

I didn't cry. My heart ached, but I didn't cry. There was too much to do. I packed all night, and left him Gentile's address sticking out of a drawer in my beautiful painting cabinet.

In the morning, Palmira was bewildered. "Is Papa coming too?"

I drew her head to my body. "I hope so. Someday."

He stayed away until after the coach collected us and our belongings, but I saw him standing alone in the Loggia della Signoria to watch us pass.

He was not a monster, only a man imperfect and unwise. Human.

Cleopatra

"Mama, take the string," Palmira said, thrusting the cat's cradle at me.

"I'd rather look out the window right now."

"Please, Mama."

"All right. Just once." I pinched the strings where they crossed, raised them over the sides of the square, and stretched the loop into another pattern held taut around the base of my fingers. I shuddered. It reminded me of the *sibille*. Holding out her perfect little fingers, Palmira daintily performed the next move. Where had she learned such a horrid game?

"Take it, Mama," she said, standing up now between the men and me in the coach. She was bored. To her, the ride was tedious and long, and the motion of the coach with its unexpected sideways lurches made her feel sick, and so she was contrary. I offered her bread to settle her stomach but she shook her head. The Tuscan countryside held no fascination for her, but for me, the moving landscape framed by the coach window made me melancholy that I was leaving it.

That morning riding through Florence, I had craned my neck to get a last glimpse of Giotto's bell tower, the one feature above all others that proclaimed, Florence, City of Possibilities! The thought made me ache. Riding along Corso dei Tintori for the last time, I had tried to imprint on my memory the brilliant silks hanging from upper windows. Umiliana was not at her vat. That was good. The city might still hold some possibility for her. Now, as we passed ochre and apricot-colored villas adorned with oleander, golden-leafed vineyards with mulberry trees among the vines, plum and pear and persimmon orchards, I felt as though I was being expelled from a Tuscan Eden.

"Take it." Palmira's voice crackled with impatience.

"No."

She loosened her fingers from the pattern made by the string and threw it at me. It caught on my bodice button and I picked it off and wound it up.

"Why do you have those little lines on your fingers, Mama? I don't have any. Is it because you're old?"

I glanced across the coach at the men who were now looking at my hands. "Yes, I guess that's why. I'm old now." Maybe that's what lost love had done to me, made me old overnight.

Palmira flopped down next to me and one of the men smiled at her. "They don't have any," she said.

"Maybe they're not as old as I am." They laughed and Palmira looked from them to me, snapping her head back and forth, trying to figure out who was older.

"Look, we're passing a town. See that fortress on the hill?"

"It's dumb to have all the towns on hills," Palmira said.

"Maybe it's so they can see who's coming. Or to save flatter land to grow things where the rivers are."

Palmira screwed up her nose in derision.

"Once there was a village named Pocopaglia and it was built on a hillside so steep that the people tied sacks under the tails of their hens so the eggs wouldn't roll downhill."

Palmira put her hands on her hips,

knowing she was being teased, and leveled at me an exasperated look. "It's still dumb."

I shrugged. "Maybe they just wanted to enjoy the view."

One of the men stuck out his thick bottom lip as if to say, "Could be." "You are a brave woman to make such a trip alone." His voice scraped with condescension.

"With your inquisitive child," the other man corrected.

I decided to take it as a compliment rather than an insinuation of impropriety. "Not by choice, but to seek employment."

"Employment?"

The question was weighted with suspicion. Genoa was a port city, so there was plenty of night employment for women on the docks. I couldn't let them think I meant that.

"As a painter. I am a painter. I have a new patron in Genoa. I imagine it's a lovely city, always with an ocean breeze."

Over the course of the day's long journey, the men unknowingly taught me a great deal — to divert a conversation, to give thin, mysterious answers about my private life, to make it clear that I had a husband, and then to close that slit of conversation by alluding to his absence as if it were a demise.

It pained me to speak of him that way, as if

by doing so I had killed any chance of resurrecting what at first seemed possible. Already I wished I had been more importunate about him coming with us.

I didn't tell the men my name. The Genoese were a talkative lot. "A Genoese, therefore a trader," was the saying, and they traded information as willingly as they traded bales and crates. I wanted to get established before news of my arrival reached Father.

How different my life was now than the last time I took a coach trip, when Father at the coach door had shaken his hands in agitation and said, "Get in. Get in." That one moment from the whole day was as clear to me now as if it were painted and hanging in a frame. I suddenly realized that I wasn't sure if he thought me innocent. Impatience was not his usual manner. Maybe Tuzia's suggestions had worked on him and made him suspicious. Maybe, behind his efforts to marry me off in a different city, he wanted to be rid of what had stained *his* reputation.

On the third day, we came into Genoa. Palmira stood up in the coach with her head out the window as we passed white villas looking clean and hopeful surrounded by terraced green hills facing the sea. "Look!"

she kept saying, which was precisely what I was doing too.

Sea air blew deep into my lungs, refreshing me from the long ride. In a semicircular bay, ships of all sorts — galleons, trading vessels and stout men-of-war with tall masts — lay at anchor. Crooked streets created an incomprehensible tangle amid hills and sun-washed palaces in bright terracotta colors.

Palmira quivered with excitement. "Which palace will we live in, Mama? Which one?"

"The Palazzo Cattaneo-Adorno on the Piazza de Banchi," I told the coachman. When the coach stopped, Palmira slumped back in her seat. It wasn't nearly as grand from the outside as Palazzo D'Oria or Palazzo Bianco, which we had passed on the way.

"You are to be polite and grateful, no matter what," I told her.

A porter ushered us into the great hall lined with carved and inlaid furniture bearing an array of fanciful objects. Two ewers in lapus lazuli in the shapes of birds caught my eye, but Palmira waved me over to a funny rock crystal fish with gaping mouth and enormous bulging green eyes, and fins and tails edged in silver. On the walls, there were only a few unremarkable paintings.

A round-bellied man in mustard-colored brocade dressing gown came toward us holding out both his arms. "I am Cesare Gentile. You are welcome in our home. Artists are honored persons in this household." A huge, loose-jowled smile widened his face and doubled his chin.

He tapped Palmira on the shoulder with a flick of a chubby, rubied hand. "Two artists? Two? *Che splendido.*" With his eyebrows lifted and arched and his lips pinched together in mock seriousness, he gave an exaggerated, humorous bow to Palmira. A tall, graceful woman came into the room. "*Santo cielo!* Bianca, *che prodigioso,*" he said. "I didn't realize I was getting two painters for the price of one!"

Palmira shot me a look of panic, not knowing what to do, and we all laughed.

"He's absolutely unpredictable," the woman said in an indulgent way.

"My wife, Bianca. Signora Gentileschi and Signorina . . . ?" He bent down to Palmira amiably.

"Palmira," she said, without letting me introduce her.

"And Signorina Palmira Gentileschi," he said, grinning.

"We are pleased to have you both," Bianca said. An elegant, dark-haired woman, she wore a dressing gown of wine-colored velvet with a pomegranate design cut into the nap.

"Palmira and I are heartily grateful, and trust our efforts will meet with your pleasure."

"These are our two daughters, Theresa and Margherita." She motioned for them to come forward.

They were older than Palmira, beautifully dressed, but not ravishing beauties. Against the wall, the whole serving staff lined up to be introduced. Signora Gentile called forward one young woman who was rolling down her sleeves. "This is Renata. All day she's been rushing to the windows every time a coach passed. She will tend to your needs."

Renata curtseyed, and Palmira, confused again, curtseyed back which made us all laugh.

"You must be tired from your journey," Bianca said. "Please, take your ease."

Renata took us up the wide marble stairs to our quarters. Palmira tugged at my skirt. "We're going to live here?" she asked in wonder. Renata giggled.

The outer room was large, light, and high-ceilinged with two tall windows. "This is your studio," Renata said with an exaggerated sniff.

"I can tell." I smiled when she pinched her nose against the smell of turpentine. There were three sizes of easels, an adjustable stool, a long trestle table, a chaise longue, and various chairs, pillows and drapes for posing. "A room just for painting. How wonderful."

"Signor Cappelini left it a mess. Paint on the floor, oil spills, and smudges of charcoal everywhere, and him being here less than a year."

I crossed myself in a frantic, exaggerated way. "*Madonna benedetta,* let me stay longer than he did."

She laughed, which is what I wanted. "He was an old grouch. We're glad you're here instead." She opened double doors to a bedchamber, equally spacious with fine bed linen, two *cassapancas* for our clothes, and a furnace.

"What's this?" Palmira asked, pointing to something that looked like a square box with a round lid.

"A closestool," Renata said.

Palmira gave her a steady opaque look.

Renata lifted the lid. "A chamber pot."

Palmira's mouth dropped to a tall oval. "Padded?"

"Only two like that in the whole palace. I'll leave it to you to guess where the other one is." Renata turned to me. "Will you be wanting help to put your things away?"

"Later, perhaps."

She curtseyed, blew Palmira a kiss, and left.

"Look, Mama, a big mirror." Above a low table laid with a linen cloth, a vase of irises, and a wash basin hung a tall polished metal mirror. "I can see myself." Palmira spun around, looking over her shoulder at the swirl of her skirt.

I did not look into the mirror to see my face worn by travel. Tomorrow I would look. Today I wanted just to lie flat on the unmoving bed, rest my aching back, and be grateful I had solid ground under me once again. I sat on the edge of the bed and took off my shoes. "The bed is plenty big enough for both of us."

With a knock on the door, Renata, her face wrung with worry, came in again carrying a tray with green glass goblets and a pitcher of water, followed by another servant bearing a majolica platter of sweetmeats, pears, and walnuts.

"Please, signora, don't tell Signora Gentile. I was supposed to have this here when you arrived, but I — we were trying to wave that smell out the windows."

"How?"

"With your bed linen," she said shame-facedly. The other girl giggled. They set down their trays and the two of them pretended they were trying to capture air by lifting a sheet like a billowing sail and running with it to the open window.

I laughed. "I wish I would have seen that. No, Renata, I won't tell. What good would this lovely platter of food have served before we came? Thank her please. And thank you too, both of you."

Renata blushed, curtseyed, and shooed the other girl out the door.

I lay down and looked at the carved leaves and tendrils edging the coffered ceiling and felt all the evidences of welcome wash over me again. There was plenty of empty wall space in the great hall. This could last a long time. What would it be like to live with laughter in the house? I closed my eyes and felt my shoulders relax. It would be good for Palmira, good for me.

The next morning Renata came early to summon me to Cesare's reception chamber to discuss my first painting.

"He certainly doesn't lose any time," I said.

"Take it as a good sign, signora. He has been speaking of nothing else but you since he came back from Florence. When you agreed to come, he was so happy he gave his entire household a holiday."

I gathered some drawings to show him as a sample of my work. "A holiday?" She nodded energetically. "And what did you do on your holiday?"

She looked down at her clasped hands. "I went to my favorite spot up in the hills above the city and tried to draw what you might look like."

"I certainly hope you made me more beautiful than I feel this morning." I wrapped my hair in a haphazard fashion and secured it hastily with a comb.

Cesare Gentile greeted me again with that wide spread of his arms which showed the embroidery on his dressing gown. "Forgive me if I called you too early. It is only a measure of my enthusiasm."

"I brought some recent drawings, just for you to take a look."

"I will be pleased to see them, but I already know your talent."

He looked at them with much interest, nodding and murmuring his satisfaction, and then ushered me out to the garden. We walked along the sandy path beside a flowering hedge.

"First, as you know, I want you to do a female. A woman painted by a woman — so that you can see deeply into the life of her. You might know some secret that we men, you understand, do not. Second, she must be beautiful, but not too beautiful — in order not to incite a touch of envy in my lovely daughters. But beautiful enough so they see themselves as art, and valuable." His hands stroked the air as if tracing sensuous curves. "And then, as you know, she must be nude." He flung his arms wide. "Show us all the glory of woman."

"And the figure herself? Allegorical or historical?"

"Historical, of course. Beyond mere beauty, art must tell us something."

"I quite agree. Might I do a Cleopatra reclining? With a mystery to solve? A beauty of the spirit as well as body? Suffering a loss as vast as Egypt?"

"Doesn't matter the subject. I am pleased to have any woman painted by you, the great woman artist of Florence."

It seemed like he cared more about my reputation, whatever version he knew of it, than my painting, yet he grinned so innocently. I had to wait and see.

He pinched off a gardenia from a bush

and handed it to me. I breathed its heady sweetness. "Beautiful and exotic," he said. "Like your Cleopatra, no?"

When I came back to my room, Renata was waiting at the doorway. "Would you like help with anything? May I put away your things?"

"Yes. Thank you."

I considered a moment using her as a model. She had a natural, artless beauty — soft, gray, thoughtful eyes and a sharply defined, curvaceous mouth. But Cleopatra's beauty was not artless, in fact was entirely self-conscious. Besides, the painting was a nude. That would be undecorous.

"Where do you think I could get a woman to model nude?" I asked.

"Easy. The whores along the docks."

"Which docks? The whole city is docks."

"At my brother's tavern. I'll take you there."

A few days later when the Gentiles took Palmira on an outing in the country, Renata led me through twisted alleyways hung with drying laundry and alive with cats and rats. We made a sharp turn to a wider street incongruously lined with palaces, and came down a stepped pathway which opened onto the busy wharf and the gray sea. Under glowering skies men hoisted bales on ropes and rolled barrels along the docks. I spotted a short piece of old rope lying on the wharf and I picked it up. It would do for an asp. An old man sat on a crate nearby.

"May I have this?" I asked.

"Not mine to give." He puffed on his pipe. "Take it."

Fishwives sold live eels and shimmery, golden-spotted bream from large glass tanks.

"Live squid," cried a woman holding a writhing one as proof.

"Oysters and mussels here," another woman shouted, leaning on her cart.

"*Frutti di mare*," a third woman called.

"What's *frutti di mare*?" I asked Renata.

"You don't know? You must try one," Renata said. "They're a Genoese specialty. Sea urchins."

Using tongs, the woman pulled a round, spiny purple thing out of her bucket, dripping with salt water. She split it with a knife, scooped out what looked to be a slimy reddish egg mass, not at all appetizing, laid it on an oyster shell, squeezed lemon over it and handed it to me.

"You'll like it," Renata said.

It slid down easily enough. "Tasty," I said, though I didn't want another one. I just wanted to please her.

Renata's brother's tavern was wedged between a warehouse and a seamen's lodging. In the smoky room, dark-skinned sailors with leathery necks and faces gulped ale and looked us over. One wearing a black beret, crimson cumberbund, and a gold hoop earring grinned and said, "Looking for work, eh? Plenty of it here for beauties like you."

"Zitto, marinaio!" Renata snapped. Her supercilious tone made him shrink back to his game of dice. It amused me that a servant girl had this commanding power.

I went to the rear of the room while Renata spoke to her brother privately. He sent his tavern boy out. After some time, a parade of whores in orange, red, and purple skirts came flouncing into the room past the ogling men. Thin, gathered peasant blouses showed their unbound breasts. Some were too old, and I felt sorry for them. One wasn't much older than Palmira, and I felt even worse for her.

A dark, wide-hipped Moroccan sauntered in, swaying her full red skirt. "Pick me, signora." She trailed her hands over her breasts and down to her waist, then leaned forward to show me more. I had the feeling that she teased men along the docks in the same way.

A lighter-skinned brunette posed sideways and lifted her orange and green skirt. "I have been painted before, signora. I am Sicilian." She raised her chin in a haughty way. Too much like Vanna.

A beauty with her black hair pulled back tightly elbowed her way to the front. "I am a Spanish dancer," she said, executing a twirl and a stomping step and clapping her hands above her head.

"Aye, aye, aye," another woman called, and the men joined in.

The women seemed to know each other and were used to such robust competition.

"And where are you from?" I asked a dark-haired woman whose expression was detached and wistful.

"Genoa."

"Push up your sleeves please." Her skin tone was pale honey. "Lift your skirt." Her legs were beautifully shaped. "Look up a moment please. No, not with your head. With your eyes. Look worried and pleading. Now look peaceful." Her face was wonderfully fluid and her figure just round enough. "What is your name?"

"Giuliana."

"Will you pose nude?"

"Yes, signora."

"Aye, Giuliana!" the Spanish woman

298

cried in hearty congratulation, and thrust her knee into Giuliana's backside, shoving her forward.

Giuliana blushed. Renata explained to her where we lived.

On the way home Renata said, "I think you picked the right one."

"Why is that?"

"She'll be easier to work with than the others."

Giuliana was not at all shy about undressing in front of me, and Palmira wandering in and out didn't bother her. As I sketched her in various compositions — reclining to the right on pillows on the chaise longue, then left, I told her Cleopatra's story — how rich and powerful she was, how captivating to men. "The queen of sensuality."

"I wish I knew her secret," Giuliana said.

"Don't we all."

I drew her placing the rope to her breast, and then thought, no. That was too common. The asp wound around her wrist? With Cleopatra deciding the moment when she'd put it to her breast? A possibility.

"Close your eyes a little, Giuliana. Make them just slits, as though you're thinking hard."

"About what?"

"Think as Cleopatra would think."

I turned when I sensed someone behind me. It was Renata carrying a tray of fruit, olive bread, cheese, and almonds.

"Oh." She backed away a few steps, but kept on looking at my drawing. "I'm sorry, signora, and signorina. I —"

"That's all right. You don't mind, do you, Giuliana?"

"No," she said, keeping her pose, her eyes almost closed.

Renata set down her tray. "It's a miracle, what you do. To make her round. When I draw, it's only a flat outline."

"It's in how you shade it." I worked a while longer to show her.

"How do you know how to do that?"

"By seeing where the light rests on her and where it doesn't." I could feel her studying Giuliana.

"It must be a different way of seeing. Like you're ignoring color and only paying attention to light and dark."

"Yes, that's exactly right. But it's more than that. It's in the shading that you can give interpretation too." I stood up. "That's enough for today, Giuliana. Here, have something to eat before you go."

She stretched, shook out the arm she'd been leaning on, and then sat completely naked as she cut a wedge of pear and ate it.

"Do you like posing?" Renata asked.

"It's all right. It's nice here. I like the quiet."

"What do you think about while you're sitting still all day?" Renata asked.

"I'm supposed to be Cleopatra, so I think about what it must be like to love real love and to be loved back so passionately that men give away kingdoms for a kiss."

Renata's eyes opened wider.

Her frankness surprised me too. "Oh, you don't have to be Cleopatra to think about that," I said with a soft chuckle. "That desire is the naked truth of us all."

We sat a moment quietly, each thinking, it seemed, of our own versions of that love.

"Easier for me to think it than for you to draw it," Giuliana said softly.

"Is that what you meant by interpretation? You have to draw thoughts too?" Renata squeezed her eyebrows together, overwhelmed by this vast new aspect of drawing.

"It's not impossible, Renata, but don't be surprised if it takes a lifetime to learn."

Months later, after Guiliana had gone home one day and I was painting the asp's head against Cleopatra's flesh, Renata was drawing my composition. Palmira pranced in, waving a piece of torn lace Signora Gentile had given her. She stopped suddenly.

"Ugh! Why is she holding that snake?" she asked.

"It's an asp. It's poisonous. This is Cleopatra, Queen of Egypt, Cyprus, Crete, and Syria, a very rich and powerful lady," I told her. "She had two immortal loves in her life, Julius Caesar, who ruled Rome, and Marc Antony, who ruled Asia Minor."

"But why is she holding that snake?" Irritation edged her voice.

"She's going to kill herself by letting it bite her. Or maybe she already has."

Palmira shook her shoulders. "She's rich and she wants to die?"

"She was defeated in war by a Roman emperor and didn't want to be paraded through the streets of Rome on display. Rome has always loved a spectacle, especially of a woman humiliated."

"It's dumb to want to die."

"Not always," Renata said. "How would you like to have crowds shouting curses and throwing things at you?"

Palmira shrugged. "Where's the bite?"

I considered each breast, an upper arm, even her throat. I hated to inflict a wound on the flesh I had painted so smoothly. "I don't know yet."

"Maybe nowhere," Renata said. "Maybe she just willed herself to die. Or maybe she loved enough in her life that she's passing to the other realm . . . mystically . . . being called there by Marc Antony before the asp hurts her."

I liked that. I turned to Palmira to see what she thought.

"She's not very pretty," Palmira said.

"But she has beauty of the spirit," Renata said.

Palmira draped the lace around her neck and twirled around in a dance step Margherita had taught her. "That doesn't count."

Cesare and Bianca loved the Cleopatra, framed it extravagantly and hung it prominently in the great hall. Later that day they came into the studio and saw me struggling to attach my *Woman Playing a Lute* to a wooden stretcher myself.

"No, no, signora. You mustn't," Cesare said. "You'll hurt your hands doing that — those wonderful hands that should only paint."

Was he making a snide remark or was it genuine? Did he know what he was saying? I didn't think so. It wasn't in his nature to hurt.

"I'll send in a joiner tomorrow to stretch

all your paintings and fit them with frames. They must hang here in your studio, since you are a permanent resident. Isn't that right, Bianca? Now you choose a subject for your next painting," Cesare said, tapping me on the shoulder with his pudgy, fluttering fingers. "We have many more walls to fill."

"Anything?"

"Anything you like." He looked at me directly, expectantly, as if I would decide right then. He clasped his hands across his paunch and waited.

"Hmm. What about a . . . a standing portrait of . . ." I made him wait, pretending I was thinking hard. "Of you! As a *condottiere*."

"Me?" A wide grin spread across his face. "Me. Yes. Me!"

Bianca laughed.

"Do you have any armor?"

"My father did."

"Good. Get it polished."

I posed him with a scabbard at his side, plumed helmet on a table, and a fringed campaign banner hanging on the wall behind. He wore the stiffest, widest, most extravagant ruff I had ever seen, with smaller versions at his wrists. I draped a lace scarf over one shoulder. One day he came clanking into the studio with four friends in tow to watch him pose. He assumed his puffed-up stance and blushed at his vanity in front of his friends which made Bianca laugh. He scowled a pretense of offense. "We're doing hard work here, so please keep silent."

"*Amore mio,* it's a fine pose, and a fine portrait," Bianca soothed. "I love it almost as much as I love you!"

After more than a year with the Gentiles, I accompanied Palmira and the two Gentile daughters to a birthday party of a child of a wealthy shipping lord. In the loggia of his villa there stood a group of men, and under a tree laden with yellow blossoms, four women were engaged in a game of whist. Not knowing anyone, I sat on a bench between the men and women and watched the children play. A burst of laughter from the men drew my attention and I heard amongst them, unmistakeably, Father. My heart plummeted. He had his back to me. I thought of slipping around the corner so he wouldn't see me, but while I hesitated, he happened to turn my way.

"*Buon Dio.* Artemisia!" His breathy voice barely reached me. He broke away from the men and came toward me with his arms opened wide.

"Father." I stood up and we embraced. His beard scratched my cheek just as it did when I was young.

"I didn't know you were in Genoa," he said. "Didn't I write you that I was here?"

"Yes, but I didn't know where you were to tell you. I have a new patron. Cesare Gentile."

"Is he good to you?"

"Oh yes. An amusing man, and very generous. I'm happy here."

His eyes became watery. "You look beautiful."

"You're combing your hair forward now, in the Roman way." I laughed softly, but there was tension in the sound. "I thought you said you never would. Too much of caesars."

"It's gray now. I have a right. Never is too long a time for mere mortals to make promises."

"Look, there, in the red smock playing hoodman-blind, my daughter."

His eyebrows lifted in high arches at their outer reaches, and even his forehead smiled. "My granddaughter?" he said with wonder. "I thought I would never be able to see her."

"Palmira Prudenzia."

"She's a pretty thing."

"And she knows it. Almost nine years old."

"She reminds me of you. Can she draw?"

"Not very well. That concerns me. Painting is the only way for her to continue to live the way we are now."

"You don't have to worry. Anyone can see that she'll be a beautiful woman."

"I'm going to have quite a time keeping her dressed the way she wants. She has become a favorite among noble families, which worries me."

Slowly he drew his eyes from Palmira back to me. "Stiattesi said you left his brother."

The sharp way he said it stung, as if I were ungrateful for the effort he took in arranging the marriage.

"There are two sides to every story."

"Why did you leave?"

I felt my jaw tighten and my back teeth grind. "Pietro could have come with me. I have written. He doesn't answer."

We stood in edgy silence.

"Artemisia, we must see each other again."

"I'm in the middle of a commission."

"All the better. Let me see it."

"I —"

"Caravaggist?"

"No, not particularly."

He stole a look at my hands and said tenderly, "Don't be afraid of me, Artemisia."

"I have reason to be, don't I?"

The lines in his forehead deepened. "You wouldn't deny an old man his grandchild, would you?" He looked wistfully at Palmira laughing and hopping up and down with the other children.

The skin of his cheek had become coarser, as if scoured by grains of sand falling grain by grain through the hourglass.

"No."

19

Renata

Father, Palmira, and I dodged a bale of cotton being lowered by a hoist onto the wharf. Men wearing loose pantaloons and black slippers guided it on top of other bales, speaking sharply in a strange language. Wind flapped their full white sleeves like sails.

"Why is their skin so dark?" Palmira asked.

"Because of the sun, *preziosa*," Father said. "Those men are from Morocco, the north of Africa."

I let him answer her questions since he took such delight in it. She deserved someone fatherly after I had yanked her away from Pietro.

He pointed to bulging sacks along the wharf. "Smell the pepper?" he asked her. "Cinnamon too." She drew in an exaggerated breath. "It's probably from Syria. Shipments of things come from many places — Egypt, Sicily, Corsica. Gold comes from North Africa." He looked down at her to make sure she was listening. "Silk from Asia. Oranges from Spain. So people from all those places come here too. Muslims, Jews, Egyptians. And they bring with them different ideas."

"About what?" Palmira asked.

"Everything. Life. Religion. Art. Government. And from here ships take away wine, olive oil, silverware, marble. The Genoese think that this port is the center of the world."

I smiled at the quaintness of that belief. After Galileo's ideas were accepted, no one could think that. There were changes to come in the world. I was sure of that.

We stopped at a ship chandlery and Father bought some dry sailor's biscuits and strong-smelling Turkish coffee. He noticed Palmira looking at a display of brass sailors' buttons and pins with various nautical and foreign symbols. "Pick one out," he said, and gave the shopkeeper a few coins.

"You pin it on me." She stood up straight while he did so.

We sat on barrels on the quay to drink the coffee. Every so often Palmira touched the pin on her cape.

"Tell me what you've painted in Genoa," Father said.

It was a safe topic.

"I started with a Cleopatra because Cesare wanted a nude. Then he let me choose my own subjects for several paintings."

I took a sip of the thick, dark liquid and could barely swallow it. I pushed it toward him, squinting my eyes. "You drink it."

He smiled. "It takes a while to get used to. Here, eat a biscuit."

I did. "Kind of tasteless."

"I like them," Palmira said, swinging her legs and knocking her heels against the barrel.

"Don't do that, *cara*. It'll ruin your shoes."

"So, what else did you paint?" Father asked.

"A standing portrait of Cesare as a *condottiere*. I suggested it, but he jumped at the idea. I did it in the style of Titian, with a dark background. It wasn't the kind of subject that bubbled up from the center of me, but I was glad to do it for him since it made him so happy. I'll probably do Signora Gentile next. I've been more prolific here than I've ever been. I owe that to the congenial home, I think."

He set down his cup on the barrel with a little thud and looked at me suspiciously.

"I mean, with meals provided, and with Palmira spending the days with Gentile's daughters, I have more time to paint."

I couldn't quite determine why I felt defensive, but I knew there was some danger in being too relaxed. Even with Father, I reminded myself, I had to be wary.

"You are making me envied," Cesare said one morning as I was cleaning brushes.

"How?"

"Plenty of gentlemen in Genoa would vie for a painting from the hand of Artemisia Gentileschi — a woman who understands women. I must treat you handsomely." He winked. "Otherwise you will go elsewhere."

"I don't even think about going anywhere else. We're happy here. You know that."

"Then it's time to discuss a new painting. My daughters will be coming of age soon. This time, let's have a Lucrezia."

"The one figure I would most dislike doing."

He puffed air out of his round cheeks. "But why?"

"I have no desire to celebrate a woman

who killed herself to escape the shame of rape."

He raised a finely plucked eyebrow. "And therefore you must."

Then he did know about the trial. Was Rome to follow me to Genoa too?

He put on a playful frown, balled up his fist and swung it in an arc upward. "Confront the enemy, and crush it dead. Make Lucrezia yours alone."

No one but Cesare could turn a frown into an infectious, all-over grin with such fluid movement of flesh. As for his request, I had no way to avoid it.

I was in misery for hours — so untalkative at the midday meal that Cesare and Bianca surely noticed. I pushed my food around my plate and only took occasional bites. Palmira kept pleading that I take her on an outing to the country.

"No, Palmira. Not today. How many times do I have to say it?"

She pounded her elbows down on the damask cloth and moped with her cheeks on her fists. "You're selfish," she muttered. "Grandpa would."

I was embarrassed by her bad behavior. After the meal, she escaped downstairs to the courtyard and wouldn't come when I called her.

By late afternoon, the studio was littered with halfhearted sketches of women in the act of stabbing themselves and women sprawled and bleeding. Renata came in carrying a huge fan of dark crimson gladioli. "These are from Signor Gentile," she said as she put them on the trestle table below the window.

"Just for me? They should be in the great hall."

"No. Signor Gentile told me to put them in your studio."

"They're exquisite. See how the play of light and shadow on the petals graduates the color from crimson madder almost to purple-black?"

"Inside the petals," she pointed, "they look like wax. How can you paint it to look like that?"

I was about to explain about Venetian amber varnish when she turned and saw my sketches. "Not another woman killing herself!"

"Not my choice. Cesare's. That's why I've been irritable. For the first time in my life, I don't want to paint something."

"Why?" She looked at me with that endearing earnestness, and sat down to listen.

I told her the history of Lucrezia's shame after her rape by the Tarquin. "According to

314

the story, she thought that if she remained alive, it would set a precedent of pardon for adulterers, men and women."

"I think it's because of Signor Gentile's daughters. He wants to scare them into chastity."

I tossed my drawing pencil onto the table. "I hate all these paintings where, just after killing herself, Lucrezia is lying in serene virtue with the painter's peace, not her own, smeared across her face. Killing yourself isn't like that."

Renata leaned forward and peered at me with furrowed brows. She opened her mouth to say something, and then sank backward.

"In Filippino Lippi's version in the Palazzo Pitti in Florence, she committed the act publically. To me, that is supreme folly. If she was an innocent victim, she didn't need to feel shame, and so killing herself was a rash, prideful act, not an ennobling one. A way out that might be appealing for a moment, but . . ."

"But what?"

"No one who loved life could willingly choose that escape."

There was still a look of concern on Renata's face. "Then it doesn't make sense."

I held up a finger, thinking. "Unless, of

course, you think that victims share the guilt, or even cause the act. Lucrezia only makes sense to those who don't want to recognize that women don't like being raped. To me, she's a false and unnecessary martyr."

"Are you going to paint her to show her thoughts or yours?"

"An important question. Mine, I think. Cesare said for me to make Lucrezia mine alone." The task seemed even more formidable now that I had put it in words.

The way Cesare had looked at me with that one eyebrow quirked up in that exaggerated curve told me he knew precisely what he was doing by letting me have the freedom of choosing several subjects, and then challenging me. And now this extravagant display of flowers to soften what he thought I ought to confront. All done with understatement and respectful, fatherly intent.

Renata laid out my sketches in a row on the floor. One of them I had torn in frustration. She held it at arm's length. "This one. You didn't want it?"

"No. It's the worst of the lot."

She examined it, scowling a little in her attempt to understand what I meant. "If you're sure you don't want it," she bit her

316

lip, "may I have it?"

"Why?"

"So I can practice in my room at night. So I can go over your lines and shadings and see how it feels."

The thought of her doing that moved me. Her spirit was pure and her mind eager and absorbent and her desire keen — all that I wanted in Palmira.

Renata waited on the edge of her chair for my answer.

I was suddenly afraid that I could give all I knew only once — that I could express it in the freshest way, at the moment of my discovery, as I was learning it with each new painting, only once. I ought to save this intimate core of my creative self for Palmira, who by virtue of the accident of birth had more claim to it and was in a better position to use it, but . . .

I stole a look at Renata still scrutinizing the torn drawing, afraid too, it seemed. Of what? That this might be the last time she'd see it?

"Take it, *carissima*. And when I'm finished, you can have them all."

A tiny, sweet gasp issued from her lovely mouth.

A rustling of skirts made me turn. Bianca was standing at the open door. I felt caught in an act of overfamiliarity with a servant, and responsible for keeping Renata from her other duties.

"I'm sorry to interrupt you." Her voice was unusually solemn.

"Come in. Please."

Renata quickly set down the torn drawing on a chair, curtseyed and left.

"Cesare's steward just returned from Florence, and I knew you'd want to know. Il granduca Cosimo has died."

"Died?" I was dumbfounded. "He was so young."

"Only thirty, I think."

"He didn't have time to finish his project, the extension of the Pitti."

"The dukedom will go to his oldest son, Ferdinando, even though he won't come of age for eight or nine years. And Giovanni, 'ruling' Venice now, is even younger."

"The poor archduchess. This will send her into years of vigils."

"Doubly hard on her, coming so soon after her idol died."

"Who's that?"

"Pope Paul."

I thought of Galileo. He had Medici patronage for life, but Ferdinando might not be so firm a supporter as Cosimo had been. And this new pope was an enigma. "This worries me," I murmured.

"Cosimo might not have been as great as Lorenzo, but he was a good man," Bianca said.

"He was generous to me, and always welcomed me at affairs at the Pitti. And now his sons are fatherless."

Bianca put her palms together. "I'm sorry to tell you on a day when —"

"When I'm selfish? Like Palmira said? That's all right. Thank you for letting me know."

Bianca moved toward the door.

"Don't leave." I removed the torn drawing from the chair. "Please, sit. I'm sorry Palmira was disagreeable today."

"Even when she's disagreeable, she's adorable."

"That's part of the problem. She knows it. I wish I could interest her in something."

"Painting?"

"Of course. But I've tried other things too. She's learning to embroider, but she won't read or practice writing unless I'm directing her, and it takes away my concentration."

"My daughters could teach her. Theresa, I mean. She'd like to."

"Are Theresa and Margherita so different from each other?"

"Different as the sun and moon. It wouldn't surprise me if Theresa became a nun, but all Margherita thinks about is picnics and parties."

"Strange, isn't it, how our children grow." I hesitated, but Bianca's open expression urged me to continue. "What we most expect of them, what we'd love most for them —"

"Interests them the least?"

"Exactly." I looked at the torn drawing. "Blood ties seem so arbitrary." I twirled a pencil in my hand. "I was just thinking of Renata. I . . ."

"Go on. You can be frank. It's all right."

"She's hungry for any shred of teaching I can give."

"She's a delight, isn't she?"

I nodded. Bianca tipped her head, encouraging me to speak.

"Which one is really my child? The one I brought forth with my own groans who has no liking for the thing I love most in all the world, or the stranger's child whom fate placed in my life, the one who is absorbing and treasuring every word I give her, whose eyes are learning every day, whom I would love to teach, except that I fear Palmira's jealousy?"

I began sharpening the pencil with a knife,

ashamed to have admitted this to Bianca.

"Maybe she's more like her father. Palmira, I mean."

A sad, involuntary chuckle escaped me. "No. He's a painter too. She inherited only his sullen, dark-eyed glare."

We sat a moment, looking absently at the drawings on the floor. I felt no hint of judgment from her, only understanding. "I have a question, if it's not too unmannerly of me."

"Please, what is it?"

"How did Renata come to be with you?"

Bianca smiled. "I love to tell that. She used to work at the flower market. Cesare adores flowers, can't live without them."

"I know!" I pointed to the fan of gladioli. "Did you know he did this?"

"Yes. He walks down the hill every Saturday morning early to pick out the best blooms. For years, he always went to Renata's stall, but then he fell ill and was bedridden for a while. She must have learned of it, and so, of her own doing, she began to bring flowers here each week, picking out the kinds and colors she knew he liked. The first time, she just left the flowers with a servant, not waiting to be paid."

"Typical of her modesty."

"When she came again, I insisted that she carry the flowers in to him, because I knew she'd bring him joy. She was devoted and so full of pleasantness and cheer, that one Saturday he made up a tale about how he desperately needed another chambermaid. 'Won't you stay, just for a week, to help an old man through a sickness?' He put on an exaggerated pout and sounded so pitiful that she couldn't say no, but when the week was over, she folded the dress I'd given her to wear and left it on the *cassapanca* and slipped out before Cesare had awakened. When he learned that she had left, he got dressed for the first time in months, and walked down to the flower market himself and brought her back to stay, both of them blushing with smiles. He hasn't been sick since."

"Do you know how fortunate you are to have a husband so — ?"

"*Gentile?* I learn it again every day. My only hope is that my daughters will have men half so kind."

"And Palmira too. And Renata."

"This is a famous Roman woman named Lucrezia," I said to Palmira who was sitting on a chair behind me swinging her legs and sucking the juice out of an orange.

I was working on the background now without the model whom I had posed in a disheveled white night shift tangled with a dark crimson velvet bedspread, the same color as the gladioli. The figure was holding my mother's dagger in one hand pointed at her full breast held firm in her other hand. Life and motherhood set against suicide and martrydom — there they were, both roads.

"Did you know her?"

"No. She lived two thousand years ago." That long ago, I thought, and some things haven't changed. I stopped painting. "Yes, I did, in a way." Maybe Palmira was old enough to know some things other than lace and ruffles. "A man violated her against her will and made her ashamed. That means he did something to her she didn't want."

Palmira sucked again. "She's got a big leg."

"That's to call attention to the tension in her knee and thigh. It goes with her expression. You see, people treated her badly. They thought she enjoyed what the man did but they were wrong. She didn't want to face them."

Palmira scraped her chair back against the floor.

"And so, she found a dagger —"

"I don't want to hear it. No more horrible stories." Palmira dropped the orange, put her hands over her ears and ran out the door.

I was stunned. I had no idea the stories affected her so. I set down my brush, thinking I should go after her, but she would only go to Margherita's room and find some distraction. There was no harm in that.

But was there harm in the stories?

One morning I didn't get out of bed. I hadn't worked on the painting for three days. I lay motionless and stared at the ceiling and saw floating above me the state I'd left the painting in. I had finished the background, the folds of her white shift, the dark crimson spread crumpled on the bed where she'd been raped, her exposed leg, her arm and her right hand holding her breast ready for the blade, but I only roughed in her left hand cocked at the wrist and aiming the dagger at her breast. I hadn't been able to go on. I had dismissed the model. For the last three days, I just sat and stared. Renata had watched me with dark, troubled eyes, unsure whether to leave the room or stay.

The dagger was the problem. I closed my eyes in bed and it swam behind my eyelids, pointing to the right, then left, then stuck in her breast, then resting, bloody, in her open palm.

Renata burst into the room and said, "Quickly, Palmira. Did you forget the picnic?"

"What picnic?" Palmira asked. Renata helped her get dressed and Palmira ran out the door with her shoes in her hand.

Renata opened the shutters to let in light, came back to the bed, and looked down at me without smiling. "Why don't you stop working on her hand and do her face? Today."

I stared at the ceiling.

"Get up. I have to wash the bedclothes." She yanked them right off of me and gestured roughly toward the studio.

I was so surprised, I did as she told me. In my night shift I slumped on the stool in front of the easel and didn't even look at the painting.

"What direction does the light come from?" she asked as she rolled up the bed linen. It wasn't that she wanted to learn. It was an easy question both of us knew already.

"From the viewer."

"Tell me what that means."

"There has to be darkness on the other

side. I have only a profile, half her face, one eye in the light, to convey the meaning."

"So, begin," her tavern voice commanded.

With knit brows, Renata stood her ground until I started to work. Silently, warily, she checked on me all day. Once I wasn't working, so she stood behind me, not saying a word until I started painting again. Then she left.

Lucrezia's face began to take on expression. Distress, not fear. I furrowed the space between her eyebrows, like Renata's. I couldn't stop darkening her eye and the skin under the eye. It became more and more troubled the more I worked it. I wanted her troubled. Disturbed and disturbing.

Now, with Lucrezia's troubled, searching eye, her roughed-in hand with her wrist cocked, aiming the dagger at her breast, seemed wrong. When I loaded flesh tones onto a clean brush, I could not make the hand hold that aim. My arm was paralyzed. Speak to me, Lucrezia. What would you have me do? The room, the whole house was quiet. I waited. *Remember,* she seemed to say with her eye.

Remember?

I cleared off my work table and set up the adjustable table mirror and picked up

Mother's dagger. It was a wicked instrument as long as my forearm, black steel with a brass cruciform handle. I touched its flat side to my cheek. Its coldness shocked me. I pushed down my shift and took my left breast in my right hand, as in the pose. I propped my left elbow on the table and crooked my wrist at arm's length to aim the dagger at my own flesh. I remembered the day of the *sibille*. I had not come this close, had not even lifted the dagger from beneath my bed, but I had thought of it.

With excrutiating slowness, I bent my elbow more and moved the point of the blade toward me. Slowly. Pausing. A little more. I looked down the edge where the gleam of light traveled up and down its length as I tilted it. My wrist ached. With my other hand I felt the beating of my heart, even now, just imagining the stab of metal through my flesh. In the mirror I could see my breast making tiny movements up and down. To stop that with one mighty thrust — could I have actually done it? Could Lucrezia? Was the world so devoid of possibility to her? I touched the point to my skin.

A piercing scream.

"No!" Renata shouted. The dagger leaped from my grasp. "Don't!" She lunged at me, flinging aside the tray, the fruit, the water. A horrendous crash. She grabbed on to my ankles.

"I wasn't going to," I sputtered. "I'm only imagining. For the painting."

She cried in great, noisy sobs. "You could have told me! What was I to think?"

"I'm sorry." I put my arms around her, stroked the back of her head, felt her heart beating against my knees, the devotion behind her panic.

"But I know now. I know! My Lucrezia is not going that far. This is not an act in progress. She's thinking hard, reconsidering what the world has told her, questioning her martyrdom, but she is not aiming. Her wrist has to be painted unbent, the dagger upright."

I kissed the top of her head.

20

Lucrezia

I washed my hair and put on a clean dress the morning Father was to come early for the grand unveiling of Lucrezia at Cesare and Bianca's anniversary. I sat in a Moorish chair in the great hall tracing the design of its embossed leather with my finger. Not wanting him to come when I was upstairs and have him see any of my paintings without me, I waited, scraping at the dry flaky skin on my bottom lip until it bled.

"I was detained," was all he said when he finally came in the afternoon.

We walked around the room and he studied each of my paintings. He nodded, looked close, then stepped back to see each one at a distance. Rocking back and forth on his heels, with one hand holding the other behind him, he seemed as approving and proud as if he had painted them himself, but I wanted more. Say something, I pleaded with my eyes.

In front of Cleopatra he asked, "Where's the asp bite?"

"Is that all you can say? After ten years of not seeing my work? 'Where's the asp bite?' "

"I —"

"Maybe she died without it. The fear of public shame in itself was strong enough to kill her."

A sound but not a word came out of his mouth at the idea.

"Don't you understand that yet, Father? How deep the fear of exposure can bite?"

When he shifted his gaze from the painting to me, his nostril wings opened.

I paused, but when he didn't say anything, I added, "She deserved the right to grieve her loss privately."

He pulled his lips inward. "You —" He cleared his throat. "You've learned more from life than I could teach you."

I said his words to myself, to hear them a second time. "Thank you."

I took him upstairs to my studio. I had covered Lucrezia with a cloth so he wouldn't see it right away. He looked again at *Judith Slaying Holofernes* and *Susanna and the Elders* and smiled in recognition.

"As magnificent as I remembered them."

That was exactly what I wanted to hear. Then I uncovered Lucrezia. He studied it awhile, and thought more carefully this time before he said anything. "You make it seem like she's afraid to do it."

"Look again. It isn't fear. It's that she's troubled. She's got to think out why, and have a reason all her own that requires it. Maybe she's not sure she needs to."

A concerned expression came over his face. "This isn't the Lucrezia everyone thinks her to be."

"I know. But it's got to be this way, that she isn't sure, so people looking at it a long time from now, women and men too, might feel badly, might even weep that at some ignorant time there was once a woman raped who was pressured, even expected, to kill herself."

I hadn't known I would say that — to him or anybody. It came from the deep smoldering center of me in a voice I didn't recognize.

"Things will change, Father. They must. And art can help create the change."

His eyes shone. "My daughter. The sibyl of a new epoch." He put his arm around my waist and gazed at the painting. "What does

Signor Gentile think of it?"

"I haven't let him see it. I've kept it covered whenever he might come into the studio." I chuckled. "He's been in a fever of excitement. 'Not even a little peek?' " I imitated how he had asked, holding up his fat thumb and index finger close together, fanning out his other fingers, and tipping his head from side to side. " 'No, not even a corner,' I said to him. His bottom lip protruded in a pout. He's so funny to watch. I like teasing him."

"Such a thing — you teasing your patron!"

"He likes it. He pretended he was going to touch the cloth draping it, but he didn't. He made the decision of unveiling it at his anniversary party without even seeing it."

"That's a strong trust he has in you."

"I know."

After Renata brought us something to eat in the studio, she and Father carried the painting, covered, into the great hall.

"You're going to love what Signor Gentile did to the room," she said as we stepped into the great hall. It was filled with roses, lilies, crysanthemums, and a huge display of gladioli on the central table. "When he sent me to fetch them this morning, he told me to

332

make sure the gladioli were deep crimson. How did he know the color of her bedcover? Did he peek?"

I smiled. "Instinct, I guess."

When the guests arrived, Cesare appeared wearing the same stiff ruff he had worn in his portrait, which he had hung above the fireplace. As the room filled with guests, their oversweet perfumes did little to disguise the musky smell of their bodies. A servant carried a platter of *crostini* with anchovies in oil and lemon. It almost made me nauseous. I had to get air. Another servant passed with a tray of goblets of wine. I took one and went outside and walked around the perimeter of the courtyard several times to calm myself. I watched Palmira and another child playing with paper dolls I had made to keep them occupied.

Cesare's steward called people back in when it was time to reveal the painting. Father came outside to get me. "We shall see what these Genoese are made of," he whispered.

Cesare stood next to Bianca with his hands raised ordering silence. Satisfied with everyone's attention, he made one of his flamboyant gestures to the steward, who lifted off the covering with a flourish. At first there was no response. My soul froze. Water gurgled in the fountain outside. Someone coughed.

"A-ha," murmured Bianca. She must have noticed I had changed the position of the dagger since she'd seen it last.

A broad, slow smile crept over Cesare's face. I let out a breath I didn't know I was holding. People clapped politely. Then the whispering began.

"I thought she'd be nude."

"No blood."

"You can barely see the dagger."

"She's not dead."

"She isn't going to do it."

Bianca came to stand beside me. In the fullness of our petticoats pressed against each other, she squeezed my hand.

Cesare swung his fist in an arc and his fingers sprang open in the direction of the painting. "*Brava!* You have done it, Artemisia Gentileschi!" he said. "A victory of ambiguity. If time stopped right then, at that moment, we would never know what she did. She is yours alone."

He knew he had something no one else did. If he questioned this interpretation, that would have colored the reputation of what I'd painted for him earlier. If he approved, that would increase the value of the rest.

Renata stood alone at the side of the room clutching her hands to her chest, dewy-eyed.

The guests were bewildered. The painting had disoriented them. *Bene.* If this Lucrezia gives them a new concept, then they might reconsider the missing asp bite on Cleopatra.

"You have baffled them, Artemisia," Father whispered.

"I know."

After a string of congratulations, some of them enthusiastic, some cool, Father escorted me out to the garden. Feeling the lightness of success, I took his arm as we walked under a rose arbor.

"It might take time for people to comprehend what they congratulated me for," I said. "And what they think today may not be what they'll think tomorrow."

"They're disappointed. They wanted blood. They expected blood. They know Lucrezia's story. You gave them doubt instead. Lucrezia in doubt."

"Everyone, Father? Is that what *you* expected?"

We met each other's eyes, as we could not do in Rome. After a long moment, he sat down on a stone bench without answering.

I allowed him the pretense that it was his

expectation about Lucrezia that I meant.

I sat next to him in dappled shade to watch the children play. The fountain opposite us was fringed with deep blue iris and orange tiger lilies. With the plop of water drops and the scent of roses, it was a pleasant place. Father beckoned to Palmira and she came to him and sat demurely on his lap. He bounced her on his knee as if she were a little girl. Her dark curls sprang. "I'm too old, Grandpa. I'm nine now." Her words burst out at each bounce and made us laugh.

That bouncing — he must have done the same to me. A surprising tenderness for him bubbled up in me, and I thought — this must be happiness. I wanted to stop time, to make the moment last. I held on to Palmira's dainty ankle.

He turned to me. "What's wrong?"

"Nothing, Papa. I'm just so happy."

He didn't seem to know what to say. He bounced Palmira again.

"Palmira, will you grow up to be a fine painter like your mama?" he asked.

She shook her head ferociously and wiggled her feet, looking at her new red velvet shoes. "I'm going to be a lady and have lots of dresses and live in a palace."

"Like this?"

Her chin pointed up and then snapped down to her chest. "Bigger. And ride in a black carriage with a footman and two white horses." She measured the size of his hands against hers but soon became distracted and hopped off to play.

"When you were her age, you'd only want the horses so you could draw them."

It was comfortable with him next to me. I felt the trust of innocent times.

"I've been trying to teach her to draw her doll, but she won't sit still long enough."

"You would sit whole days trying to get the baker's boy just right, rubbing it out and starting over."

"When I was her age?"

"Beginning then. That's what amazed Agostino, you know. Not just your early accomplishment, but your determination."

I tensed at the name. It had been years since I heard it, even in my own head.

"When I failed at painting something, you'd say, 'There's always tomorrow. Start again in the morning.' Sometimes I still tell myself that." I touched the back of his hand. "But I always hear it in your voice."

A cloud passed and sunlight came again. Palmira splashed water in the fountain.

"We have become friends again," he said softly.

"Yes, Papa. We have."

He looked alarmed. "I meant . . . Agostino and me."

A razor edge sliced me to the bone.

"I have invited him for the summer. He'll be here next week. He's between commissions now and —"

"Here? To Genoa?" My voice rose shrilly.

He held up his open hands toward me as if to stop my reaction. "Yes." He spoke quickly. "He has a keen sense of perspective and we did fine things together in Cardinal Borghese's Casino of the Muses. You should see it someday. And in the Sala Regia of the Quirinale too."

"How could you? You *invited* him? He nearly ruined me!"

Father could not look me in the face. He waved his hand dismissively. "A brief unpleasantness, Artemisia, between old friends." Heat shot up to my head and made me reel. He cleared his throat. "I thought he and I might work together here for a while, and then go to France. He has letters of introduction in Paris."

"You still don't understand, do you?"

"I . . . I thought he and you might make amends."

"Father!" I stood up. "How could you even think that? My peace and happiness

338

here mean nothing to you. My *patron* is more of a father to me than you are."

He grabbed my arm. I wrenched it away.

"Artemisia, don't —"

"Bastard!"

I called to Palmira and dragged her upstairs, ignoring both of their objections.

I took out writing paper. I had to move on, and quickly too. If I had received just one letter from Pietro, I'd go back to Florence, but I hadn't. So I wrote:

Most High and Honored Lordship Don Giovanni de' Medici,

Please accept my deepest sorrow and condolence at the death of your illustrious father, Cosimo de' Medici. I am ever grateful to him for his solicitous regard for my work, and now, in accordance with his wishes, I herewith put myself at your service in Venice. I will paint anything, work for any offering. I will arrive within a fortnight in the hopes of finding you well and happy. I kiss your hand.

Your most humble and grateful servant, Artemisia Gentileschi

Ridiculous to write that to a ten-year-old. His counselors would make the decision anyway. He probably wouldn't even see this letter.

I took my paintings in the studio out of the frames and rolled them.

"Why are you doing that?" Palmira demanded.

"Because the frames aren't mine."

I tightened the lids on my amber varnish, turpentine, and linseed oil, and opened my painting trunk.

"Mother! What are you doing?"

"Help me. Put your clothes in your trunk."

"No!" she screamed. "Why?"

"We're leaving."

"Why?"

"Your grandfather." I wrapped Mother's oil lamp in paint rags and laid it in my painting trunk.

"No! I won't go." She stomped her way into the bedroom.

Her cries brought Renata, Cesare, and Bianca rushing into the studio.

"I'm dreadfully sorry. I'm afraid we have to leave."

Confusion spread over Cesare's face. "Have we displeased you?"

"No. Never." My throat swelled. "You've been the kindest man I have ever known."

"We love you," Bianca pleaded.

"I know. I love all of you too." I choked.

"Then why?" Bianca asked.

"My father is bringing the man who raped me to Genoa," I said too softly for Palmira to hear. Bianca gasped. "He thinks I'd want to, to . . ."

Renata screwed up her face as if piecing things together. Big, glistening tears spilled down her cheeks.

Cesare folded me against his round, soft belly. "We can keep him from you," he said in my ear. "There are ways."

I shook my head against his shoulder. "I wouldn't put that obligation on you."

All of us stood for a long moment looking at each other, stunned and aching. Renata was the first to move. Weeping softly, she dropped to her knees before my trunk and began to pack my painting things, handling each item with reverence.

"Keep out that stack of drawings of Lucrezia. And an empty drawing album and some pencils. For you, *cara*."

21

Palmira

Almost a year later, Palmira and I climbed the Pincian hill to Santa Trinità, both of us out of breath. "Only a little more. You can make it," I said.

"Why don't they make stairs here? If this were Venice, it would have stairs. And statues too."

"All the more reason that the sisters will be happy to meet you. They'll know you climbed this to see them."

"What will I say to them?"

"Anything you want. They know all about you. They even know about us floating them as paper dolls in our wooden bowls."

"Mother!"

"It's all right. They thought it was funny."

At the top, I looked up at the left bell tower. A large clock had been installed. I

342

wondered what other changes I'd discover.

"It will be Sister Paola who will answer the door. That's part of her duties."

When Paola saw us, she let out a squeal that reached to Heaven. *"Cara mia!"* She pulled me through the doorway and hugged me. *"Grazie a Dio,* you've come."

"This is Palmira, my daughter."

"The blessing of saints!"

Paola stretched her arms wide to hug Palmira and smothered her in her black habit. "Sister Graziela will be in ecstacy."

"Like Saint Theresa?" I said.

"Oh, she's been so despondent. The last year has been hard for her. Why didn't you write us that you were coming?" Paola took a dozen quick steps, then stopped to look at us. "Ooh!" she squealed again, shaking her hands, unable to contain herself. Palmira giggled. Paola hurried us along to the work-room where Graziela was painting. "Graziela, look!" Paola cried.

"Santa Maria! I don't believe it," Graziela murmured. She stood up, knocking over her stool, and came toward us with open arms. "I had a dream the other night about you." Her face showed surprise, happiness, relief, gratitude, all in one fluid movement of lines. "You must be Palmira. You look just like your mother did when she first came to us."

Palmira performed a pretty little curtsey. "Mother told me all about you. Your name was the first word I ever wrote."

"My! I feel honored."

Graziela's face looked a little thinner, a little more lined, but she was still a mature beauty worthy of any painter's canvas. Paola was as plump as ever.

"We thought you were in Venice," Graziela said.

"We were. For almost a year," I said.

"Why did you leave? You didn't like it?" Paola asked.

"*I* liked it," Palmira said, still a bit defiant about the move.

"What did you like about it?" Graziela touched Palmira's cheek.

"I liked the palace we lived in."

"Ooh, was it beautiful?" Paola asked.

Palmira's head bobbed enthusiastically. "And I liked the gondolas and the boat races."

"I think she began to love me again on our first gondola ride." I smoothed back her hair. "You didn't want to leave, did you?"

Her eyes, so much like Pietro's, flashed at me coldly. "I didn't want to leave any of the places we lived."

"*Allora,* that must mean that you liked them all," Paola said, clasping her hands together under her chin.

"And what about the Commedia dell' Arte?" I prodded.

"It was funny."

"And the lace-making?"

"I had lace before we went to Venice," she said, a hint of braggadocio in her voice. "In Genoa, Signora Gentile bought me lace." She lifted up her skirt to show the narrow lace edging on her petticoat.

"Che meraviglia!" Paola said.

"And she gave me her old clothes to play in," Palmira continued.

Anything frivolous or extravagant or exotic suited Palmira's taste. Had we come to Rome directly from Genoa, or had we gone to any other city, she would have nursed her anger longer, but the dense beauties of Venice had softened and enchanted her.

"What about you? Why did you leave?" Graziela asked me.

"Venice will always be a gorgeous city, but to me it was a cold, damp, unfriendly disappointment."

"Why?" Graziela asked in astonishment.

"The art, the whole city, is self-consciously extravagant. Tintoretto's enormous oil painting of Paradise shows Christ and Mary surrounded by *five hundred* saints. A sea of saints. It's just too much. There was no place for me there. The Venetian School is played out anyway except in its crafts."

"That's too bad."

"I don't blame the city. Any city would have difficulty winning my affection after Genoa and Florence."

"Who did you paint for?"

"Giovanni de' Medici, Cosimo's son. Imagine, a duke at ten years old. His counselors made the decisions, and they weren't particularly receptive to me. And then Giovanni died too. The fall of the Medici."

"Are you here to stay?" Graziela asked.

"I hope so. I heard in Venice that Scipione Borghese and several other cardinals are buying more art to decorate their villas here."

"Pope Urban has many new projects too," Graziela said.

"Where will you live?" Paola asked.

"In the artists' neighborhood where I used to live. I need to find a place tomorrow. We stayed at an inn last night, but I don't want to pay for it any longer than I have to. Our things are still at the coach house." I felt them wanting a longer visit, but I had to pull away. "We'll come back after we get settled. I just wanted Palmira to meet you right away."

They both walked us to the door, hugged

us each again, and we set out to see Porzia Stiattesi.

Nothing had changed on Via del Babuino. Still the same apothecary shop where we had bought pigments, and the same *vinaio* on the corner of Via della Croce, my street. I straightened my back. I wanted to walk down my street dry-eyed and dignified, as pure and confident as a child, loving every remembered paving stone I'd hopped upon. I took Palmira's hand. "This is where we lived," I told her. Children playing in the narrow street were singing in French. It was a tune I knew, so I sang it with them in Italian. They looked up at me in wonder, and then giggled.

"I was born right here in this house," I said softly to Palmira in front of our arched doorway. The stucco had broken off in places making the wall patchy.

"It's not very nice." She touched a loose flake of stucco and it fell off.

I yanked her away. "One has to be born somewhere." The left shutter was missing and the right was hanging sadly by one hinge. "Things happened in that house. Things that changed my life."

"Kind of small too."

"Were you expecting a palace like Cesare's or Giovanni de' Medici's? We're on

347

our own now so you'd better get used to it."

I pushed her ahead of me and pulled the bell thong next door.

"We had a bell just like this," I said, sorry already that I'd been sharp with her. "My mother kept it polished because she thought a shiny bell tinkled more happily. This is your aunt and uncle's house. Your papa's brother."

Porzia came to the door and threw up her hands. *"Mamma mia!* Artemisia! I — *Dio mio."*

I laughed. "Don't be that surprised. I'm not a ghost."

"No. No. You look the same!"

"So do you," I said, but we both knew it wasn't true. I was heavier and she was worn and one shoulder was higher than the other. I'd never noticed it before.

"This is Palmira. My daughter."

"By Pierantonio?" she questioned in a low voice.

"Of course." What did she think — that I'd bring a love child to her doorstep?

"Che bellina. You have your father's curls and dark eyes and your mother's skin."

Porzia opened the street door wider and we crossed the small courtyard into her house. She limped so badly now that it pained me to watch her walk. She spooned out three bowls of polenta from an iron pot hanging over the fire, poured two small tumblers of wine, and held up a smaller glass. "A taste for her? With water?"

"A little."

"Are you going to stay in Rome?"

"As long as there's work. We have to accept the fact that painting is an itinerant occupation, don't we Palmira?"

"What's that mean?"

"Traveling about. Just think. Not very many grown-ups get to live in three cities."

"Does Rome have boats?" Palmira asked Porzia.

"No, but it has other things you'll like. Things from a long time ago."

Palmira screwed up one side of her face and swung her legs. I'd be glad when she would be too tall to do that incessant leg swinging. It wouldn't be long.

"It's a good time for any artist to be here," Porzia said. "No one can believe the money the pope is pouring out."

"The question is, will any of it pour in my direction. Maybe not if my reputation is still stained. Have people forgotten here?"

"The trial? Yes. Life goes on, and new misfortunes claim people's attentions. You coming back might remind them, though."

"Agostino isn't in Rome, is he?"

"The last we heard, he'd gone to Genoa, and eventually Paris."

"With my father, probably. You don't have to hide it from me. I know."

She scraped with her fingernail at some hardened candle wax on the table. "It made me sick to see them together, arm in arm weaving down the street. My heart ached for you each time —"

I held up my hand. I didn't want to hear it.

"Do you know where we can rent two rooms, cheaply? Near here."

"There are always people moving in and out between here and the Piazza del Popolo."

"We'll have to walk the streets tomorrow." I leaned back in the chair, trying to feel comfortable here again.

"The plague has threatened Florence, you know," Porzia said, her eyes searching for my reaction.

"No, I didn't know. We came south on the coast. I thought it was only in Milan."

"Processions of flagellants have been going from church to church. They even cancelled the *calcio* for fear of contagion."

"Is Pietro . . . ? Have you heard from him?"

"That's how we learned this, but that was a month ago."

I drank the wine, wondering.

"We were sorry to learn that you left him."

"Not by choice. I loved him as much as he let me."

"Then why did you leave?"

I tried to discern if there was accusation in her question, but I couldn't tell. "To find work. What did he tell you?"

"The same." She tore off a hunk of bread and brushed the crumbs off her lap primly. "We just thought it might be something else."

Either she knew about Vanna and was sympathetic, or she believed some justifying story from Pietro. I could find out if he was still with her, but I didn't want to in front of Palmira, so I hesitated. Porzia hesitated too, probably for the same reason. It would have to wait for another time, we told each other with our eyes.

The next morning Palmira and I set out to walk every street between Piazza del Popolo and Via della Croce, the artists' section. We asked the apothecary for suggestions, pulled bell ropes, and followed where people pointed. One landlady on Via dei Greci scrutinized me and said, "I don't rent to lone women with children."

"Just one child?"

"One is one too many."

After that, Palmira trailed behind me sullenly kicking a stone on the ground.

"Don't do that. You'll scuff your shoes." It was a constant effort to keep her in presentable shoes.

She sent one more stone flying and then walked silently by my side.

"The world will pinch you if you let it, so don't let it."

Lone women. I thought of Pietro. If he was still making his living as a painter, it was no easier for him than for me. But for us together, I wondered.

On Via Laurina, I asked a woman, "Do you have two rooms to rent? I am a painter, and this is my daughter." I stood straight and dignified and held Palmira's hand.

"*Sì,* two rooms. Third floor. Other painters live there too. You go and look. First door to the left at the top of the stairs."

Each flight up, the smell of turpentine grew stronger and the heat more oppressive. There were no curtains in the room. Shabby bed linen covered a sunken mattress.

"This is awful, Mama."

"*Stai zitta!*" I yanked her arm.

The afternoon was wearing on and my feet hurt. We went back down.

"I'll take it. May I move in now?"

"*Sì.* Your name?"

"Artemisia Gentileschi," I said. "And my daughter Palmira."

Immediately one side of her upper lip twitched, fighting whether or not to form a sneer. "Wait here," she commanded, and turned back into another room. When she came back, she said, "No. It's not available. My husband rented it to someone else this morning." She held open the door for us to leave.

I had realized that returning to Rome might be revisiting old griefs, but I had hoped I wouldn't have to face scorn.

A building on Via Margutta near where I used to live had a room I could afford. A whiskered, wizened man whom I thought I recognized took us up two flights of stairs to a spacious room with large windows on two sides.

"This is very nice," I said. "We'd like to move in this afternoon. May we?"

He nodded. "What's your name?"

"Artemisia Lomi, and Palmira."

Palmira shot me a look of confusion. "Gentileschi," she corrected.

The man's wrinkles showed the workings of his mind pulling out from the past a memory of the name. He looked down at my hands, and then with suspicion and disgust at Palmira. My stomach cramped.

"No. Not for the likes of whores." He closed the door in our faces.

"*Madre di Dio. Che villano.* We didn't want to live there anyway, did we?" I muttered to Palmira and hurried her down the stairs.

"Why was he so mean, Mama? What's a whore?"

"I'll tell you tonight. After we find a place."

As we waited for our belongings to be delivered to the rooms we finally found, I heated water over the corner wood stove and poured it in a basin and we soaked our feet and ate cheese and bread.

"Those people talked funny, Mama."

"That's because they're trying to learn our language. They're Dutch. I think the man decided to rent to us when he saw that I loved his paintings."

When our trunks were delivered from the station, we were too tired to unpack, but I did write a letter to the academy in Florence.

If it please your honored gentlemen, is there any news of my husband, Pietro Antonio di Vincenzo Stiattesi? Is he alive? Is he painting? In memory of my former member-

354

ship in your illustrious academy, would you grant me any information about his condition?

I doubted that they would answer. I looked over at Palmira in her shift half asleep on the bed. "You were a good girl today. I know it wasn't fun for you."

I took off my bodice and skirt and lay down next to her. She turned onto her back and opened her eyes. Together we watched the light in the window dim, and felt very close. There were the two of us, and there was the world. My eyes grew heavy. "I think we'll be happy here," I murmured.

"You said you'd tell me," Palmira said after a time.

"Tell you what?"

"Why that man called us whores."

"He said that because it was the worst thing he could think of, but since it isn't true, it doesn't have to bother you."

There in the darkening room, both of us looking up at the cracks in the ceiling, it would be easier to tell. Palmira would be having her first blood soon. It was time.

"Do you remember in the Loggia della Signoria in Florence where I drew that statue of a man carrying that woman away? Remember I was drawing it on that rainy day when we ran home?"

"No," she said emphatically, as if the expectation were unreasonable.

"When a man forces a woman to do what husbands and wives do when they love each other, and the woman doesn't want to, that is rape. That sculpture showed it about to happen."

"So?"

"So that did happen to me, here. I didn't want anyone to know, but my father found out and accused that man in court. Then people thought I wanted it, but I didn't. When a woman wants it with anyone, not just a husband, they call her a whore."

Palmira was quiet. Maybe she was trying to understand what men and women did together. That would have to come another night. So would the trial and the *sibille*. When she was older. When it would be no more to me than a story — like Lucrezia's or Cleopatra's, or someone else's from a far-off time. I was almost there now, I thought, barely able to stay awake.

Later, out of the darkness of exhaustion, came the timid question, "Was it Papa who raped you?"

"Your papa? No, *cara*. He never hurt me that way. It was my father's friend. Agostino was his name. They painted together. That's why we left Genoa so quickly. Your grandfather invited him there."

"Did being raped hurt?"

"Yes. For a time. Not forever."

"What husbands and wives do, does that hurt?"

It was a crucial question. I did not want her to live a life of fear.

"No. Think of Cesare and Bianca, how loving they were to each other. If the man is gentle, and if the woman wants it, it doesn't hurt. That happens when they are in love."

"Will I ever want it?"

"Yes."

"Does every lady?"

"Most every lady."

"Does Sister Graziela?"

"She did once." I rolled onto my side toward her and kissed her ear. "I'll tell you about her some other time."

22

Graziela

Most Reverend Eminence Cardinal Scipione Borghese,

In the hopes that my father, Orazio Gentileschi, pleased Your Eminence in painting the ceiling fresco in Your Eminence's Casino of the Muses, I, Artemisia Gentileschi, likewise a painter, having been under his tutelage and having been graced by the patronage of His Lordship Cosimo de' Medici, offer Your Eminence my services.

If it please Your Eminence to grant me permission to see my father's work, I would be most grateful, as I have never had the opportunity to do so. Respecting your privacy and your holiness, I patiently await your reply.

Embracing the purple of Your Most Reverend Eminence, I am Your Eminence's

humble and obedient servant,
                    Artemisia Gentileschi

I sealed it with candle wax, pressed in my bracelet cartouche of the figure of Artemis to leave an impression, and started on another letter while Palmira continued the unpacking. By the end of the day, I had finished letters to five cardinals and three noblemen recommended by the apothecary and my Dutch landlord.

A short time later, I received two responses. A secretary from the household of Cardinal Borghese wrote back, giving me permission "for a brief time to look at the work of Orazio Gentileschi, but do not assume," he said, "that this is to be an audience with His Eminence. His Eminence is not available." And a nobleman wanted "as soon as can be accomplished one of your monumental Judiths like those at the Palazzo Pitti."

I was grateful. I needed the security and joy of being in the next painting. Right away I tried out compositions on little scraps of paper while Palmira watched the soup for me hanging in a pot over the fire. Living here, she'll do some growing up, I thought.

"Who's this going to be?" she asked.

"Another Judith."

"Don't you ever get tired of making Judiths?"

"Not if they're all different. I haven't painted one in, let me see, five years. I'm different now, so the painting will be too."

"Does it have to be a bloody one?"

Her voice sounded so earnest, and she was taking an interest, for once. Maybe it was the fault of the gruesome subjects I'd been doing — the head, the hacking, the snake, the dagger — that made her not attracted to painting.

"No. Just for you, *cara,* it won't be."

Maybe it wasn't just for her. Going back to displaying that violent act seemed retrograde. It held no interest for me now.

I let my mind imagine as I sketched. This Judith ought to be a heavier, middle-aged woman, made wiser by experience — not a mere temptress and killer, but a more reasoning individual. Here in Rome where Caravaggist technique was appreciated, I could indulge my love for dramatic chiaroscuro of light and shadow, even on her face. Judith could be holding out her hand to block light coming through the tent opening so she could concentrate on hearing noises. The body of Holofernes wouldn't even be in the composition, only his head in deep shadow, hardly noticeable in Abra's sack. No blood. No gore. But just outside the tent, out of sight, Judith could hear rumblings. There would always be danger. She must be intensely vigilant.

"There," I said after I worked awhile. I handed Palmira a rough sketch of a possible composition. "No blood."

She looked at it and then at me. "None streaming out of the sack?"

"None."

"Good."

"Yes, good." I patted her hand. "I'll tell you what. Because you've been so helpful in unpacking, tomorrow we'll go to a beautiful building owned by a cardinal. Scipione Borghese. A very powerful man. Your grandpa's work is there. We'll go take a look."

I wasn't sure where Cardinal Borghese's Palazzo Pallavicini was, somewhere near the Quirinale, so we had to ask three people before a coachman told us it was set back a long way from the street by a carriage courtyard and stables. With my letter from Cardinal Borghese's clerk, the porter admitted us into a lush garden of hedges, arbors of fragrant flowering vines, sprawling oleander, pines, and plane trees.

At the door of the palace an orderly lowered his staff in front of us. "What is your business?" he asked.

What did he think — that a woman and a girl were going to storm the cardinal's residence?

"I am Artemisia Gentileschi. My father, Orazio Gentileschi, painted the ceiling fresco in His Eminence's Casino of the Muses. Is this the right building?"

"Yes."

"I wish to see it, I and my daughter."

I showed him the letter from Cardinal Borghese's secretary. He glanced at it and let us in. "Ask the clerk." He pointed to an old man sitting at a carved and inlaid writing table.

The clerk was reading a document, squinting, head down. He did not look up, even when we stopped right in front of him. His face was so long and narrow it looked as though it had been pressed between boards when he was an infant. It made him look like a weasel. I placed the letter, open, on his writing table. He read it with no expression. He didn't move his head, but his eyes looked to the right and then left.

"Gentileschi, eh? I know about you. I was here when your father and Tassi were. You've come back to Rome to ask for more rape, have you?"

Palmira blew out her breath.

"I've come back to Rome because it is my home. And I've come back to paint. I am a painter too. As such, I wish to study the work on the ceiling."

"You didn't learn enough from Signor Tassi himself and now you want to learn from his paintings?"

"From my father's." I steeled myself against what he might say next.

"A painter, eh? You paint pretty pictures of whores, then, I suppose?"

"I paint heroines."

"You paint out of your own whoredom." Spoken under his breath, but like spit in the face.

"That's not true!" Palmira blurted. "She does not!" I squeezed her hand so she wouldn't say any more. She looked up at me to retaliate. The man smirked, enjoying the flash of her outrage.

"I paint out of honor and pride and rapture and grief and doubt and love and yearning." I spoke evenly, but quickly so he wouldn't interrupt me. "I hope I may live so long as to paint out of every emotion felt by humankind."

He snorted and went back to his reading.

"It is customary to let painters study the works of other painters, even if they are held privately by the Holy Mother Church," I said. "If this is an inconvenient time, I will come again. Just tell me —"

"Go on up. Go on." He waved his hand toward the stairway, bored with baiting us. He'd already done what he wanted.

We walked upstairs, and I put my hand on Palmira's shoulder. "I'm sorry you had to hear such rudeness."

"Rome is awful. I hate it."

"It's not all awful. Just think what we're about to see."

A fat woman whose upper arms hung over her elbows was mopping the floor in shiny wet arcs. I asked for the Casino of the Muses. She waddled across the anteroom and opened one of a pair of doors.

I took Palmira's hand as we entered. An enormous, vaulted ceiling rose over a grand entertainment hall. Above the actual cornice molding where the ribs of the vaulting curved into the arched ceiling, an elaborate illusionary stone cornice was painted with many consoles supporting a painted overhanging balcony. Behind the balustrade of the balcony, there were painted columns and a loggia of arches.

"It's so real." Palmira stretched out the last word.

Under the arches and in some places along the balustrade, handsome men and buxom women were playing lutes, violins, bass viols, tambourines, drums. Others were singing or listening, an arm resting on the balustrade here, a shawl flowing over it there. Above the delicate shades of pink, green, and yellow of their clothing, a blue sky was patched with clouds, making it seem as though the phantom balcony were ascending to Heaven. All the complex parts — the pillars, capitals, arches, the rosettes in coffers, the consoles supporting the balcony, the chins, elbows, noses, torsos, the bass viols and other instruments positioned as if seen from below — all were correctly proportioned to make a unified whole. The effect was dazzling.

"How can it look so real?" Palmira asked.

"This is what they call illusionist architecture painting," I explained. "You can't quite trust what you're seeing, what parts are the real building and what is the painted illusion. It seems real because the shapes and the figures are foreshortened. They're painted with shorter proportions than they really have and from a viewpoint below. It's very, very difficult."

"Have you ever done it?"

"No."

She dropped my hand to turn in a circle and count. "Nineteen people!"

"Creating such a complex work, with all parts working harmoniously together, must have taken constant, absorbing thought."

Father's mind had to be in the work, in its problems, searching for solutions as he was walking home, eating, getting dressed, grinding pigments, sitting in court. The postures of the figures had to be with him as his thoughts took shape upon waking every morning. My dilemma must have been only on the periphery of his mind, even on the morning of the *sibille*.

"This was painted by Grandpa and that man?" Palmira asked.

"Yes. They worked well together, didn't they? Grandpa painted the people and musical instruments and sky, and Agostino painted the structures."

Where Orazio was weakest, in architectural perspective, Agostino determined the correct angles, the vanishing points, the shadings. Agostino structured the space as a showcase for Orazio's figures, each one an individual, ardent in his performance, or enraptured by the music. Orazio knew his weakness. Agostino knew his. Separate, their art and reputations would be forever limited. Together, they were magnificent.

"It must have been profoundly exciting

for him to have seen it take shape," I murmured.

I understood now, with perfect clarity, why Father wanted the trial over. It had nothing to do with me.

I understood, but understanding was not forgiveness.

"Look, Mama!" Palmira pointed over my right shoulder. "It's you!"

I whirled around. "No."

"It is. It is. You always stand that way, with your hand on your hip."

"I do?"

"Yes. When you're angry with me."

"Maybe it's your grandmother." Just as I said it, I noticed in the painting that untamable lock of hair spiraling wildly at my right temple. It had given me grief ever since I had learned to comb my own hair. My mother's hair was smooth and straight, pulled back into a knot like Spanish women.

"No, it isn't. It's you. Look at that fan in your hand. You're always complaining about the heat."

There I am, looking down on me, the same age as I am right now, but painted thirteen years ago. How had he known how to age me? An eerie sight to see myself as a matron annoyed by something, distracted, looking down over the balcony instead of watching the musicians, unable to relax into an easy enjoyment of the music. Unable to relax. Yes. How had he known?

I was dizzy and my neck hurt, yet I couldn't stop looking up. I had posed for Father many times, but I never knew he was going to use one of the drawings here. Then I *was* on his mind in those afternoons after court adjourned. And furthermore, he had imagined what the trial and the years ahead would do to me. I reached for Palmira and held her against me.

"You're right. It *is* me," I murmured.

After Palmira went to sleep that night, I sat sipping wine and wondering if Father thought of me often. If he ever talked about me. To Agostino, or to anyone. If he were ever lonesome. If he were lonesome right now. If he ever thought of Mother. I hoped he was happy, or at least was painting well . . . even with Agostino. I leaned out the window to feel the night's deep blue, the same dark air that surrounded him in Genoa or Paris or wherever he was. I would give a great deal to know what he was thinking right at this moment. If a person could know for certain what the other person was thinking or doing, then loneliness might cease to exist in the world.

I thought of Pietro and tried to imagine what he was doing right now. Was he with Vanna? Had he given himself completely to her now that I was gone? Could he? Did he ever think of me?

Had I done something similar to what Father had done, sacrificed a person for my art? I was filled with a longing to apologize to Pietro. To apologize to Palmira. Had I hurt people out of selfish impulsiveness? I yearned to apologize to Cesare and Bianca and Renata, and put our lives back the way they were, but that was impossible. Love is so easily bruised by the necessity of making choices.

I'd heard once that an English queen had denied herself suitors in order to wed England, and I understood at what cost.

A moon of startling brightness rose over the rooftops, lifted on a divine, invisible thread, like a paper circle held before a cat. What I had seen at the Borghese casino made it impossible to sleep. I took out writing paper but I didn't know where Father lived now. Instead I wrote:

My Most Illustrious Friend, Galileo,
The sky tonight has a clarity that I have not
known for many years. The moon is a perla

barocca, a trifle God flung in our direction to tease mortals with unanswerable questions. I can see its hills and valleys, as you described. I never see it without thinking of you, never see stars without wondering which one is your Venus.

I am afraid for the world tonight. Whirling, as you say, on the edge of the universe instead of resting stable in its center under God's watchful eye, we are not central to God's concern. Things happen. We take missteps without knowing we have done so, and cannot go back. How difficult it is to rely on our own best selves for the issues of our small lives in order to leave the Father of us all to concern Himself with greater matters.

Take care, *amico mio*. Although you say that Pope Urban has great affection for you, Rome is as ruthless as I discovered it to be in my youth. Do not think, in your country villa with your citron trees, that Rome's fingers cannot extend to Tuscan hills to pluck its most illustrious fruit. One pope is not all there is to the Roman hand.

Yet, even while I say this, I know that you will speak truth as you see it, though it might bring you to danger's edge. With your permission, therefore, if only to ease my concern for your well-being, I will ask my trusted *friend, Sister Graziela at Santa Trinità dei Monti, to pray for you.*

Ever yours,
Artemisia

I heated water and washed my hair and Palmira's in the stone sink.

"Ouch, you're digging too hard," she cried.

"Doesn't it feel good to have your scalp scratched? Makes you feel more alive."

"But you're hurting me. Let me do it."

Reluctantly, I stepped back to relinquish this pleasure of motherhood, but I couldn't take my eyes away from the sweet, slender taper of the back of her soapy neck.

"Let's go see the sisters today," I said. "I want to give Graziela some pigments. Take your embroidery to show to Sister Paola. If she isn't busy, she can teach you a new stitch."

"She knows how?"

"Of course. She's made beautiful vestments for the monsignori. With gold thread, too."

I braided her hair wet so it would keep the waves, and I wound the braids on top of her head. "There. Now you look like a little lady."

We found Graziela sitting on the L-shaped

bench in a corner of the cloisters, doing nothing. I'd never found her doing nothing before. "Is she praying?" I asked Paola.

"No. Just brooding."

Her face came alive when she saw us.

"Are you all right?" I asked.

"I am as God wishes. Did you find a place to live?"

"After some trouble. People still remember. It's been thirteen years and they still remember."

Graziela looked with concern at Palmira and then back at me.

"I told her. She knows." I sat down next to Graziela. "People didn't want to rent to us. Yesterday we went to Cardinal Borghese's casino to see my father's work, and the cardinal's clerk was rude to me, right in front of Palmira. He asked if I came back to Rome for more rape. People are still beasts here."

"Those with more sublime faith than ours would see even in this, the working of His loving hand."

I looked at her in disbelief. Where had her compassion gone? "He said I painted out of my own whoredom! Where is God's love in that?"

Immediately Paola tried to get Palmira to go out to the herb garden with her, but Palmira plopped herself decisively on the

372

other angle of the bench and Paola sat beside her.

"God's love is in how one reacts to that," Graziela said. "When Constantine was told that the Roman rabble had stoned the head of his statue, he raised his hands to his head and said, 'How remarkable. I don't feel the least bit hurt.' A woman your age whining over what some mean-spirited clerk says is not an attractive picture, however you paint it."

I was hot with embarrassment for her saying this in front of Palmira.

"Look what you've done in those years," she went on. "You've lived in three magnificent cities and seen the greatest buildings and sculpture and painting in Italy. You've had the experience of love with a man. You bore a beautiful, healthy child. You have earned your own way and had your talent recognized by one of the most prestigious courts in the land. Other women would thank the Lord on their knees for even one of those things."

Palmira looked from Graziela to me. I felt small and selfish. "I know. I know."

"I had hoped you would have let that go, Artemisia."

"I thought I had, until my father betrayed me again, in Genoa."

"So? There's got to be a time when daughters tear themselves loose from their father's shortsighted mistakes. Believe me. I know."

I felt the reminder of her own father's betrayal as sharp and hard as a tack in my throat.

"I wouldn't wish resentment on my worst enemy. It's a killing thing. Don't tell me you haven't progressed beyond that in thirteen years."

"I have."

"Then sit up straight and tell me what you've learned."

"From what?"

"Start with yesterday. Borghese's casino."

"Stupendous. It's a ceiling fresco of musicians and listeners on an illusionary balcony." I saw it again in my mind and it made me proud.

"Yes. And . . ."

"Father and Agostino painted together magnificently. Father could never do that complicated architectural perspective without Agostino, and he knew it. He would have ruined the project and his career would have been over. He had to end the trial." With an even voice as free of hurt as I could make it, I added, "He sacrificed my reputation and art for his."

Graziela searched my face.

"I'm not saying whether it was a despicable or a noble choice, only that it was a choice that showed a willingness to pay the inevitable price."

"Given a similar choice, wouldn't you have done the same?"

I watched Palmira swinging her legs.

"Yes."

"What does that tell you?"

"At some times in our lives, our passion makes us perpetrators of hurt and loss. At other times we are the ones who are hurt — all in the name of art. Sometimes we get what we want. Sometimes we pay for another to get what he or she wants." I looked at Palmira apologetically. "That's the way the world works."

"And forgiveness?"

I uncrossed my ankles, planted my feet as if at the edge of a precipice. "I learned that forgiveness is not easy."

"But it's possible."

"Yes, it's possible."

After a moment, I said to Palmira, "Show Sister Paola what you're working on." She lifted her embroidery out of our drawstring bag.

"Ooh, that's lovely!" Paola said, and engaged her by naming stitches after saints.

I reached into the bag and brought out the small cakes of pigments wrapped in paper. Graziela's eyes welled up as she opened them. "They're beautiful colors, and they'd make brilliant pages. It's just that . . . without seeing anything new, I keep painting the same things."

I understood that. Art builds on art. I'd be stifled and repetitive too if I couldn't see new forms and new combinations of colors and new compositions.

"Tell me about Venice," Graziela said. "Paint a picture for me right now."

Some quiet desperation in the forward lean of her body made me comply.

"In Venice every shape of pinnacle, dome, spire, cupola, and parapet rises above the rooftops — flat roofs with balustrades for viewing the city. Statues on one palace roof look across the canals to statues on another roof. Above the keystones of palace arches, the carved masks are tilted downward in order to be more visible from gondolas. Everything's for show."

Graziela's unfocused eyes were staring at the paving stones in front of her but I felt sure she was seeing canals and cupolas. She curled her fingers toward her chest, urging more.

"Crooked alleys suddenly open onto

hidden piazzas. Narrow canals turn unexpectantly. We were always lost."

I looked to my side. Palmira was intent on learning a new stitch from Paola.

"Genoa was all right to be alone in," I continued more softly, "but Venice — every loggia, every bridge, every stone in Venice was designed as a setting for moonlit trysts, clandestine meetings, hot clasped hands."

Graziela's long fingers stretched beyond her black sleeve and rested on my knee. Palmira's legs came to rest.

"And Florence?"

What was behind this urgency?

"Every small or insignificant church in the city has masterworks hardly seen that any other city would boast of as their *opera più importante*." I gave her more detailed descriptions than I had in my letters in case she was searching for an idea for an illuminated page, but the more I told her, the more desperate she was for more.

Graziela scowled when I paused. "Tell me again about Masaccio."

I looked at Paola for some guidance. She only winced and lifted her shoulders.

"What a genius. Masaccio wrenched my heart when I saw his Adam hiding his tortured face, and Eve wailing a cry that reached right into my soul. I couldn't sleep the night after I saw it."

"Was that your favorite thing?"

"No. Giotto's bell tower was. Next to Santa Maria del Fiore, self-standing, taller than you can imagine, like God's own reliquary reaching toward Heaven. It has rows of narrow arches separated by twisted pillars to give it lightness, and it's faced with marble. In rain it has the sheen of white, rose, and pale green satin. Beauty enough to break your heart."

"And Rome?"

"Rome you know."

"Not anymore." Her voice cracked. Shiny rivulets trailed down her cheeks.

Paola, Palmira and I looked at each other, perplexed, not knowing what to say.

Graziela shook her head apologetically. "The hardest thing for me is the confinement. Not to see the beauties of the world. Oh, I remember cypress trees and sunset on the Tiber — vaguely, as a blind person would remember them. But the beauties made by man are harder for me to conjure. They're made by God too, you know."

She tried to dry her tears on her wide, coarse sleeve, but they kept coming.

"Beautiful art is all around me, and I'm destined never to see it. To die without . . ." A burst of sobbing shook her.

Paola stood up in front of her, so that no one might see.

"Would it be such a crime for a nun to . . . It wouldn't take away one dust mote of my love for God for me to see a carved fountain, or a loggia of marble figures, or a painted ceiling."

Delicately Palmira put her hand on Graziela's knee, just as Graziela had done to me. Her hesitant, soulful little gesture stopped up my throat.

"What I would do to see the view from that tower, or Eve wailing in the garden." Graziela's voice rose and trembled. "To feel the cool smoothness of a marble thigh, or the glide of a gondola. Just once before I die."

The pity of her longing and deprivation made me feel I had been insufficiently grateful for all that I had seen.

The Mother Abbess and another nun came toward us under the arches. I uttered a warning. Paola turned, opened her arms to spread her sleeves, and walked toward them to divert their direction.

"What would happen if you just did it?" I whispered. "If we, the three of us, just took a walk? You'd come back, of course. Paola would unlock the door. What would happen?"

"I don't know. Confinement and enforced silence for a while."

"So? What's more confined than you are already?"

A bitter chuckle. She sniffled and wiped her face with the back of her hand. "I'll think about it."

I took her hand in mine. "In the meantime, I have a task for you. I have a friend in Florence, a scientist, Galileo Galilei."

"Oh yes. We've heard of him. Women in convents are not unaware of the controversies of the outside world. Cardinal Bellarmino —"

"Galilei needs your prayers, Graziela. For his protection. He is a learned and honorable man, and he does believe in God, regardless of what they say."

She sniffled again. "I understand. I will."

I kissed her on her forehead as I stood to leave, and when Palmira came to stand in front of her knees to say goodbye, Graziela kissed *her* on the forehead. Palmira tugged my arm for me to bend down, and, grinning, she aimed a noisy kiss on *my* forehead.

Outside the convent, Palmira and I stood on the high platform before going down the stairs.

"Do you think she will? Take a walk with

us someday?" Palmira asked.

"I don't know. I hope so."

We looked down the Via de Condotti and at the city's rooftops. "Look, Palmira. That dome in the distance, the big one, is Saint Peter's in the Vatican. This view is all Graziela ever sees."

Apparently it was not enough. It wouldn't be for me either.

"It's so high up here," Palmira said. "I love it."

I was seized with regret for not having taken her up Giotto's bell tower. I undid her braids. "Shake out your hair and feel the breeze. It comes all the way from Spain."

I took the pins out of my own hair and let the wind loosen it.

"Look and look and don't ever forget. Now, close your eyes. Here, give me your hand. And just feel. Can you feel the Earth move?"

"No."

"Hold onto the balustrade and lean forward. Imagine us speeding through the sky like sparrows at sundown, like the bats over the river in Florence. Wooosh!"

"Yes! Yes, I can!"

I knew right then that no matter what happened in her life, she would be all right.

As for Graziela, I began to worry.

23

Naples

"The stonecutters first, signora. The bishop's orders."

"But why must a painter wait until every lowly stonecutter has his due?"

"They have families to support."

"And I don't?"

The priest's polished ivory fingernails fluttered just beyond his wide sleeve, as if to discount my claim.

"Have you forgotten, Monsignor, what the Apostle Paul declared? In Christ there is neither bond nor free, Jew nor Greek, *male nor female*."

"I'm sorry, signora. Come again after All Saints Day."

I wasn't going to beg. I turned to Palmira, whose dark eyes burned, and gestured for her to go through the door. Outside, the Naples sun glared down on us.

"Mother, how could you just let him —"

"Ssh. Wait."

I marched across the piazza leaving the church behind me, and snapped my hand over my shoulder at it as though shooing a fly. "Priests!" I said with a puff of air on the *p*. "Four years building a strong reputation among the patricians of this city, and this lowly priest thinks he can treat me like a common laborer."

Palmira hurried to catch up. "What will you do?"

"I'll have Francesco write to the bishop. Or I'll write to him myself." I addressed the air in front of me. "What do they want? Sackcloth and ashes? Repentance that I was born a woman? I'm glad I'm a woman, and I want you to be glad you are too." I raised my voice with bravado. "Living as a painter would be too easy if I were a man."

"Now how will we pay for my ball gown?"

"Little by little. Delia can keep the dress until I pay it all."

"But Andrea's *ballo!*"

"Andrea. Andrea. All I've been hearing lately is Andrea, as if he arrived fully formed and gorgeous, a mortal Adonis standing naked on a seashell."

One look at her young face drawn into

desperate worry, and I softened. How pure and lovely it must be to be swept away by uncomplicated desire, dreaming of a fancy ball.

"All right. We'll get the dress today and eat bread and broth until the bishop makes that churl of a priest pay." I smiled at her wryly to let her know we wouldn't starve. Her face relaxed.

We turned up a narrow lane that kept changing direction, threading up the crevices of rocky hills of the squalid neighborhood where Delia, our seamstress who charged less, lived. Tall mean houses were piled askew on top of one another, and yellowed bed linen flapped from balconies. We held our sleeves to our noses against rank odors issuing from puddles and doorways.

Neither of us liked Naples as well as Rome where we had enjoyed four good years before the commissions ran out. Yet Naples was where Don Francesco Maringhi lived, my clerk and agent. He had secured commissions for me from the Duke of Modena, Don Antonio Ruffo in Messina, and the Spanish Count of Monterrey who was ruling Naples. Francesco was even negotiating the sale of my first Judith. He was a valuable aide and had become a good friend, and so we stayed.

An old crone whose flaccid yellow wrinkles were grooved with grime slumped on a stool under an arched passageway milking a goat. She would be a good model for some allegorical figure of age, but no one wanted realism now. Buyers saw no courage in age or unpleasantness. They didn't understand that ugliness caught in real emotion would speak through the centuries. They wanted only ideal beauty. In another time I might have been able to paint her, but I had no more courage for *invenzione*. I had learned to bow to what paid for ball gowns and bread.

Delia's house up a narrow stairway was cleaner than I imagined the others to be in this neighborhood. A doublet lay in pieces on a trestle table, and someone else's unhemmed skirt hung from a ceiling hook. Palmira looked around quickly for hers.

"It's ready and waiting, child. Don't fret," Delia said, and went into a rear room. She came back holding high a billowy silk gown the color of the Bay of Naples on a sunny day. It had slashings in the full sleeves to show puffs of white satin. Palmira's enraptured expression was priceless. Delia turned it to show a row of small white satin bows down the back.

"How will we tie those bows just like that?" Palmira asked.

"You don't need to. They're sewn that way. Put it on."

Palmira hurried to get off her bodice and skirt and stand in her shift with her arms up to let the skirt float down around her. Delia helped her on with the bodice, attached it with hidden hooks to the skirt, and pulled tight the laces. It fit perfectly.

"You're an artist, Delia, as fine as they come." I slapped the money on the table and Palmira kissed me on the cheek.

Walking up to our own doorway, both of us carrying parts of the dress, I saw the corner of a letter sticking out from the bottom of the door. It had the seal of the Lyncean Academy.

My Dear Friend, the Gracious and Brilliant Artemisia Gentileschi,
I fear you have given up on ever receiving a letter from me again, and I beg your forgiveness so that you may read this with the open mind and gracious spirit I remember yours to be.

I have been sorely beset by just what you had foreseen. Two years ago, having finally completed the Dialogue which uses sunspots and tides to validate the argument I told you of so long ago, I made a trip to Rome to se-

cure permission of the Holy Office of the Inquisition to publish it. His Holiness Pope Urban granted me such permission with all good will if I would change the opening and closing and title so that it would appear a hypothesis, which I was willing to do, knowing that the arguments in the middle were strong enough to convince God Himself. Since I didn't want to stay in Rome during the heat and plague of summer, I returned to my villa at Bellosguardo and found my faithful glassblower to have succumbed to the pestilence in a wretched manner.

I secured permission from the Florentine inquisitor to publish the Dialogue in Florence, and early this year, I presented the first copy to il granduca Ferdinando at the Pitti. One disappointment accompanied this momentous event — that you were not at the Pitti to witness it.

I am forced by Pope Urban himself, now that his political fortunes have changed, to appear before the Holy Office of the Inquisition. Rome is as you have said, capricious and dangerous, and since my health is precarious, I am spending the weeks prior to my departure in settling the affairs of my estate and informing my good friends of my extremities.

Hold me ever as a man trustworthy and inquiring, as I hold you a woman unimpeachable and courageous.

Ever the seeker,
Galileo Galilei
Twenty November 1632

Astonishing courage. I set the letter down to keep it from shaking and read it again. The handwriting was not Galileo's usual smoothly arched script. On the first line, ink had dripped sideways. Was he writing this in bed? The issues of Palmira's gown and a nobleman's coming-of-age party were inconsequential when Galileo was in such jeopardy. I could do nothing. The black hand of the Inquisition would have its way. And where that stopped, the other black hand, the plague itself, was ripe with horrors.

It had taken four months for the letter to reach me, because of the blockages to contain the plague, I surmised. Judgment of his case was imminent, if not already executed. I sat down to write what encouragement I could to him.

My Most Honored and Cherished Friend,
Only a few moments ago I received your letter and am much distressed for your sake.

Remember, as you once told me, we only experience the illusion of standing still. The world is changing even though in our lifetimes it seems as immoveable as stone. Even stone bears the footprints of many men. Yours will someday lead to undreamed-of truths. Let my loving and high regard for you comfort you if it can. You have my prayers.

Ever yours,
Artemisia

I sent it to the Tuscan embassy in the Villa Medici in Rome.

On Sunday I went to church with dread. At mass the monsignor announced with arrogant glee that the faithful need not fear the erroneous claims of Signor Galilei, that the Holy Office justly convicted him of heinous crimes against the sacred Canons, that he abjured, denied, and cursed under oath his former theories as errors and heresies, and that he now detested such claims and would willingly do penance daily in mitigation of his crime.

A stroke as swift and inexorable as the plague itself. I thought I would be sick. I left Palmira with Andrea in the church, went straight home and lay down in my darkened bedchamber. It was all bigoted treachery.

His recanting had to be false. He would never willingly betray his passion unless he was threatened with torture. I knew the hot-to-the-bone panic of that, and I didn't judge him. That loathsome priest had smirked through the announcement. Trying to control my imaginations of Galileo's suffering, I spent the afternoon in feverish restlessness.

The next few days I was sullen and sick. Palmira paid me quiet attentions, took over the work in the kitchen, and urged me to eat. She fretted that I would still be morose at Andrea's ball that Saturday.

"I'll pull myself out of it by then. I promise. Just leave me be for a while," I said.

On the sweltering, breathless night of the ball, we got ready together like sisters, tying the side laces of each other's bodices and winding each other's hair. When I finished hers, I touched her on the shoulder. "Wait." I found my mother's bloodstone and pearl hair ornament in my memento box.

"Don't you want to wear it?" Palmira asked.

"You wear it." I fastened it on the back of her head. "There. Mother would be pleased."

"Do you think he'll notice it there?"

"Silly. His dreamy eyes will caress every

morsel of you, from every angle." She giggled, and the melody of her anticipation helped to lift my spirit. "Stand up."

She stood and performed a dance turn. Her skirt swirled out around her like a shimmering wave, and the bows on her white satin shoes peeked out from under her hemline.

"You look stunning."

Francesco Maringhi called for us in his carriage. I had never seen him so elegantly dressed — black velvet doublet with white satin sleeve inserts and an understated white ruff. He bowed and kissed first Palmira's hand and then, lingeringly, mine, his eyes looking up at me.

"I am deeply honored to escort such a pair. Palmira, you look like your namesake, the Greek queen, and your mother puts to shame the goddess who bore you."

"You are too kind, Francesco," I said. Palmira and I smiled together in the glow of his adoration, which dispelled my moodiness and reassured Palmira.

"Will you ladies dance the Spagnoletto tonight?" he asked.

"Palmira will. All week she's been practicing the steps while holding a dance book."

"Mother! You don't have to tell that."

"It's only Francesco. It's all right if he knows."

The palace was lit with torches on the roofline and at the entrance which was crowded with carriages, their lanterns flickering. A pale yellow glow issued from the palace windows. A liveryman opened the door of our carriage and greeted us. Blithely Francesco got out and offered his hand for us to step down. "My beauties." With one of us taking each arm, he ushered us to the door, humming.

Palmira asked him, "You're not going to hover like an uncle all evening, are you?"

"On the contrary, I suspect I'll suffer the loss of you as soon as we step inside."

Two palace doormen opened the double doors, and suddenly music, light, perfumes, and a hundred voices poured out. Up the stairs the great hall was ablaze with candles, the crystal sconces reflecting pinpoints of light. Musicians played violins, cellos, and a bass viol at one end of the room, and guests gathered around long tables laden with trays of meats and other delicacies.

The postures of people shifted when Palmira glided into the hall. From the crowd, Andrea bolted toward us. "Signora, signor, welcome." He kissed my hand, but in an instant, his eyes were fastened on Palmira. He executed a low, elegant bow. *"Che bella.* I am honored."

Dressed in midnight blue, with his black hair slicked back and parted down the middle, Andrea looked suddenly older than when I'd seen him last. He offered Palmira his arm to make a *passeggiata* around the hall, and Francesco and I followed at a respectful distance, greeting those people we knew, paying our respects to Andrea's parents and the Count and Countess of Monterrey, and watching the dancing.

The Spagnoletto was the highlight of the evening. Every time the musicians played it, more foursomes joined in. Francesco and I watched in admiration as Palmira and Andrea completed one quadrangle. One moment the four were in a circle with hands joined, doing quarter-turns one way, half-turns the other, the ladies' skirts billowing about them while they gave flirtatious looks first to one man and then the other in their quadrangle. The next moment, after a rapid leap sideways, a flourish and a seductive lunge, their four hands were joined in a pinwheel. Palmira was graceful, coquettish, and captivating.

Later we saw Palmira and Andrea slip out to the balcony and kiss under the moon hanging over the Bay of Naples like a plump, Egyptian fruit. To see my child do the very thing I yearned to do myself made me ache a little, tenderly, for her, for me, I didn't know. Perhaps the music, the gaiety coming after Galileo's letter made me too sensitive.

"No sadness on such as night as this," Francesco urged.

"No. It isn't sadness."

"Then what were you thinking of?"

"Palmira. She's like an apparition floating unknowingly into her future," I said. "Here for too brief a time." Francesco listened intently. "I've done the best I could for her, but the injustice I did to her in depriving her of her father and grandfather, the sudden uprootings, the long coach rides between cities with all our world packed into a few trunks, I'll pay for someday, here or hereafter."

"How?"

"She'll leave me, for one thing, and I'll have to live alone someday."

"Alone? That doesn't have to be." He raised my hand to his lips. I withdrew it.

"Rumors, Francesco. I must be vigilant. Rumors hound me everywhere."

"That poet in Venice? Loredan? He was only a rumor?"

"*Madonna benedetta,* he was only a boy

with a hot imagination."

"Rumors make me jealous, and jealousy makes me bold. You are still young. You can have another daughter." He looked at me with fawn's eyes.

"I can hardly pay for this one. You must work harder, Francesco, to obtain larger commissions for me. Someday I'll have to produce a dowry, you know."

As a gentle hint, I looked over at the homely black-haired Countess of Monterrey commanding a circle of women in the alcove near us. Francesco followed my gaze.

"Perhaps she would condescend to have another portrait painted, as a figure from Spanish legend," Francesco said.

"You read my thoughts exactly."

"That's *my* art, Artemisia. That's why you need me."

"I see she even fidgets with those yellowed fingernails when she isn't sitting for her portrait." I stifled a chuckle. "Once when she was posing in our rooms, Palmira ridiculed her behind her back. She draped her own head in a black shawl like a Spaniard, stretched out her face, sucked in her cheeks, widened her eyes and twitched her fingers. I had a hard time to keep from laughing right in the countess's face."

Francesco smiled at me indulgently.

"You know, don't you, that in her portrait I heightened that dark ribbon of her forehead and separated her one eyebrow into two? It made her look less furtive for her grandchildren to adore someday."

"Very intelligent of you. For that, she owes you a favor."

Just then, the musicians called for a Florentine Venus Tu Ma Pris, the dance Lorenzo de' Medici had invented. I leapt forward to join another couple as the extra lady in the threesome. The room swirled with colors and the sweep of music. I felt Francesco's eyes on me during the entire dance. When it was over, he and Palmira and Andrea applauded.

Out of breath, I leaned against a pillar. The countess was standing across the room, momentarily unengaged.

"Yes. She does owe me a favor," I said to Francesco. "Why don't you go see if you can collect on it?"

Dutifully he approached her and I turned away so as not to be found watching.

Ravishing and dreamy-eyed, Palmira took Andrea's arm to make another *passeggiata* around the hall. Other men watched her as she passed. When had she become a woman? Those extra-long walks along the bay, were they with Andrea? I must have been blind to the looks that passed between them at court affairs. She was as unwary as a lamb at the edge of a precipice, even after she knew about rape. I worried about her.

Besides warnings, what did I have to give her? The understanding of color and the principles of creating shape. The appreciation of beauty. An example of determination. And love. That above all.

So now, at eighteen, the very age when I was sweating in a Roman courtroom, she was queen of the ball — beautiful, confident, unstained, ripe for the picking. Free to make her own choices.

24
Bathsheba

"If you're going to paint, then you'll have to learn the female nude," I said just after I bathed one morning not long after the ball. "That's what they want out of a woman painter. Don Ruffo wants a David and Bathsheba. We'll do one together. Let's see if he can tell whether Bathsheba is painted by you or by me." I put wood on the fire, took off my dressing gown, and positioned myself on a low bench. "Draw me."

"Mother!"

The shock of seeing flesh, my flesh, so unexpectedly startled her, and for a long time she couldn't begin, couldn't even look.

"Forget it's me. Pretend I'm a hired model. Remember how you used to run in and out of the studio in Genoa when I was painting Cleopatra?"

"That was different. She wasn't you."

"She was a fine model because she was comfortable being studied nude. And I am too. I have nothing to hide. This is the body that bore you, *cara.*" I paused and then added softly, "Take a look."

Tentatively, she let her gaze travel over my body.

"Looser than you've known me bound in laced bodices, yes?"

She nodded.

"Is it too real a glimpse into your own future?"

"Kind of."

"What you see is all right, Palmira," I soothed. "It's just part of womanhood."

She took a few strokes and then froze, gripping her pencil. "I can't."

"Start by marking out the proportions, like any other drawing. Then begin at the head oval and work downward."

She began again, slowly.

"Notice how the weight of flesh makes shapes asymmetric," I said.

"I'm afraid of what will come on the page."

"Be faithful to what your eyes see, and you won't have anything to fear. Don't try to compliment me. Don't ignore folds of skin. Let your eyes study what happens to a woman's nipples after she has nursed a baby. That's the story my body tells. We, you and I, are in the business of painting truth. Let them find the beauty in that."

I was quiet after that, and eventually she became immersed in her drawing. It was a close, contemplative time, and for the weeks she worked on the sketches prior to painting, we spoke only in soft tones to each other.

One afternoon while Palmira was painting and I was posing for her, we heard a knock at the door. She opened it a crack and reached through.

"It was a courier," she said, and handed me a letter.

It carried the seal of His Majesty's Royal Mail, in English. I slid the handle of a paintbrush through the fold to break the wax. Father's script. I read it to myself.

Dearest Artemisia,
Porzia Stiattesi wrote me that you are in Naples. I am hard at work on the ceiling of the great hall of the Queen's House in Greenwich, near London. It is An Allegory of Peace and the Arts under the English Crown, done in quadro riportato. There's work here for you if you want it. King

Charles has asked me to petition you to come at once. The Stuart court is friendly to me. A few people speak Italian here. Inigo Jones, the royal architect, spent a few years in our cities. The court would welcome you, as I would. In hopes of receiving a "yes" in your hand, I am saving the female figure of Strength for you.

> *Your loving father,*
> *Orazio Gentileschi*
> *I am alone.*

Leave my clients I had worked so hard to get? Wrench Palmira away from someone she loved? I could not, would not do that to her again. I laid the letter on the glowing embers in the fireplace. A worm of incandescence crawled toward the word *alone.* Palmira looked at me curiously. "Nothing important," I said, and resumed my pose.

As soon as the parchment burned to ashes, phrases sounded in my head. *Dearest . . . welcome you . . . I am alone.* The word *dearest* made me ashamed that I had destroyed it without at least showing it to her.

Only a few weeks later, when we were both painting, another letter came. He hadn't even waited the length of time a reply would take to reach him, had I sent one.

My only and most beloved daughter, Artemisia,
I am lonely. I am dying. Forgive a foolish old man. Help me finish.

Papa

I felt my heart split. Just the word. *Papa*. It unearthed what I thought was dead to me. I saw him swinging me by the arms so that my feet flew over the tall grasses along the Via Appia on our picnics. Weeping as he told me Mother had died. Squeezing each other's hands in awe before the great paintings of Rome. Teaching me to draw the symbols from Ripa's *Iconologia*. Showing me when I was a mere child which pigments needed more oil, which needed less to make smooth-flowing paint. Which could be made ahead, and which would lose their suspension. Which should be ground very fine, and which left coarse to preserve their intensity. *Alchimista di colore,* he called me. Papa, who made me want more than anything to be a painter, and then made it harder to become one.

I slipped the letter up my sleeve and went back to painting.

Palmira groaned at her canvas. "It's not coming right."

"*Cara,* the pleasure in painting *is* that

hurting sense that you're not getting it right, and so you try something else, and you try and you try until you get it. It may not be perfect, but it's comfortingly better than when you started, and when that happens, it's one of the grandest feelings in the world, because it's earned."

Her expression turned pitiful, and her eyes were moist. Maybe she needed to stop for a while. I set down my brush and read the letter to her.

"Grandpa!" she cried. The years dropped away. She grabbed the letter like a greedy child. "That letter you burned, that was from him too, wasn't it?"

"Yes."

She glared at me. "Why didn't you show me? He says he's dying."

"He didn't say that in the first one."

"Still, you had no right not to show me."

"What are we to do? Give up everything we've worked for? What about Andrea? Leave right now when —"

Palmira's hands flew up to her mouth. Alarm shot through her dark eyes.

"— when you're so happy? I wouldn't do that to you." I laid my hand on hers.

"There's another side to your grandfather you don't know. I thought maybe I'd never have to tell you. He isn't thinking of us in that letter. He only thinks of himself."

Palmira's face clouded. She had happy times with him in Genoa. "How can you say that?"

I spoke softly, evenly, factually. "He agreed to pardon my rapist because he needed him. They became friends again. How do you think that made me feel?"

She said nothing.

"Now that you're old enough to understand, I'll tell you something else. When I was your age midwives examined my pudenda right in court and he let it happen — sat there and watched right along with strangers who came for entertainment, because he wanted a painting back. He was holding out for its return. Otherwise he would have stopped the trial sooner."

She said nothing.

"Is this the man we're going to give up everything for?"

Nothing. She didn't ask a question, didn't even tighten her brow. Not a single sound or gesture.

I scraped back my chair and stood up, still waiting for her to say something. I took the letter back from her, went into the other room and poured a glass of wine, sat there alone and drank it all, quickly, three gulps. My cup of bitterness. I had a daughter with no feeling for others.

The letters and numbers of the date, *24 December 163–*, were smeared and crowded together at the right edge of the paper so that I could not read the last figure. That was a bad sign for a painter who ought to plan spacing better. There was something pitiful about those disfigured numbers.

I read it again. *I am lonely. I am dying. Forgive a foolish old man. Help me finish.* Loneliness I understood. Dying I did not. Though I had painted it, and imagined it, I did not know it. Help him put a finish to what? It couldn't just be the ceiling fresco.

He wanted me there to help him die. It was permissible somehow for him, for anyone, to long to die in the presence of love, such as it was, such as he hoped it to be. I would want the same thing, to die in a daughter's arms, or a lover's. If a stranger were to be with me, that might be enough, if only for that person to hold Michelangelo's brush and stroke my temples with its softness, to remind me that one man thought me worthy of such a gift. We prepare ourselves for death by treasuring such moments when we feel that even the least of us has been necessary for the full expression of God. Maybe Father needed someone to whisper that in his ear, in Italian.

Let that man with the strange name, Ini-something, whisper it.

I went back into the main room. "Let's get back to work," I said as gently as I could. I picked up my brush and tried to concentrate and let her work out her painting problems on her own. In a little while, Palmira slammed her brush down onto the table between us. I jumped at the noise.

"I can't do this. It's too hard," she cried.

I looked at her Bathsheba. The proportions were right but the figure was wooden. Bathsheba's gesture was meaningless. Palmira had been working on her face, but it conveyed nothing. My own daughter, and she had no gift for expression.

"You need to convey her emotion by defining the shape of her cheek with —"

"Lights and darks." Mockery tinged her voice. She gave me a look I'd seen a thousand times — sharp, narrowed eyes, hardened jaw, throat stretched taut — the look I'd hoped time and teaching would dispel.

"Well then, you already know this."

"Yes, but I can't *do* it. Not like you can."

"You will."

"When? When I'm thirty? I don't want to be married to painting like you are."

"Think what you just said!" My voice turned shrill.

She looked sheepishly at the bottom edge of her painting.

"All right. Decide first what you want her face to convey, and then we'll find a way to express it. You know the story. What kind of woman was she, displaying her voluptuous body to David? What has she just been thinking?"

"I don't know!" Her hands flew up like Cesare Gentile's. "I can't make up something like you can. I don't care."

"Enough. You don't care enough. But to be a painter, you've *got* to care for people, and for their feelings. You've got to understand human feelings in order to convey them. And — you — don't." I snapped my brush at her once for each of the last three words.

"How do you know?"

"Because I tell you about the humiliation and pain of my life and you say nothing. Nothing! You have no sense for other people, for their pain or the drama of their lives."

"That's different. It's people in paintings I don't care about."

"People are people whether they breathe now in front of you or lived a long time ago. You've got to care for each person you paint as if she were real, as if getting her expression right and true in that painting is the most important thing in the world at that moment. If you can't care for a real person standing before you, then how can —"

"Who said I don't care?"

"Your silence said it. Just now. When I told you what they did to me in court, what your grandfather let them do. It's not that I want to open old wounds. That's ancient history for me. I'm tired of thinking about it. But for you, you just learned this and yet you've said nothing."

"What am I supposed to say?"

"Say what you feel."

For a moment, we just stared at each other, numb. I tried to swallow, but my throat seemed filled with sand.

"See? You don't show any feelings with words or with paint. But an artist's feeling is the white-hot core of painting. Do you want to be limited forever like Agostino? He can't paint people because he has no heart. That's why he'll never last. What's inside you? A heart, or only dresses and dreams? What is a heart but the working of the imagination in behalf of another person? Think. What white-hot passion is going to make Bathsheba betray her husband? Feel it yourself." I touched her belly. "Right there. What passion is burning in you for Andrea? You've got to use your own emotions and paint with your own blood if need be in order to discover and prove the truth of your vision."

"That's crazy. No one would do that."

"Renata would!" I snapped. "She would have done anything to paint well."

"Renata was a little whore. Pleading 'take me with you,' like a baby as we left the house."

"That's exactly what I mean. Desperation. You've got to want it enough that the thought of it being taken from you *would* make you a little crazy. I should have brought her with us. She'd never give up, whining that it was hard. Of course it's hard. If it weren't hard every washerwoman would be painting. But they wouldn't paint with their own hands bleeding onto the canvas. Like I did!"

"When? You never did that!"

I threw down my brush and splayed my fingers right in front of her eyes. "Take a good look, Palmira. A nice — long — look." I said it slowly, separating the words. "Harder to look at than my nakedness now, isn't it? What do you see?"

"Lines."

"Yes, well, use your puny imagination and tell me what they're from."

"You always told me they were age lines."

Her voice quavered.

"Because I didn't want you to see the ugliness in the world. That was my mistake. These are not age lines, Palmira. I got them when I was your age."

I moved toward her, bending forward, one slow step at a time, my hands still thrust in her face. She backed away.

"They're torture lines, scars from wounds inflicted in court the day a rapist called me a whore. So don't you *ever* use that word lightly."

I grabbed her by the elbow and marched her over to stand in front of my *Judith Slaying Holofernes*. "That's my blood on that mattress, and it's my pain that started this career that kept you in bread and ball gowns, so don't you dare say it's crazy."

I stormed outside and slammed the door. Let her wonder whether I'd come back. Her life had been too easy, and in an easy life, the imagination doesn't grow.

I strode down the lane ripping leaves off bushes. Palmira. Oh, Palmira. What mistake did I commit in raising you that made you so unfeeling? Not even a murmur of condolence. Not a touch of your hand to mine. Not a ripple of compassion across your features.

I remembered when I'd given her Michelangelo's brush on her last birthday, telling her that of all the things I owned, that brush was the most valuable to me. She'd turned it over, stroked her wrist with the brush hairs, pretended she was painting with it, and then had passed it back to me saying, "You keep it, Mother." I thought at the time that it was reverence that made her give it back to me. No. That wasn't it at all. She had no feeling for the gift.

Walking seemed my only comfort. Winter dusk came early, turning the houses inward. I came to the little rise where I knew I'd see a sliver of bay, and stopped to slow down my breathing.

No, Palmira's life wasn't easy. That wasn't completely right. She saw how the rich live and then went to bed cold. Four times she'd been uprooted. I swore I would not do that to her again. Now that she knew my whole history, would she forgive me for denying her a father for the sake of art? Or, in her mind, was the sacrifice I imposed on her too great? Why was it that art had to cost so much to achieve?

I had to accept that the stories behind my paintings meant nothing to Palmira even though to me, those women were as real as sisters. At least there were some patrons in the world intrigued by a woman artist painting women. But if my own daughter didn't care about the women I painted, who, beyond those few patrons, would? Down the sweep of years and centuries, would what I'd done matter? I had to believe that there was a purpose in painting every Bathsheba, every Judith, Lucrezia, Susanna. Not thinking so would mean a lifetime of futile work.

I watched the oval moon rise over the bay, lighting a wavy swath of liquid pewter just beneath it. It lacked luster. Galileo's night pearl, dull and flat as a dirty plate. Had he felt his work was futile when he had to recant his beliefs?

I waited until I felt calm, and then I opened the door quietly. Palmira was staring at the tile floor, a piece of bread in her hand. Some cheese and two slices of sausage were left on a plate. She pushed the plate toward me. I poured more wine, took some cheese, and sat down.

I stared into the ruby liquid. "What is it that you really want?" My voice sounded hollow.

"I want to marry Andrea."

I tore off a piece of bread and sopped it in olive oil. "More than anything else in the world? It must be that, you know."

She nodded. Her rosy hands rested in her lap, palms up, curled like shells. They were, as yet, unmarked by work or pain.

"Not just the idea of being married, any more than the idea of being a painter."

"I know, I know." She sighed loudly, annoyed. "I want to be really married. To a man, not a job."

I couldn't respond to that or we'd start all over again.

"Andrea wants to, too. He told me so at the ball." She spoke in the same petulant voice I remembered from our years in Florence.

I thought of how Pietro and I had carried her as a young child into the great churches and galleries of the city. How we had breathed as one when we held her out to the bishop in the Baptistry. How the beauty of Pietro's body had made me want love again. And how Palmira must be longing for the same. How could I expect her to choose my passion over hers? She had a chance for what I'd longed for — to marry out of love.

"All I want is for you to want something so deeply you ache for it as I ache to paint well." I took a sip of wine and smiled at her. "I will make inquiries."

"You will?"

"Negotiations don't usually start with the

bride's family, but Francesco will help us. Andrea's father is a courtier to the countess. She owes me a favor, Francesco says. He'll know what to say to make her think it's her idea."

Palmira flung herself at me and hugged me on her knees.

"That's only part of it. There's the issue of the dowry."

She let go and leaned back on her heels.

"I'll have to work a long time before I'll have the money Andrea's family expects," I said. "You'll have to work too. It might be easier for you when you're working for a goal that's important to you. You're not too young to sell that Bathsheba, so tomorrow we'll *both* get an early start."

We drank from the same glass and let the idea settle. I noticed Father's letter on the table. I read it again. I could go to England alone, after the wedding, if there was one. It might be my only chance to — to do what? I didn't know.

I passed her the letter. "What do you think I should do about this?"

"I think you should go."

"Disrupt my whole life here for him?"

"Not for him. For you. To tell him he was selfish. Did he ever take responsibility for what they did to your hands? Or for humiliating you? Did he ever say he was sorry?"

Surprised, I inhaled slowly and deeply, looking at the word *Papa*. "No," I whispered.

"You should go."

"It will only make your dowry even smaller. Your trousseau too."

"I know."

"That means fewer linens, dresses, night shifts. A simpler wedding."

"You should go."

25
Palmira

On Palmira's wedding morning, I pinned a gardenia in her hair, and then stepped back to look at her. Delia had made a pale lavender overskirt of the sheerest silk I'd ever seen which floated over Palmira's blue ball gown and trailed on the floor in the back as lightly as froth. Delia had replaced the white bows with lavender ones, and at one place in the front she had gathered up the overskirt to show the blue underneath matching her bodice.

"The colors are lovely. You look like dawn in Heaven."

"Do you think Andrea will think so?"

"Everyone will. I wish Pietro could see you. He'd be in awe, and very happy. And Father. He'd be so proud."

"Don't get soft-hearted, Mother. You're

supposed to tell him I think he was selfish."

"A person isn't all good or all bad, Palmira. He would still love to be here. Let's have only happy thoughts today, so you'll remember your day of days untarnished."

I sat on the edge of my bed and lifted the lid of my mother's wooden box where I kept my few important mementos — her blood-stone hair ornament, Galileo's letters, precious little notes from Palmira from when she was learning to write. Under the bottom one, there was the small drawstring bag. I held it to my nose. Oregano. Faint but unmistakable. They hadn't been worn since Umiliana had posed for the Magdalen. That was good because Umiliana was loving. And Graziela's love for her husband had surely erased any stigma of the imperfect pearls given to her as false love tokens.

"Come here, *cara*."

She spread out her skirt as she sat next to me on the bed. "What, Mama?"

I chuckled. "You haven't called me Mama for years." She blinked at me, smiling with high expectations of what lay ahead for her. "Open your hand."

She held her palms up.

I let the little bag drop. She felt with her thumbs. Her eyes opened wide and she recognized the bag. "Mama! Really?"

"Untie the string."

She let the earrings tumble out into her palm, and sighed at their beauty. She turned each one over, looking at their humps and hollows, and then held them up to dangle.

"Put them on. They were Graziela's, remember?"

"She wants me to wear them?"

I turned my face away so she would not detect the lie. "To have them."

"Truly?"

"I already told Francesco to add them to your trousseau inventory. Put them on." I brought over my table mirror. "See? They look beautiful on you."

She looked at herself, first one side and then the other.

"Graziela would be so happy to see them on you today. She was married once too."

Palmira's hands fell to her lap. "I didn't know that."

"The earrings were a gift from her husband, a man named Marcello. Graziela . . ." I caught myself. I couldn't tell her their story today, even as gentle advice to be wary. Only happy thoughts today. Besides, if Palmira couldn't feel Graziela's sorrow, that would be more than I could bear.

"Graziela what?"

"Graziela has told me many things over

the years, but of all that she told me, I want you to promise you will remember these words: Do not believe in illusion."

Waiting for Don Francesco to escort Palmira down the nave, I sat in the first pew looking at the small arrangement of red roses on the altar. The wedding wasn't as lavish as Palmira had dreamed about ever since she was a little girl, but it was certainly grand compared to mine, stark and furtive in a nearly empty church. I looked behind me and smiled at the people I'd invited — a few artists, people for whom I had painted, my apothecary, my joiner, and Delia — but my contribution to the congregation was modest. I so wished Graziela and Paola could have been here.

In his black velvet doublet with lace collar and cuffs, Francesco appeared at the back of the church and held out his arm for Palmira. As they came down the aisle, he looked as proud as if he were her father. I felt a surge of gratitude. He had managed the negotiations masterfully. Affirming that Palmira's purity was without question, and promising that I would give Andrea's parents a painting when I returned from England, he had gotten them to accept a modest dowry. The important thing was that she had had a proper *impalmamento* with the banns published three times at parish masses. Now, in the Mass of the Union, the organ left its last powerful chords suspended under the stone ceiling as Francesco gave over the bride to Andrea whose young face shone with love.

When the priest invited the bridal couple to the altar, Palmira's gaze was fixed on Andrea, her eyes dewy with adoration. I felt a warmth radiate through me as unmistakably as though I were the one to be wed and loved tonight. She repeated her vows in a voice that rang with innocence. When the priest entoned, *"Ego jungo vos in matrimonium,"* and joined their hands, she swayed under the heady weight of love. And so did I.

The prayers and responses of the mass seemed interminable. All I wanted to do was to hold her in my arms and whisper some sage advice, but what? Think every day of some new way to please him? Ignore any indications of infidelity and go right on loving him? Keep peace between you by obeying your mother-in-law? I felt a sharp pang. Now Palmira was more that mother's daughter than mine.

At the supper afterward, Francesco, looking down the table to the bridal couple, leaned toward me and asked in a low voice,

"Wouldn't it be nice to think they'll always feel about each other as they do at this moment?"

"They might, if she's clever enough to keep him tantalized and feeling manly, and if she doesn't demand too much."

"And if she's not?"

"If not, she'll survive. There's always painting."

Feeding me an artichoke heart on the tip of his fork and grinning, he said, "And so, my lovely, talented, gracious lady, you are, from this time forth, free of motherhood. Free to be completely you. Free to —"

"Never free of motherhood. She will always be my child, to me. *Grazie a Maria,* she has had the privilege of choice. Tonight and always, I pray that she'll remain mindful of that."

"And to whom else are you grateful, tonight, that she could marry the man she chose?"

I rolled my eyes sideways toward him and touched my glass to his. "To you, Don Maringhi, my brilliant negotiator."

"Negotiator? Only that?"

I closed my eyes, smiled, and lifted my shoulders.

"Just so you don't forget while you're in England on that fool's errand that I await your return . . . to serve you faithfully."

"Not a fool's errand."

"Then what? A filial obligation?"

"I'm not sure."

"Then why go?"

"To find out what I'm capable of, for one thing." I took a drink of wine, turning my shoulder to him slightly. "Don't forget it was my father who taught me the skill that you benefit from."

The priest came downstairs from the bedchamber above the dining hall where he'd gone to sprinkle holy water on the marriage bed. "It is ready," he announced.

Andrea's friends became suddenly boisterous, teasing Andrea and Palmira, singing rousing love songs and holding glasses of wine aloft. Young women, not permitted at the nuptial mass but present now, laid red rose petals up the stairs to their bedchamber. I realized with a start what they stood for: the blood of Palmira's purity. The young people gathered around Palmira and Andrea to whisk them upstairs. I rushed to Andrea's side and took his elbow. He bent down so I could say in his ear, "Take her gently, Andrea. Such a flower bruises easily."

I only had an instant to hug Palmira and whisper, "It's easier if you relax. It's all right to ask him to go slowly."

"Don't worry, Mama. He loves me."

"Laugh a little together every day, *no matter what.*"

"*Sì*, Mama."

In a moment, Palmira and Andrea were hoisted aloft on young men's shoulders and borne high above the crowd up the stairs. Palmira looked back at me with her gardenia hanging loose and her face marked by exhilarated trepidation. My throat constricted in a spasm of happiness. I blew her a kiss.

26

Paola

The coach delivered me to the central livery station in Rome. Only two weeks, and I was already missing Palmira fiercely. Until her wedding, there had not been a day in all her life that we'd been apart. I stored my trunk and carpetbag at the station, and from there, I walked to Santa Trinità.

Paola answered the bell. Her face turned white. She didn't step back so I could enter.

"What's wrong?"

"I have something to tell you."

"About Graziela?"

She nodded and looked to the right and left. "There's nowhere we can go," she fretted. Apparently she wanted a place where Graziela wouldn't discover us.

"To the church?"

"No. Over here, I guess." She pointed to

the cloister and we sat on the L-shaped bench. She inhaled deeply, as if gathering energy or fortitude.

"Just tell me."

"She died."

I was stunned. I couldn't comprehend it. Nothing prepared me for this.

"When?"

She waved her hand backward over her shoulder.

"How?"

Paola's whole face puckered. "She went outside."

"And that killed her?"

"Out of the convent. More than once."

"How often?"

"Many times. Usually between matins and lauds. To see Rome."

My part in this crept into my consciousness like a snake. *Come, taste the forbidden pleasure. Disobey your holy order.*

"But how did that kill her?"

"The pestilence."

"I can't believe it. The plague? Didn't she know?"

"She knew. But her need outweighed her fear. Once she went out the first time, she couldn't stop. She saw things that made her happy." Fear that I wouldn't understand flooded Paola's eyes. "She was always better for a while afterward."

I felt dizzy, and braced myself with my hands on the bench. I tried to comprehend the magnitude of her yearning, and the effects of my feeding that passion.

"Why didn't you write me?"

"My shame, Artemisia. I couldn't."

"How did she get out?"

Paola fingered her rosary. "I heard her weeping at night. Such gasping, choking sobs. She tried to muffle them. I couldn't bear to hear her." Her voice took on a tinge of defensiveness. "She was my dearest friend for twenty years. The purest spirit I ever knew. How could I deny her?"

"So you let her out?"

Her head tipped forward. "I prayed every minute she was gone."

"And stayed awake to let her in again?"

A cry burst from Paola's pale lips. "I did penance the very next day, and haven't missed a day since."

"The plague — and you didn't get it from her."

"Not by my own will or wishes. I would rather it had been me," she cried.

"I didn't mean that as a recrimination," I said softly, put my arm around her, and let her weep against my bosom. "Just the strangeness of it."

"Our Father has seen fit to chastise me with sleeplessness, and a festering conscience."

A weight bore down on my chest. "You are not the only one responsible."

"She saw Michelangelo's *Pietà*," Paola said with a hint of her usual brightness, lifting her head. "And Bernini's new altar canopy in Saint Peter's. Imagine, as tall as an eight-story building. And your father's ceiling."

"Bless her, that she wanted to see that too, for my sake. Then she had to go in the daytime."

"Between tierce and sext."

"Was she punished?"

"For a long time no one knew, as long as she went at night, but when she went in the daytime she was caught. The punishment of confinement and silence only allowed her the privacy to think over every detail of what she saw. She was always calm afterward."

"That's good. At least we have that."

"The last time, she stayed out all night and walked all the way out the Via Appia. It was a full moon. She thought she found the spot where Peter saw Christ. She said her feet felt the warmth of his love. On the way back she saw a dying man under the Arch of Constantine and crouched next to him to say the Lord's Prayer in his ear and touch him with the sign of the cross." Paola's voice rose high and thin as a thread. "I think that's what killed her. Her own charity."

All the air leaked out of me and I felt crumpled in on myself, like a dress in a hump on the floor without me in it.

"Did she suffer horribly?"

"Just three days."

"Wasn't she treated by a doctor?"

"For the first two days I kept the buboes covered so Mother Abbess wouldn't see."

"And then?"

"I had to tell her. Mother Abbess feared any doctor coming into the convent would bring the plague with him. Besides, if a doctor knew, he'd have to report it. They would have quarantined us, and might even have boarded us in." She spoke more quickly and softly. "If Graziela were the only one to die in the convent, we could call it a natural death by divine will and bury her here and not have to give her up to the House of Plague — or the trench." Her voice cracked on the last word, and she squeezed her eyes shut.

"No priest gave her last rites?"

"The Mother Abbess did. We buried her between matins and lauds. Within the hour. On her straw mattress. By lantern light.

Ourselves. I didn't let anyone else touch her."

"So she's here? In the cloister?"

"No. In the herb garden. Unmarked, in case inspectors come."

"Show me where."

Silently we walked under the arcade, through the ground floor corridor to the enclosed herb garden in back. Paola's hands covered her mouth and pressed palm to palm. "Forgive us, Artemisia. She's under the oregano."

I knelt down and smelled its earthy, spicy scent, an aroma I knew I would never smell again without grief. I stroked several of the spade-shaped leaves with my thumb, picked off a sprig, and tucked it into my bodice lacing. My tears bounced on the leaves.

"See? I planted a row of rue all around her." Paola knelt down next to me. "I'll never forgive myself, even if Our Gracious Lord does." Her voice was a mere squeak. "Never."

"You acted from compassion. Remember that. And she always advocated forgiveness. Graziela told me once not to pray as a penitent. I think she meant not to pray in abject self-hatred. Don't punish yourself with this, Paola. She wouldn't want that. She did what she wanted, knowingly."

Paola nodded, her round face pinched. "She would have touched the leper's hand just the same as the Virgin's."

"Remember what you taught me when I was young? 'Charity suffereth long' . . . ?"

" 'And is kind . . . Charity beareth all things.' "

"It just takes a lifetime to learn how."

The world seemed to stop, and we were quiet for a long time.

"Maybe she did touch the Virgin — in marble. Michelangelo's *Pietà*. You should have heard her describe it." Paola smiled sadly at the memory. Then words poured out in a flood. " 'A Heaven ordained sculpture, the Passion of Christ. The deep, sad, helpless love in Mary's face looking down at him on her lap. His smooth, unperturbed cheekbone bearing all selflessly. The stiffness of his marble arms so freshly taken from the cross. Her tender, strong fingers supporting his riven side. The sweet, small folds of cloth at her neckline.' Graziela was so full of rapture describing it, she could have been lifted to Heaven right then."

Paola's thinking made me smile. A certainty settled over me. "That's what great art is supposed to do — help us to live in the spirit and die at peace."

After a long pause, Paola murmured,

"Thank you for saying that."

"What about the letters I wrote to her since?"

"I read them to her. Right here, just before I go in to vespers. Beautiful letters. I read them more than once. I've saved them all."

"Then I'll keep writing." We stood up and stepped out of the garden. "I'm going to England. I'm on my way now. To see my father."

"You have forgiven him?"

I lifted my shoulders. "How can I be sure?"

"By going. You'll know when you see him."

"I hope I won't disappoint you."

"You won't if you remember the rest of what Paul the Apostle said. Charity is not easily provoked. It comes naturally with the putting away of childish things so we can see face to face."

I nodded, still doubtful that I could achieve that.

She tipped her head toward the herb garden. "Tell her, *cara*."

"I'll leave that to you."

We took a few steps back toward the building and she stopped. "One thing Graziela wanted you to know. She prayed for Signor Galilei."

"I knew she would."

"He was kept just there," she pointed over the wall, "in Villa Medici, except when he was in a cell in the Holy Office of the Inquisition. And later he was at the Convent of Santa Maria Sopra Minerva." She lowered her voice. "Don't worry, Artemisia. I have taken over praying for him."

"Thank you."

Putting one foot in front of the other was never so hard as now, walking out through the cloister, seeing again every crack that Graziela knew like the veins in the back of her hand. Slowly, to the door, and the dark key in Paola's hand, the instrument that let Graziela love the world, and leave it.

"One more thing," Paola said at the door. "When she died, she passed silently into the Lord's arms. With ease, at the last. I do believe at that moment she saw the city of God and she thought it beautiful. Full of domes and spires and loggias with marble angels."

"How do you know?"

Paola's chin quivered. "There was a tiny, lovely gasp, hardly a breath. Her eyes opened brightly, and then she was gone."

27

Orazio

For the second evening I lay down with strangers on a single-deck packet boat at anchor off Calais waiting for fog to lift so we could cross the British Sea. A faint flicker of light from a refuge tower brooding over the ashy gloom made me conscious of the frailty of human craft. There was no certainty in this world. Shrouded forms emerged and then retreated, playing wicked tricks. Across the deck, was that a stanchion or a crouching nun? A mast and spar or a crucifix? Was this vagueness the way Graziela remembered Rome before she took her nocturnal walks? Did one dear thing after another become hazy until the oppression of blank, foggy sameness grew too much for her? The creak and wallow of the vessel and the clanking of wooden blocks against the rigging were the most melancholy sounds I'd ever heard.

I wrapped my cloak around me, but still I shivered in the dampness. A man emerged from the fog and came toward me. With words I couldn't understand, he draped his blanket over me. Or was it only the trick of the fog? The feel of the wool against my palms and its weight on my shoulders were real enough. Were we enacting a parable from the Bible urging me toward Christly charity in a time to come?

The third day was clear enough to make the crossing, but night descended so early it seemed only half a day. How could Father paint here at all after midday meal? Despite my fear of the passion that might boil up in me when I saw him, I felt pulled across the water by an invisible bloodline, a vein strong enough to tow the boat.

The next morning I boarded a river craft to sail up a broad, muddy estuary. The land lay flat and uninteresting, the trees leafless, the air thick, heavy, and cold. This, the great Thames River of a proud nation with a glorious history, was foul-smelling and sluggish in brown and gray. The croaking of monstrous ravens did nothing to welcome me. Raw wind cut through the threads of my cloak. The craft beat up the river against all impulses of the land to repel it. Now that I

434

had come this close, I faced a wind, a river, a nation that did not want me to enter.

Ships and barges moved slowly past brick warehouses and shipbuilding yards. Farther inland, sheep grazed in meadows surrounding country estates. Where was the famed city that ruled the seas? Only a single man-of-war was anchored opposite a tall, brown, heavily turreted palace on the south bank, dark and forbidding, more like a fortress than a residence.

"Greenwich, madam," the steward said.

Was Father in there? Maybe I was too late.

"Is that the Queen's House?" I asked in the only language I knew.

The steward stared at me, not comprehending. I showed him the outside of Father's letter where he'd written in English, "The Queen's House, Greenwich." Wind threatened to snap it out of my hand.

He pointed beyond the dark, turreted palace to a small white building upon a rise, the only white building visible. While my trunk was being unloaded onto a dock, it started to rain. The steward carried my carpetbag weighted with jars of olive oil, artichokes, olives, and a bottle of wine. I followed him down the gangplank and he showed the letter to a hackney driver, spilling out words I couldn't understand.

A short carriage ride on a glistening cobbled street took me past the brown stone palace, up the rise to the white building. I leaned out the carriage window, and showed a guard the letter. He nodded and pointed to the white building behind him. "Orazio Gentileschi? *Pittore italiano?*" I asked. He shook his head and directed the driver back to the brown palace near the river.

By now, torches were being lit at the palace gatehouse. What would I do if they wouldn't let me in here either? I leaned out the window again. "Orazio Gentileschi? *Pittore italiano?*" This time a guard repeated the name to a porter who went inside.

Somewhere in that wet stone building Father breathed and painted, but he could not see through walls. I could tell the driver to turn around. No one would know. I could go home, back to warmth and people I knew. To Genoa. To apologize to Cesare and Bianca. To take Renata to Florence, to the academy. Look Signor Bandinelli straight in the eye and say, "Pay attention. Train her. Nurture her. She will do great things." I could give her Michelangelo's brush.

But that was not what one did. Instead, one muddled through, fretting about what to eat each day, trying not to think of one's last brushstroke. What color would it be?

What brush? What effect?

The porter returned and allowed me to enter and the trunk to be set down in the gatehouse. I picked up my carpetbag and, with a stride that belied my uncertainty, I went inside. A woman led me upstairs, chattering words I didn't understand, harsh sounds echoing against the bare stone walls of the staircase. Her expression seemed a reprimand for not coming earlier. We passed through room after room until she finally opened a door and he was there.

Orazio Gentileschi, with his shapeless coat draped over his shoulders, coughing and holding his chest. Something between a grunt and a whimper escaped when he saw me. He took a few steps toward me, then stopped.

"You did ask that I come," I said, my pulse beating in my throat.

"I had given up thinking that you would."

"I couldn't come earlier. Palmira wanted to get married. It took me a long time to earn a dowry."

"You should have asked."

Our sentences came between awkward pauses. We stood apart from each other. I was still holding my carpetbag. He gestured for me to set it down.

"She married a nobleman. For love. They chose each other. She'll never lift a brush.

She hates painting."

He looked hurt. "She was a beautiful bride, I imagine."

"Yes, but beauty isn't everything. It's better to have a hunger and appreciation for beauty than to be merely beautiful. In the end, life is richer that way. She may learn that."

He puffed air out his nostrils. "So, the years have made you wise."

"They've made me realistic, and content. I'm glad she's happy."

"And Palmira's father? Was he at the wedding?"

"No."

"Pity. It would seem an opportune time for a reconciliation." Judgment shone in his eyes. "Did you try?"

What business is it of yours, I wanted to say. "It's not as simple as you think."

"He didn't help with the dowry?"

"I didn't ask him to."

We looked at each other warily, as if we both recognized that any misstep might unleash fire.

"Can't I sit down? I'm exhausted."

He emptied a chair of paint rags and dragged it toward the fireplace. Not a word of thanks for my coming.

"The palace is so empty. Furniture and tapestries, but no people. Just a few servants

and caretakers. You live here all the time so
. . . alone?"

He closed his eyes, screwed up his face,
lifted his chin.

"What's the matter? Are you in pain?"

"Just hearing Italian again." He blew his
nose on a rumpled handkerchief.

"You said that fellow with the strange
name speaks Italian."

"Inigo Jones. *Uomo vanissimo,*" he said
scornfully. "The expert of all arts. He is everything and everywhere. Clever, with a
good sense of design, but mightily full of
himself. Flaunts his position as a favorite of
the king. So does a Flemish painter. Van
Dyck. An ill-mannered and jealous boor
lapping up the king's luxury."

He stirred the fire roughly, and placed
more wood on it.

"So there are people here?"

"The king and queen hold court here in
the palace twice a year, for hunting. The
queen comes more often to follow the progress of the decoration of her own house."

"That white building?"

"Yes."

"What's her name?"

"Henrietta Maria. Her mother was Marie
de' Medici."

"You can speak French to her?"

"Five years in that court ought to have taught me something."

"And English?"

"Some. Badly."

Now what? What to say next? I couldn't tell him about Graziela. No stories of dying. Not with how thin he was.

"I brought you olives and artichokes." I dug into my carpetbag for the jars, happy to have something for him that he'd like. "I saved them for you from Palmira's wedding supper." He pried open the wax seal on the olives with a palette knife and ate one, then two more.

"Do you have any bread?" I asked.

"Yes. Awful stuff."

I brought out the wine and olive oil. He drew over a chair for himself, and watched my every move, curious, it seemed, about what was in my carpetbag. He poured the wine and we huddled by the fire and ate artichokes on the moistened bread. He closed his eyes when he chewed, to concentrate on the taste.

"Too many years I have lived here. And in France. Too many."

"Yes. I know." I felt the warming path of the wine in my body while the fire thawed me from the outside. I held my hands up to the flames and let out a slow, deep breath to

440

try to relax from days of cold.

"And for what? For hard-hearted courtiers swarming here twice a year?" he continued. "Men of duplicity who eat the king's meat and then plot against him? They wear quilted doublets here, but not for warmth in this frozen land. They're to ward off poignards." He made a gesture with his bread in his hand, and an artichoke fell off. He picked it up and ate it. "For a scheming, supercilious queen?"

I didn't expect such bitterness. "For all time, Father."

"No, Artemisia. Most of the world's people will eat their bread while watching whippings, hangings, burnings, spectacles of any kind" — he drummed his fingers on the wooden arm of the chair at every word — "and not care a whit that there are painters in the world quietly working, for all time."

"But you wrote that the court was friendly to you, and would be to me."

"To get you to come."

"You mean you lied to me?" I felt my back become rigid.

With a disdainful wave of his hand he disregarded my question. Was this another betrayal? Would there be no work for me here? If I reacted, we'd surely get off to a bad start.

"They tolerate me because I can bring

them a little visual drama instead of their stiff, boring portraits." He took a draught of wine, stretching out his neck to savor it. "Artemisia, there's none of *la dolce vita* here." He balled up his fist and brought it to his heart. "No conscious, appreciative enjoyment of fine things. Their gentility is self-serving and manipulative. They don't care about art. They care about hunting and horses and ships."

"But we care. Every painting gives us joy."

He looked up from his wine as if the thought startled him. "You're doing . . . well?"

"It varies. I have a clerk now who acts as my agent. He sold my first Judith."

"Finally someone smart enough to recognize your genius. Who bought it?"

"Prince Gennaro of San Martino."

"Lucky for him that fools before him passed it up."

"I still have to explain again and again that I charge the Roman way, a set price. They think I operate the Neapolitan way, asking thirty scudi and then settling on four." It was an odd thing to say, but I was tense. We didn't trust each other. And I didn't trust myself.

"I've been working for a patrician from Sicily, Don Antonio Ruffo, and for the Count of Monterrey. But only portraits for him. Nobody wants *invenzione*. All they want is ideal femininity. I haven't done any heroic women since I came to Naples. Time bled the torture out of me."

His eyes flashed resentment that I'd said that word, that I'd reminded him so soon after arriving. I only meant . . . I didn't know what I meant. I just said it.

"Still angry?" His voice turned icy.

"No. I've stopped painting violent Judiths. I guess that shows I'm not angry, except when mean-spirited people in Rome brought it up in front of Palmira when she was younger. But that was only feeble, short-lived anger at them, not at you or him."

"I thought that finding a husband for you made up for it anyway. Considering your reputation —"

"*My* reputation. If reputation was on your mind, why didn't you look into the reputation of the man you were paying to take me?"

"He was Giovanni's brother."

I squeezed the arm of the chair. "Giovanni's brother had a string of lovers before and after I married him. That's why I didn't reconcile, if you must know. And that's why he was willing to marry someone sight unseen. He had to go out of Florence to find a wife ignorant of his reputation." I kept control of my voice, but only by a hair. "He married me for the dowry, which he used to rent a room to entertain his women. A closed box of a man, incapable of real love. Oh yes, Father, a careful choice you made."

"Me. Always me to blame." He stood up and walked away. "Just what I was afraid of," he muttered. "I shouldn't have written you."

"Do I still need to tell you how I might have been chosen by a man who loved me if I had not been exposed in Rome?"

"It was necessary."

"Necessary that everything else come first? Your friendship with a bastard? Your sickly need for him?" Words I'd said to myself a thousand times and promised I wouldn't say to him came gushing out. I leaned forward in the chair. "So necessary you couldn't stop yourself from inviting him to Genoa?"

"How many years does a man have to live in penitence? For twenty years you've treated me like a leper." He was pacing now.

"And for twenty years, you never acknowledged that you betrayed me. Never said you're sorry. You want forgiveness but you're unwilling to say you're sorry."

"There'll come a time, either here or hereafter, when you'll say that things just happened, not that I made them happen." His fingers pounded his chest at the "I."

"You expect too much of me. Nothing less than what I did would have stopped Agostino. I know him, Artemisia."

For an instant, I had the sense that he actually believed what he said. Still, I plunged ahead, my nails digging into my palms. "You send me a self-pitying letter asking that I come and forgive you. Can't you see how selfish that was? Can't you, for once, look at my life from my perspective? No family blood runs in your veins. I'll tell you what runs in your veins. Orazio Gentileschi, first, last, and always."

His trembling hands grasped the back of his chair. "If you felt so bitter, you shouldn't have come. Do you think an old man wants to be slapped down again by hearing everything he ever did wrong? God will judge me, Artemisia, on my day of dying. Not you."

I stood up. "But I can say —"

"No!" he bellowed and waved me away. "Leave me alone. Get out."

I was dumbfounded. He wouldn't even look at me. "Get out." He took a few steps toward me as if he would push me.

I couldn't move.

"Eh, *porca miseria.*" He grabbed his doublet and left.

28

Artemisia

Get out. Where? I stood alone in his room, shaking. After traveling for a month, *get out.* After dismantling my life again, *get out.* The ingrate. I shouldn't have come.

I walked around the room in circles. I wasn't going to get out. I had nowhere to go. I couldn't make anyone understand me even if I left. Let *him* spend the night somewhere else. Getting me to come here under false pretenses and then shoving me away. He'd become an embittered old man.

I gulped down some wine and flopped into the chair by the fire, feeling torn and drained. Only one thing Father had said made sense — that Agostino would have continued using me unless Father exposed him in court. Probably true. One dreary month of travel to learn that.

I ate an olive and looked around. The room was cluttered. A waistcoat and breeches hung on an easel. Books, plates of half-eaten food, jars of brushes, his worn copy of Ripa's *Iconologia*, small sketches on scraps of paper all lay haphazardly on a long worktable. Between a pair of oil lamps there was a stack of large drawings. I was curious but too tired to get up and take a look. I tipped my head back against the tall chair and closed my eyes.

After a while I heard a noise. Maybe he was standing outside the door waiting for me to apologize. I opened it and walked through a few other rooms. Empty. And cold. I went back into his room and put more wood on the fire.

My curiosity was too much for me. On a portfolio cover he had written, "Allegory of Peace and the Arts Under the English Crown." I looked at the whole stack of drawings. They were muses and allegorical figures holding their various symbols taken from the *Iconologia* — book, helmet, sphere, flute, palm frond, sheaf of wheat, laurel wreath, cornucopia. He still had a fine sense for composition and form. It looked like a huge project. I wondered how far along he was on it.

I picked up a small parchment page of

profile and three-quarter sketches. To think that this late in life he was still studying how to do faces. I was moved by the humility in that. Like me still struggling to do feet. On the back of it was a letter, full of ink blotches and scratch-outs, addressed to il granduca Ferdinando.

I am taking the liberty to transmit to Your Highness this small example of my painting in order for you to determine if I am able to merit employment in your service for the little that remains of my life, if this weak talent of mine might be sufficient to fulfill my ardent desire to return to my beloved homeland, submitting myself to Your Very Serene Highness, to whom with devoted affection I make a reverent bow from England.

If he had actually sent it, and this was only a draft, he had apparently received no answer. He'd probably yearned to come home for a long time, yet was afraid to leave secure work. I understood that. It sprang from the same source as my own ache at being uprooted. His exaggerated self-abasement saddened me. To practically beg for a commission from a boy duke after a lifetime of painting for cardinals and queens. A knot swelled in my throat. He'd suffered humiliations too.

His *cassapanca* was open and clothes lay in disarray. A sick shock pierced me. His undergarments were all in shreds.

On a window ledge was his carved wooden memento box, the other one of the pair I had always kept with me. I went to the door and listened a moment but didn't hear anything, so I opened the box. My letters from Florence were on top, brittle and faded. I read them again — Palmira's birth, Cosimo's first acceptance of my work, my admission to the academy. The last one pricked my conscience. I'd barely thanked him for writing to Buonarroti, yet that had started my acceptance in Florence.

Underneath the letters were a few Roman coins, cold to my touch, probably kept in the hope of returning, and my mother's wedding ring. The large ruby I remembered had been removed. I didn't like to think what that meant. A child's drawing was folded to fit the box exactly and show the face of a woman. On the back was written, *Amore mio, Artemisia drew this portrait of me for you on her tenth birthday. See that she is happily married, as we are. Prudenzia.* How Mother would have grieved if she had witnessed the scene just past.

The pity of his life, his last thirty years

without her, more than a decade outside his homeland, his communication always limited by language. How long has it been since anyone touched him, other than a slap on the back, a touch that would convince him that his heart was still alive? I marveled at the courage of his loneliness. Would I be able to command it when I was alone at his age? If, for his time in France, Agostino had been with him, I could not begrudge him that.

I set my father's things back in his memento box the way I had found them, put on my night shift, and finished the wine in my glass. I could not shake the humiliation and longing of his letter to Ferdinando, yet I'd written letters nearly as desperate. Both of our lives seemed to consist of piercing humiliations, some victories, and brief moments of sweetness. We both ought to count ourselves fortunate if, in the end, the sweet and the sour were of equal weight.

Coming here meant nothing if I had made him wish I hadn't. The journey I'd made was easy compared to what lay ahead — to complete the gesture, not just to come here but to enact the full measure of compassion, bigger than offering a blanket, as formidable to me as Christ touching the leper, Graziela touching the dying man. It was frightening, not because of what might happen, but because, if I were fiercely honest with myself, I would distrust my sincerity.

I loosened my bodice laces, lay down on his bed and pulled his blanket over me. Maybe he'd come back tomorrow morning, ashamed, as I was.

No sounds in the neighboring rooms roused me until late in the morning. I stirred up the few embers to ignite a fire, and stood close to it. I was famished. I ate more artichokes and olives and the rest of the bread while standing there. I poured water from a pitcher into a washing bowl and dipped my hands in to wash my face. It was so cold I cried out at the shock. I managed to tie up my hair, dirty from weeks of travel.

I looked out the window. The rain had stopped. The sky was what I imagined English people took for blue. On the other side of an enclosed meadow stood the Queen's House where the carriage had taken me first. From here I could see its classical lines, its fine sense of balance. It had a balustrade for viewing the countryside from the roof, and a loggia on the first story. There was nothing to do but walk across the meadow and see if he was there. I dug into my carpetbag to find Michelangelo's brush and tucked it in the inside pocket of my short cape. I found the stairway and a door. The long wet grasses soaked my shoes. I lifted my skirt to try to keep it clean and dry.

At the door of the Queen's House, workmen were carrying in a large unfinished wooden framework. "Orazio Gentileschi?" I said. They looked at each other, said a few words I couldn't understand and shook their heads. *"Sala grande?"* I waved my arms to convey a large room and pretended I was painting the ceiling. They took me inside past plasterers and carpenters working on a cornice and pointed to a grand staircase. Upstairs, the rooms had none of the flourishes and ornamentation common in Roman or Florentine palaces.

In the great hall, I recognized Father's dramatic figures already installed as coffered panels in the ceiling. It was an enormous project — nine panels and a central roundel of eleven women surrounding the figure of Peace bearing a staff and a leafy garland made of an olive branch. She was dazzling in power and beauty. I counted twenty-two figures so far, all female, even Pittura and Scultura, against a background of clouds and sky. Four panels were left to do. And him so frail and old.

A gorgeous ceiling except for one thing. The colors. Predominantly greens, pale violet, light blue and gold, they were so subdued compared to the paintings he did in the bright light of Rome that it seemed as if the life of the figures was waning.

"English taste is more conservative than ours." I twirled around at the sound of his voice, edged with apology. His anxious eyes pleaded. "I still have four panels to do."

"I'll help you."

Slowly, tentatively, as if afraid to hurt me, he reached out his arms for me. I felt my body soften in his embrace, like Palmira's used to when she was a child just relaxing into sleep.

I pulled away from him and looked up. "These are exquisite, Father. You can't deny that they have given you joy. I see it in every face, even if it's only private contentment at what you've done. Haven't you ever felt like shouting, 'Look! Look and let this beauty transform your heart'? A few practically split me with happiness. Hasn't it been so with you?"

He blinked at me with eyes the deep brown color of need.

"We've been lucky," I said. "We've been able to live by what we love. And to *live* painting, as we have, wherever we have, is to live passion and imagination and connection and adoration, all the best of life — to be more alive than the rest."

"Than who? More alive than who?"

"Than my own daughter, for one. I feel life more intensely than she does. I take its bite as fully as its beauties. I hope that means I'll come to die contented that I have really lived."

"You don't have any regrets?"

It was the most dangerous thing he'd ever asked. I respected his bravery, his willingness to edge right up to the injury.

"Of how I lived after I left Rome the first time?"

"Anything." I could see his jaw tightening, his shoulders preparing for what I would say.

Should I tell him I've too often felt like a bundle of false starts, like wet sticks being struck with fire only to burn out pathetically when something goes wrong? Should I complain that I wasn't able to keep the man I learned to love? Should I explain to him Galileo's discovery that we are not what we thought — that our lives are made smaller by the unimportance of our dwelling place on the periphery, like a touch of color at the edge of a painting, contributing to the whole but unnoticed by most? Should I admit that my mark on the world means everything to me, but my work is a mere trinket to the Medici?

Holding onto the back of a chair, Father waited for my answer, an old man trying to fortify himself for the onslaught.

He'd had enough of his own humiliations. He didn't need to hear me whine about mine.

"No. No regrets." I sucked in a long breath, in and out like the tide. "Only I've never been able to relax."

A squeezing around his eyes told me he was trying to understand what I meant.

"There's been only painting, and Palmira. If I'd had a lover or a loving husband, there would have been something else — someone with whom to enjoy *la dolce vita*."

He bowed his head in thought. "Only painting and a daughter," he murmured.

Like him, I suddenly realized. He'd had the same two. Only I had denied him the joy of one in a way Palmira had not denied me. We looked into each other's eyes at the same instant, both of us awash with sorrow and recognition, seeing each other face to face. I felt the cords of connection tighten.

"I am my father's daughter."

"How's that?"

"We have both chosen art over our daughters," I said softly.

"Only time will tell whether it's been worth the price." In a moment, he added tentatively, "You didn't find love?"

"Love." I grimaced. "To love is to stand willingly in the noose of illusion, adoring someone while you wait to choke."

His face contracted.

"Yes, that I found, if you can call it love. But even one-way love, fleeting love, is better than no love at all. I'm grateful for having had the feeling. So I guess, no regrets."

I patted his arm awkwardly. Slowly his expression softened. He teetered a bit and had to sit down. I pulled a second chair close to his.

"I have something to show you," I said, and handed him the wrapped brush. He let it roll out of the cloth onto his hand. "It was il divino's. Buonarroti the Younger gave it to me."

Looking at it lying in his open palm, he drew in a long, rasping breath. "With this he painted souls, Artemisia. Me, I only painted skin."

"You painted *your* soul, Father. You remember the Magnificat? 'My soul doth magnify the Lord.' That's what you've done — made the Lord's beauty larger with your life's work."

"Do you really think so?"

"With all my heart."

"But the price."

I lifted my shoulders. " 'Recompense belongeth to God.' Sister Paola told me that a long time ago. It's out of our hands."

After a moment he held the brush up to the air and pretended to be using it on an imaginary painting, smiling and glancing at me as if I were the model.

"You painted me, didn't you? On Borghese's ceiling. The casino."

"You saw it?" His face brightened.

"A magnificent work." Say it, I told myself. "A magnificent collaboration." Pain slicked over his eyes, desperation that I would understand. "You worked together as one."

"The worst and best thing I ever did. It has grieved me ever since."

"How did you know I'd be distracted, twenty years later?"

"It wasn't distraction that made that figure look over the balcony instead of at the musicians." He chuckled softly, sadly. "It was you glaring back at me in accusation while I was painting you."

He handed me the brush.

"I've never used it," I said.

"I can understand why. Anything less than his brilliance would be a desecration."

I could take offense at that. I was about to say Buonarroti meant me to use it, until I looked into Father's eyes and saw only reverence for an ideal.

Father arranged for a room for me next to his and brought me wood from his own supply, carrying it stick by stick, to build up a fire. Then he brought in Mother's footrug from his room and laid it next to my bed. In his studio, we looked at his drawings and decided which of the remaining paintings I would work on.

"Let's prime all of them," he said, suddenly animated, dragging out four enormous stretched canvases.

"All four at once?"

"Why not?"

We set them up in a row and mixed a thin gesso out of gypsum, horse glue, and white lead. He grinned mischievously as he found his wide priming brushes and handed one to me. "Watch this and guess," he commanded, his eyes sparkling. He loaded his brush and swooped on a huge S on the first canvas, stretching it from edge to edge, and then widening it. He stood back and pointed to each of the other three. "Do you know yet?"

"No."

He chuckled and moved to the second canvas. It was good to see him so happy. Sloppily he painted a large P. "How do you like that, eh?" With impish glee, he gestured for me to do the remaining two. "They'll never know."

I wasn't quite sure what he meant me to paint, but I loaded my brush and executed a large O.

"*Sì, sì,*" he said, watching.

I gave the letter a curving tail, making it into a Q.

"*Bene!*" he shouted. "*Eccellente.*"

On the last canvas I painted an R.

"*Che meraviglia.* There we have it! SPQR. The Senate and People of Rome." Chuckling, he said, "Under the English claim for Peace and the Arts is Rome, will always be Rome."

"The foundation," I said.

He kissed me on both cheeks. While we widened the letters until they filled in the canvas, he sang one of his Roman love songs.

How slowly he painted. How tentatively he mixed his colors. Sometimes we worked on the same canvas, he painting one figure and I another. I often found him watching me. Every morning he took longer before he began to paint. He stopped earlier in the afternoon. But every day, he did something, if only a patch of background. During his afternoon naps, I worked against time, always with an ear alert to his slow, uneven, rattling breaths.

I often hummed the melodies I was sure he knew just to get him to join in with the words. We began to relax with each other in a new way. A curious, unexpected lightness lifted me. Before this I had always held back, had never lived freely, not with Pietro, not even with Palmira, but here, where nothing was known, I did not fear judgment, and because Father and I shared the same sensibilities, all the rigidness of my living melted and I felt myself coming into myself. If it was genuine, if it would last, it was a wonderful feeling.

I had lived too gravely, had hugged judgment to my chest too tightly, had let the fear of it make me stiff. No wonder my back ached all my life. I should have done certain things — put more secret messages behind my paintings, taken Palmira up the bell tower, visited Galileo in Bellosguardo, painted him and given him the painting, danced more, enjoyed the attentions of Francesco instead of guarding against them. I should have taken that stone I found on the Via Appia the day of the verdict and hurled it — not against anyone or anything — just to let it sail out over the open countryside, fall somewhere unknown and mix with the elements — just for the feel of swinging my arm.

It was my own fault if I hadn't enjoyed *la dolce vita*. Francesco had said that now I was free to be me. Yes. Naples would be different when I went back.

One morning Father said he had business in London and was going by riverboat. He wouldn't let me go with him. It was the second time he'd done that. I worried about him, a frail old man traveling alone. I tried to get as much done as I could while he was gone. When he came home out of breath that evening, he sank into the nearest chair and looked at what I'd been working on. "You're a fine painter. Better than I am now." His chest heaved.

"You were my teacher."

"Yes. I taught you suffering."

"You taught me to see, and to use my imagination. You spared me a life of needlework and picnics."

"I'm sorry you missed the picnics."

"Plenty of time yet for picnics. Maybe even with grandchildren. Remember the blue cornflowers along the Via Appia?"

"Your mother threaded them through

your hair and made a chain of them around your neck. You looked like a goddess."

"To you."

"Come here." He reached inside his cloak and drew out a small drawstring bag and placed it in my hand. "I had this made for you. Open it."

The giddiness of girlhood rippled up in me. I untied the string and tipped out a bronze medallion shaped like a stage mask on a long gold chain.

"Do you know what it is?" he asked.

"Something from the *Iconologia*?"

"Go get it, there on the table."

I brought it to him and he showed me the allegorical figure of Painting — a beautiful woman with a brush in one hand, a palette in the other, and around her neck a gold chain with a medallion of a stage mask.

"Painting. A woman after all. I had forgotten." I looked from the medallion to him. His eyes shone with love. "It's beautiful."

He pressed his hands on his knees to stand up, took it from me and lifted the loop of chain over my head. "There. Just where it belongs."

"I've never had such an important gift," I whispered.

He collapsed one cold damp morning in

the great hall with a sheaf of sketches in his hands. I rushed to him and gathered him in my arms, his torso on my lap. I supported his lolling head in the crook of my elbow like Michelangelo's *Pietà*.

He winced and pressed his hand against his breast. His voice scraped softly. "Artemisia."

"Where does it hurt?"

"A brief unpleasantness. It will pass."

The bravery of those words moved me. And the horror of dying unforgiven. His hand clutched mine and his eyes burned with a question he was too embarrassed, even now, to put into words.

"*Sì*," I said. I felt a twenty-year knot release in my chest, and I finally understood that what he had wanted was not just forgiveness for him, but healing for me.

He seemed to let go then. I couldn't tell whether his eyes focused on me, or on his ceiling. Before they closed, I hoped he recognized his figure of Peace above him, soft and light and luminous, holding an olive leaf garland and floating on a cloud.

I thought he was gone. Gone, and I had not called him what he longed to hear. Then his chest lifted. His flaccid bottom lip quivered and curled inward with a breath.

"Artemisia?"

"I'm here, Papa. I'm holding you."

"Use his brush. Do a self-portrait," he whispered slowly. "An Allegory of Painting. For all time."

"*Sì*, Papa." I kissed him lightly on the forehead. "I will."